A Crossed Reality

by
Gerald Pruett

CCB Publishing
British Columbia, Canada

A Crossed Reality

Copyright ©2009 by Gerald Pruett
ISBN-13   978-1-926585-20-8
First Edition

Library and Archives Canada Cataloguing in Publication

Pruett, Gerald, 1963-
A crossed reality / written by Gerald Pruett – 1st ed.
ISBN 978-1-926585-20-8
I. Title.
PS3616.R837C76 2009   813'.6   C2009-901728-8

Publisher: CCB Publishing
              British Columbia, Canada
              www.ccbpublishing.com

To my son Joseph Pruett.

I know that he would rather that I have spent my time playing video games with him than write.

Chapter One

At Harvard University on Tuesday, October 5, 2010, 10:05 A.M., Professor Blumberg, a science instructor, was returning graded assignments.

Randy Miller, a twenty-one-year-old student in the class, was the tenth one to get his research paper back, and when he glanced at the front cover of his paper he saw a large red 'F' across the front page of his work. He couldn't help but to let out an audible groan for his initial protest.

Randy was half Mexican from his father's side. He was of an average height and weight. His mother Phyllis had never married Randy's father and he had disappeared from Phyllis' life just after he found out that she was pregnant with Randy.

Once Prof. Blumberg handed back the last assignment, he walked up to the head of the class. He stood in front of his desk, and as he panned the room of where his students were sitting, he asked, "Okay, does anyone have any questions of the grade he or she received?" Randy's hand quickly shot up. "Mr. Miller, I had a feeling that you would be the first to raise your hand. Mr. Miller, your paper is a joke and I will not entertain joke papers, so your grade stands."

Randy abruptly stood up and uttered, "Prof. Blumberg, I must protest. I have scientific facts to back up my paper."

"Mr. Miller, science fiction is not facts."

"There's nothing in my paper that's science fiction," Randy insisted.

Alexander (Alex) O'Brien, another twenty-one-year-old

student and a childhood friend of Randy's watched the exchange of words with great interest. He had short red hair and green eyes. He stood taller than Randy by only an inch, but weighed a few pounds less.

"Okay, Mr. Miller," Prof. Blumberg said. Randy sat back down. "Let's get your fellow students involved in this. Everyone, Mr. Miller's paper was on the alternate reality theory. In his paper, not only does he agree with the alternate reality theory, but he also states that more realities are spawning each day. In his paper he states that with each crossroad event that a person comes to in his or her life that event will spawn more realities. How many realities will depend on how many possible outcomes there are to each crossroad event. According to Randy, four possible outcomes means that four realities will be spawn. He had even claimed that he has come up with a way to identify different realities from each other with the Alpha realities being the same or similar to ours while the Beta through Omega realities being completely different. Correct me if I'm wrong, Mr. Miller, but our reality is known by you as being Alpha followed by seven zeros."

Randy stood again before answering, "Actually there should be a decimal point between each of the seven digits and it is an address of a particular reality. Each home reality would share the same home address. It's only to us in this reality that another reality address would be different. When a person would travel into another reality, the address of the two realities would be flipped so that person would have to use the same address that was originally used in the initial jump to get back." He flipped to a certain page of his papers. "Here are the examples I gave for my address system." He slowly panned the page for his fellow students to see.

The students who were sitting next to him were able to make out the following:

A crossroad event is a pivotal moment to where the future of a person or a group of people is determined by the outcome of the event. There are two types of crossroad events.

Type 1: is where a person's life changes by the person's own choosing. (A person can receive a unique set of circumstances by making a choice to a multiple-choice scenario.)

Type 2: is where a person's life changes that wasn't of the person's own choosing.

An example of a type1 crossroad event:

Tony has been presented with three possible choices after coming to a six-foot fence with a narrow hole in it.

1. *Tony goes around the fence and nothing bad happens.*

2. *Tony tries to climb over the fence rather than going around it or squeezing through the hole and falls and breaks an arm. Later at the hospital he meets his future wife Michelle. (Giving that each of Tony's future crossroad events led to marriage)*

3. *Tony goes through the hole in the fence and gets cut by a rusty metal object and eventually develops tetanus. (Giving that the crossroad event led Tony into thinking that he didn't need a tetanus shot at the time.)*

An example of a type2 crossroad event:

1. *Tony's flight was delayed an hour. While waiting he met his future wife Liz.(Giving that each of Tony's future crossroad events led to marriage)*

2. *Tony's flight was on time and he had never met Liz.*

Examples of the reality address system.

(#)is any number from 0 to 9; (#>0) is any number from 1 to 9. 0 being no magnitude and 9 being the maximum magnitude.

(Greek alphabet) #.#.#.#.#.#

Reality home address is Alpha 0.0.0.0.0.0.0

The reality address Alpha 0.0.0.0.0.0.(#>0) almost completely identical to the reality home address. The differences would most likely be missed.

The reality address Alpha 0.0.0.0.0.(#>0).# is less identical to the reality home address. The differences might or might not be missed.

The reality address Alpha 0.0.0.0.(#>0).#.# is even less identical to the home address. The differences would be subtle, but apparent.

The reality address Alpha 0.0.0.(#>0).#.#.#. Half of the events in the world are no longer identical to the reality home address. The difference would easily be seen.

The reality address Alpha 0.0.(#>0).#.#.#.#. More than half of the events in the world are no longer identical to the reality home address.

The reality address Alpha 0.(#>0).#.#.#.#.#. Hardly any events in the world are identical to the reality home address.

The reality address Alpha (#>0).#.#.#.#.#.#. None of the events in the world are identical to the reality home address.

The Beta addresses are the closest addresses to the Alpha addresses while the Omega addresses are the furthest away.

Each home reality would share the same reality home address. It's only to the AR Traveler (Alternate Reality Traveler) that another reality address would be different. When the AR Traveler would travel into another reality, the addresses of the two realities would be flipped so the AR Traveler would have to use the same address that was originally used in the initial jump to get back; however, the addresses will start deviating from each other if the AR Traveler would remain in the alternate reality for more than twenty-four hours.

Beta through Omega addresses are where the realities of Earth had gone in an entirely different evolutionary path.

As Randy was showing the page, Prof. Blumberg said in a sarcastic tone, "Thank you, Mr. Miller, for sharing that." Prof. Blumberg looked over the class. "Besides me, who else in this room feels that the alternate reality theory is a joke and it should remain in the science fiction stories?"

Twenty-five of the forty students raised their hands. Doug, Alex's fraternal twin brother and roommate, was also in the

5

class and had raised his hand.

Doug had short brown hair and blue eyes. He was the same height and build as Alex. Although Doug and Alex weren't identical, they looked very much alike in the face. Everyone who met them for the first time knew that Alex and Doug were brothers without being told.

Alex was among the fifteen students who didn't raise their hands. A friendly debate broke out, and during the debate, Alex and ten others switched sides.

Prof. Blumberg allowed the debate to go on for a short time before stopping it. Once he had reclaimed order within the classroom, he said, "Mr. Miller, as you can see most of your peers agree with me that your paper sounds like science fiction nonsense and therefore, the grade I've given you stands."

While enraged Randy stood quickly and hastily gathered his things. As he was storming towards the door he uttered out, "Then I will prove it to you. I will prove it to all of you." Everyone just watched as Randy furiously left the room.

Saturday, October 9, 1:45 P.M., Alex was parking his car in front of Randy's rented house when he saw Amanda, Randy's girlfriend, near a cab. Amanda was watching the cab driver as he loaded her suitcases.

After Alex parked his car he walked over to Amanda and asked, "Are you going on a trip?"

Amanda looked at Alex before saying angrily, "I'm going to the airport. I'm going home to stay."

Alex shot Amanda a shock look while asking in a disbelieving tone, "You're quitting Harvard?"

"Alex, I'm only attending Harvard because of Randy and I broke up with him."

"You broke up with Randy?" Alex shockingly asked. "Why?"

Amanda took a deep breath to calm herself before saying,

"Alex, since Tuesday, Randy has shut me out of his life. He's completely obsessed with that alternate reality theory of his."

"Amanda, before you leave in a haste, let me go in the house and talk to Randy."

"Don't bother. He's not even home. He's at the electronic store buying things."

"That's good, isn't it? I mean he has his mind focused on something else; something other than that theory of his."

"Alex, Randy had a break though this morning on his theory. So he believes anyway. He now believes that he can create a device that can open a wormhole into other realities. He is now at the store buying the things that he needs to create the device. As he was leaving I told him that I wasn't going to be here when he got back. His words were, 'You'll return when you see my name in the paper after winning the Nobel Prize.' Alex, I'm done. I can't handle this."

The cab driver stepped up and asked, "Are you ready, ma'am?"

Amanda faced the cab driver before saying, "I'm ready." She turned back towards Alex. "Goodbye, Alex. You are a good friend." Within seconds Amanda got into the cab and closed the door.

Alex watched as the cab driver got into the driver's side of the cab and drove away. Alex then waited for fifteen minutes for Randy to return. When he didn't return Alex got into his car and drove away.

Tuesday, October 19 at 11:10 A.M., Alex rang Randy's doorbell. He waited for Randy to answer for only a short time before knocking hard. After a few more seconds of waiting he reared back and as he was ready to pound, Randy opened the door. Randy didn't look at Alex when the door opened, but stood in the doorway while writing in a notebook. Randy was ten days unshaven and his hair was a mess.

"Randy, you've been absent from school for two weeks," Alex pointed out. When Randy didn't respond Alex tapped Randy's notebook. "Hey!"

Randy looked at Alex before saying, "I'm glad you came by." Randy then walked away from the door while not paying attention as to if Alex was going to follow. "There is something I want to show you."

"Randy, I just came by to give you a warning from Prof. Blumberg," Alex said as he did follow.

Randy faced Alex before saying, "I'm not concerned about his empty threats."

"Randy, I don't think he's threatening. He's tired of your absentees and your joke science papers that you are emailing him as your assignments."

"Those papers I send him aren't jokes. I'm very serious about those papers." Randy gestured into the direction of his makeshift lab as he continued to say, "In fact, come with me. I want to show you a breakthrough I had."

"As long as it is not on your alternate reality theory I will see your breakthrough."

"Alternate reality is real and I can prove it within a day or two."

Alex gave Randy a curious look while questioning, "What do you mean you can prove it?"

"If you come with me I will show you what I mean."

"Randy, we've been friends since the first grade so I'm saying this as a good friend. You need to come back to reality before it is too late. Now you are the best science student Harvard has seen in a long time, and if it wasn't for those papers you are sending Prof. Blumberg even he would see that, but as it is, you are about ready to be expelled."

"Alex, come with me and I will show you what I learned."

"No, I won't," Alex said while taking a stand. "Prof.

Blumberg is right. Traveling into another reality is nothing more than a science fiction writer's imagination. A person can not travel into a different reality like in that TV show."

"You're wrong and I will prove it."

"Randy, you need to see someone about this obsession of yours. I see now why Amanda dumped you."

"Amanda just didn't understand why this was important to me."

"She's not the only one. Now I'm going back to Harvard and I suggest you do the same before you are no longer a student there."

"In a day or two I will prove to you that alternate reality is not just a science fiction story."

Alex shook his head in frustration before turning towards the door and walking out.

Randy walked back into his makeshift lab. The lab had a dry erase board with an equation written on it. Not too far from the dry erase board was a workbench with pieces of a remote spread about. He sat down at the workbench, placed the notebook to where he could see it, picked up a small resister and soldered it to the main portion to the remote.

Thursday, October 21, at 12:35 P.M., Randy knocked on Alex and Doug's dormitory door.

Doug opened the door and when he saw Randy standing there with a remote in his hand he said, "So you didn't fall off the edge of the universe as the rumors have been saying."

"Very funny," Randy said before holding up his remote, almost at eye level. "I did it, and I want to show Alex. Where is he?"

"He is at the library."

"Thanks. I'll see you later."

When Randy went to leave, Doug uttered while stepping into the hallway, "Wait! I'm going with you."

In the library, Alex and four others, Kenny Johnson, Brandy Harrison, Cindy Hartford and Benjamin Bell were sitting at a table not too far from the exit.

Randy and Doug saw Alex and the others as they entered. As Randy and Doug stepped up, Alex faced Randy and said, "Wow, your record in solitude is fifteen days."

"Alex, I did it," Randy said as he again held up the remote. Everyone at the table gave Randy a confused look. "I haven't tested it yet, but I didn't want to test it without a witness."

Alex shook his head while saying, "Test it right here and now. And when it fails, I want you to drop this obsession with AR traveling."

"It won't fail," Randy said before pointing his remote towards an open area and pressing the button.

At first nothing happened, but then all of a sudden an intense feeling as though their bodies were being ripped apart came over Randy, Doug, Alex and Alex's study group. Within seconds everyone blacked out from the pain.

In the reality Alpha 0.0.0.1.0.0.0, at the library, Kenny, Brandy and Cindy were together at the same table, but on the opposite side of the library. They were faced down, passed out on their books. The librarian walked up to the table and as he shook them awake, he said, "Hey, wake up. You three can't sleep here."

After waking up, Kenny looked around before asking, "What happen to Alex, Doug, Randy and Ben?"

Brandy had a confused expression on her face before asking, "How did we get at this table?"

In Ben's hometown of Atlanta, Georgia, Ben woke up at a local tire and auto shop while wearing the shop's uniform. Other workers and customers were standing over him while giving him a deeply concerned look.

Doug woke up in his dorm room with Richard Hawkins

standing over him with a worried look on his face.

When Doug saw Richard hovering over him, he sat up and asked, "What happened?"

"Dude, you just collapsed to the floor for no apparent reason," Richard answered.

Doug looked around without standing up and saw that he was in his dorm room. After refocusing on Richard he asked, "Okay, I've seen you around campus, but who are you and why are you in my dorm?"

Richard stared at Doug as if he had lost his mind, before asking, "Did you hit your head when you fell, Dude?"

Doug thought about his condition for a moment before saying, "My head is killing me. Who are you though?"

"I'm Richard; your roommate," he pointed out. "I think you better go and get checked out at the hospital."

"You're not my roommate," Doug said with strong certainty in his tone.

"Yes, Dude, I am," Richard corrected. "We have been roommates since our freshmen year."

"My brother is my roommate."

"What brother? You don't have a brother."

Doug said sarcastically, "My twin brother Alex. We have been roommates all our lives."

"Now I know you hit your head when you fell if you're thinking that Alex is your twin brother."

"He is my twin brother," Doug insisted.

"No, Dude; Alex is your twin sister."

A shock expression flashed across Doug face while uttering, "What?!"

"Alex is your twin sister," Richard repeated. "I know you can't think of her as being hot, but come on; even you have to admit that she is a knockout. She stands five feet, five inches tall; she has the most gorgeous body with beautiful red hair that flows midway down her back. She has the most beautiful green eyes. She's a snob though so she could really use a personality makeover."

Doug thought for a second before blurting out, "Randy Miller, I'm going to kill you when I get my hands on you."

"Who is Randy Miller?"

"Never mind," Doug said as he shook his head. "Richard, you're right, I think I did hit my head and I'm having memory lapses. So can you take me to my sister?"

"Sure, Dude," Richard said before reaching his hand out to help Doug up.

Minutes later, Doug stood next to Richard as Richard knocked on a dorm door. Trudy Appleby opened the door and when she saw Doug, she said, "Thank God that you're here, Doug. Alex fainted a moment ago and when she woke up she went hysterical. She acted shocked that she's a woman."

Richard gave Doug a perplexed look before asking, "Is there a twin thing going on between you and Alex?"

Doug looked at Richard as if he had lost his mind for a moment before shaking it off and facing Trudy again. "Where is Alex now?"

"She's in her bedroom," Trudy answered while gesturing. "She's looking into her mirror and repeating, 'I'm dreaming this. This is not happening.' Doug, you need to go in there and talk to her."

"I will," Doug said before walking into the dorm.

In the common room there was a couch, a coffee table and an entertainment center. The entertainment center held a TV, a combination VCR and DVD player, and a small stereo system. There were two bedroom doors.

Doug stepped up to the closed door and knocked. "Alex, it's me; Doug."

Alex opened the door and said sternly, "You are not real.

This is all a dream."

Doug lustfully gawked at Alex for a moment. He then shook it off and whispered, "You're not dreaming, Alex. We jumped into another reality."

"We jumped?" Alex confusingly questioned just as the reality of the situation had hit her. "We jumped!"

Alex walked back into her room and looked into the mirror.

Inside Alex's bedroom was a small wardrobe closet, a twin bed with a purse setting near the head of the bed, a dresser and a small desk with a chair pushed in. On top of the desk was a laptop computer. The mirror that Alex was looking into hung on the wall over Alex's laptop.

Doug stepped into the bedroom and shut the door behind him.

As Alex looked at Doug's reflection, she said, "I'm going to kill Randy Miller when I see him."

Doug amusingly grinned while saying jokingly, "You know, I have to admit that this is a great look for you."

Alex looked at Doug with a distasteful grin while uttering, "I'm glad you are enjoying this. Look at me. I'm a woman."

Doug said in a lustful tone, "Oh believe me, I definitely see that you're a woman."

Alex said sternly, "Stop that! And stop looking at me like that. Although, I'm not Alexander on this side of the twilight zone, we are still siblings… at least I think we are."

"We're still twins, but apparently in this reality you were born a girl. Mom must really like the name Alex for that to be your name in this reality." Alex checked her pockets. She then looked around the room for a second. "What are you looking for?"

Alex pointed to a purse on the bed while saying, "That. Most likely that would be mine and I want to check to see what Alex is short for." Alex walked over and took out a wallet from the purse. When Alex looked at her driver's license Doug saw a disturbed expression on her face.

Doug moved closer while asking, "What is it?"

"My name is Alexandra Nicole Larson," Alex said while standing there with a confused expression across her face. Doug went to pull out his wallet. "Am I married in this reality?"

Doug looked at his driver's license before saying, "No; you're not married. My name is Douglas Christopher Larson." Alex saw an uncertain expression on Doug's face as he looked at her. "Alex, we don't live on Victoria Place anymore."

Alex looked at her driver's license before saying, "The street name on my driver's license is Wild Deer Road. The city is still St. Louis."

"That's what I have too," Doug said as he gazed at his license.

Alex went to put her license and wallet away while saying, "I don't know why our last name is Larson or why we live on Wild Deer Road, but we need to be concentrating on a way to get back to our reality."

Doug was putting his wallet away when he said, "I believe our first step on that is to find the one person who's responsible for us being here."

Alex crossed her arms while saying, "Randy Miller."

"Exactly. We should check his house." Doug motioned towards the door as he continued to say, "Ladies first."

Without attempting to move, Alex said with a smirk, "You're enjoying this way too much."

"Okay, I'll go first," Doug said as he made a slight move towards the door.

"Well, before we leave, I want to check something," Alex said before turning towards the dresser.

"What do you want to check?"

As Alex walked towards the dresser, she said, "Since mom keeps a diary, perhaps I would too."

Alex pulled open the top drawer; searched it thoroughly and then closed it. As she was going onto the next drawer, Doug checked underneath the mattress.

Alex was opening the third drawer when Doug said, "You can stop looking. I found what you're looking for."

Alex faced Doug before asking, "How did you know to look underneath the mattress?"

Doug held out the diary for Alex to take and said, "That's where mom keeps hers."

As Alex took the diary, she asked, "You read mom's diary?"

"No," Doug quickly answered. "I just saw her placing it there one day."

Alex glanced at the diary before questioning, "How come I get the feeling that you might've read my diary in this reality?"

Doug gave Alex a concern look before asking, "And you are becoming sensitive about the mere idea of the Doug of this reality reading your alternate's diary?"

Alex thought for a moment before saying, "You're right. This is not our reality and we shouldn't get too focused on what the us of this reality did or didn't do." Alex put the diary in her purse and then put her purse over her shoulder. "Well, we better get going. I'll read this diary on the way. Oh, you wouldn't know my roommate's name by any chance, would you?"

"I sure don't," Doug said while shaking his head. "I never even saw her in our reality."

Alex gestured towards the door while saying, "Well, let's go and maybe we can find out what her name is without appearing that we lost our memories."

Trudy and Richard were having a casual conversation in

the common room and they abruptly stopped talking when Alex and Doug stepped out of the bedroom.

Trudy faced Alex before asking, "So how are you feeling?"

"I'm good," Alex said with an embarrass grin. "Well, Doug and I have something to do."

"You're leaving now?" Trudy quickly asked.

Alex gave Trudy a curious look while asking, "Is there a reason that I shouldn't?"

"We have a class in ten minutes," Trudy pointed out.

Alex asked in a tone as if to make a point, "I'm not failing this class... am I?"

Trudy, with a confused expression across her face, answered, "Well, I know you're not failing. But what does that have to do anything?"

"Well, if I'm not failing then missing this one class won't hurt my grade." Trudy continued to give Alex a perplexed stare as Alex continued to say, "I'll see you later." Trudy was slightly baffled as she watched Alex and Doug leaving the dorm.

Chapter Two

As Alex and Doug were walking towards the parking lot, Doug reached into his pocket and pulled out a car remote. When he saw that the car remote was for a Jeep vehicle, he said, "Well, I don't own a Mustang in this reality."

Alex saw what kind of remote Doug was holding and questioned, "You own a Jeep in this reality?"

"Apparently so," Doug said before noticing that Alex was deep in her own thoughts. "Is there anything wrong?"

"Dad wouldn't approve if one of us bought a Jeep, Chrysler or a Dodge vehicle," Alex said as she and Doug were walking into the parking lot.

"Maybe Dad didn't get hurt at the Chrysler Plant and sued the company in this reality."

"Doug, I'm getting an uncomfortable feeling." When Alex saw that Doug was giving her a concerned look she asked, "Why are you staring at me that way?"

Doug stopped walking and said, "You are beginning to sound like Mom."

"Doug, I'm serious. This reality is totally different. Our last names are Larson; we live on Wild Deer Road and you own a vehicle that was made by Chrysler. Aren't you curious to know why things are the way they are?"

"No, I'm not, Alex. This is not our reality, and I for one am not worried as to why things are the way they are in this reality."

"Well, I am, so I hope you don't mind that I investigate

some."

"As long as it doesn't hinder us getting back to our reality, investigate all you want." Doug then looked over the parking lot and when he saw a Jeep Wrangler a few cars from him, he pressed the remote. Nothing happened when he pressed the button. "Well, that's not it."

Alex looked around and saw a Jeep Liberty at a distance. She pointed to it and said, "There's a Liberty over there. Perhaps that's it."

Alex followed Doug to the vehicle and again nothing happened when Doug pressed the button. "Do you see any more Jeeps around here?"

As Alex and Doug were looking in all direction, Alex said, "We might have to check the other parking lot."

Doug looked at Alex with an amuse grin before saying, "I didn't think I would ever say this to you, but check your purse. See what kind of car keys you have."

Alex rummaged through her purse and pulled out another Jeep vehicle remote. Alex grinned before saying, "Apparently I own a Jeep also." Alex then pressed the button, and the Jeep Liberty locks popped up. "Hey, it appears that this Liberty is mine."

"Good, we'll take your Jeep and worry about mine later."

Alex held out the keys for Doug to take while saying, "You drive; I want to read the diary."

"Okay," Doug said while taking the keys. As he was opening the driver's door, Alex walked to the other side to get in.

After Alex put on her seat belt, she pulled out the diary from her purse and flipped to the first page. As Doug was starting the car, Alex read aloud, "Personal diary belonging to Alexandra Nicole Larson; fourteenth volume. The first date of entry is July 9, 2010."

As Doug was backing out of the parking spot, he said, "The date of our twenty-first birthday." Doug stopped, put the car into drive and drove away. Alex set the diary to the side and opened her purse. "What are you looking for?"

Alex pulled out a cell phone before saying, "I saw this phone when I was looking for car keys. I'm going to call mom and subtly inquire about the other thirteen volumes along with seeing what I can do about getting my hands on them."

"I don't think that's a wise idea."

As Alex scrolled through the numbers that were stored on the phone, she asked, "Why not?"

"If you call mom and start asking bizarre questions, you're going to get her thinking that something is wrong."

"I know how to handle it," Alex said while seeing a phone entry that was titled 'mom'.

After Doug saw Alex pressing the button he asked in disbelief, "You're calling her, aren't you?"

Before Alex was able to respond, her mom, Beverly, answered the phone. Alex just nodded as she was saying, "Mom, it's me. Alex."

"Sweetie, if this is not an emergency, can I call you back. I'm about ready to go into surgery."

Alex uttered in a concern tone, "Oh my god, Mom! What's wrong?! Why are you going into surgery?!"

Beverly said with a confused tone in her voice, "Since I'm a surgeon, going into surgery is my job."

Alex said in a delightful tone, "You're a surgeon."

Beverly asked with a concerned tone in her voice, "Alex, sweetie, are you okay?"

"I'm fine, mom. I'll just call you later… or you can call me when you're not busy. Bye."

When the call ended, Beverly curiously looked at her phone before shaking it off and putting it away.

19

After Alex had ended the call, Doug sarcastically said, "Real subtle."

"Okay, I'll admit it. That could have been more subtle, but mom is a doctor in this reality."

"Well, in our reality, mom was in her second year of medical school when she got pregnant with us. After giving birth to us, she never went back and finished."

"I know that, but I'm really curious to know why she was able to finish medical school in this reality and not ours."

As Alex scrolled through the numbers again, Doug asked in a worried tone, "Who are you planning to call now?"

"Dad's phone number is stored in the phone too, and I'm going to try him."

As Alex made the call, Doug said, "You are going to get a net thrown over us if you aren't careful."

As the phone was ringing, Alex said, "Relax; I'm just trying to get some answers to a few questions. Besides, we may not get back to our reality right away, so we will need all the information we can get."

"Just don't get us sent to the funny farm."

"I won't. Oh, uh, your name is also listed on my phone, so you also have a cell phone."

"I'll look for it when I get back to the dorm."

The phone rang a few times before the receptionist, Tiffany Lydell, answered the phone with, "Dr. Avery Larson's office. How can I help you?"

Alex asked in a confused tone, "Who am I talking to?"

Tiffany asked in an inquisitive tone, "Alex, is that you?"

Alex cringed before responding in a cautious tone, "It's me. Who am I talking to?"

Tiffany said in a confused tone, "It's me, Tiffany. Are you okay?"

"I'm fine. It just didn't sound like you. Can I talk to my

dad?"

"He's with a patient. Is there anything I can do to help?"

"Have you ever heard of a man name Nicholas Christopher O'Brien?"

"I can't say that I have. Who is he?"

"Never mind, Tiffany; I'll talk to you later."

As Tiffany was hanging up the phone, Avery and Mr. Taylor were leaving the examination room.

When Avery and Mr. Taylor stepped up to the receptionist's desk, Avery said, "Schedule Mr. Taylor to come back for a follow up visit in two weeks."

"Yes, Doctor," Tiffany said.

Avery patted Mr. Taylor on the back and said, "I'll see you in two weeks."

"Thanks again, Dr. Larson," Mr. Taylor said.

Avery just nodded and as he was about to step away, Tiffany said, "Oh, Dr. Larson, Alexandra called a short time ago."

"What did she want?"

"She really didn't say, but she was inquiring about a man named Nicholas Christopher O'Brien." Avery stared at Tiffany as if she was a ghost. "Doctor, are you okay?"

Avery broke the stare he was giving Tiffany before saying, "Yeah-yeah, I'm fine. Did Alex say why she was asking about Nicholas O'Brien?"

"She wouldn't say."

Avery pondered over a thought for a moment with a worried expression across his face, before he told Tiffany, "Let Mrs. Jones know that I'll be a few minutes."

Tiffany stood up and said, "Yes, Doctor."

Avery turned and walked into his office. After sitting down at his desk, he picked up the phone and dialed it.

At the hospital, Beverly was just about ready to scrub in

when her cell phone rang. After looking at the number, she answered, "Hey, Honey, this isn't a good time to talk. I'm about ready to scrub in for surgery."

"Did you tell Alex about Nicholas O'Brien?"

Beverly said in a confused tone, "Of course not. Why would you ask that?"

"I didn't get a chance to talk to her, but she just called here and asked Tiffany about him. Beverly, before we got married we agreed not to say anything about Nicholas."

"And I didn't. Honey, I don't know how Alex heard the name, and I will deal with it later, but right now, there's a man on a table who needs a surgeon."

"All right; goodbye," Avery said before hanging up. He then stood up and walked out of his office.

On the road to go find Randy, Alex was reading the diary. Alex had read a few pages before saying, "Guess who Alex of this reality dated."

Doug thought for a second before saying, "Myron Bennett."

"You can't be serious. Myron in our reality is a nerd and is in desperate need of help with clearing up his acne."

"Who is it then?"

"Stephen Keith."

Doug slightly grinned before questioning, "You dated Harvard's first string quarterback?"

"No, the Alex of this reality dated the quarterback. Stephen broke up with Alex on September 15th and started dating Becky Steward."

"I don't know Becky Steward."

"I don't know her either, but Becky and the Alex of this reality used to be good friends before September 15th. There is also another woman who I don't know. Her named is Catherine Weis. She's a friend to Alex and Becky. Catherine is even remaining a friend to both of them in spite that Alex and Becky are no longer friends."

"Interesting; what else did you learn from that?"

"Not too much, but I'm still reading," Alex said before flipping to the next page.

A short time later, Doug parked in front of the house. After Alex and Doug stepped up to the front door, Alex knocked. Seconds later, Alex was stunned to see a ten-year-old girl answering the door.

"Hi; are you here to see my mom?" the girl asked.

"I'm sorry," Alex was the one to say. "I believe I have the wrong house. I was looking for a man named Randy Miller."

Before the girl was able to respond, the girl's mom stepped up behind the girl and asked, "Hi, may I help you?"

"I'm sorry to trouble you, Ma'am," Alex said. "My friend Randy Miller was supposed to have moved into this neighborhood just recently, and when he told me the address, I must have gotten it wrong. Again I apologize for troubling you."

"If this helps, I did see a moving van and two men three weeks ago two blocks up the street," the woman said while gesturing in the direction.

"Thank you for the information," Doug said. "Bye."

The woman and the girl just waved. Alex and Doug waved back before they turned and walked back towards the Jeep.

Before reaching the Jeep Alex questioned, "Doug, what are we going to do if Randy isn't attending Harvard?"

"Randy is the one who had talked you and me into applying to Harvard, so if we're here then he has to be here."

"I hope you're right," Alex said as they were approaching the Jeep.

"Of course I'm right. So do you still want me to drive?"

"Yeah, I want to read more of the diary."

As Alex was opening the passenger's door, Doug was walking towards the driver's door.

Alex and Doug didn't speak to one another while Alex read the diary. After Doug parked the Jeep in Harvard's parking lot and turned off the engine Alex looked up. When she saw where she was she put the diary in her purse.

Just before Alex was able to reach for the door-latch to get out, Doug asked, "So have you learned anything else from that diary?"

"I have. My roommate's name is Trudy Appleby. Apparently she and I became best friends after Stephen broke up with me to go out with Becky."

"Is that all you learned?"

"That's all I learned that I'm willing to share with you. There is a lot of private and personal stuff in here that I don't want to share."

Doug amusingly grinned before saying, "Okay." He then opened his door to get out. Alex followed suit.

As Alex and Doug were walking away from the Jeep, Kenny, Brandy and Cindy were approaching them. Alex and Doug watched them with uncertain expressions on their faces.

Kenny was leading and when he stepped up he stared at Alex while saying, "Doug, we need to talk to you for a minute in private."

"What about?" Doug asked.

"This is a private matter and I don't want to discuss this in front of your friend," Kenny said.

Before Doug was able to respond, Alex blurted out, "Does it have anything to do with reality being changed?"

Kenny gave Alex a curious look before saying, "That's right. How do you know about it?"

"Kenny; Brandy; Cindy, let me introduce you to my twin sister Alexandra."

Brandy stared incredulously at Alex while asking, "Alex?"

Alex grinned before saying, "It's me. How do you like my makeover?"

"Doug, what's going on?" Kenny asked.

"I'll give you one hint; Randy Miller," Doug said.

"What about him?" Cindy asked.

"He was working on the idea of traveling into different realities," Doug said.

"You can't be serious," Brandy said.

"Brandy, look at me," Alex said with her arms spread out wide. "This makeover wasn't my doing."

"So what do we do to correct this?" Cindy asked.

"We find Randy," Doug said. "Since all of us had traveled... jumped... or whatever the hell we did, I'm going to say that he did too. Alex and I were on our way to the admission office to find out what dorm he's in."

"He wasn't living in the dorm in our reality," Brandy pointed out.

"We just came from where he lived in our reality and he doesn't live there," Alex said.

"Okay, let's go to the admission office," Kenny said. "Oh and when we get there, we need to ask about Benjamin also."

Doug sighed before saying sarcastically, "Of course we do."

Minutes later, the group walked into the admissions office. The worker at the desk gave the group a confused look as they stepped up. In an uncertain tone, the worker asked, "May I help you?"

Doug pulled out his student ID before saying, "I'm looking for a fellow student. His name is Randy Miller and I want to know what his dorm number is."

The worker typed for a second at the computer. When the search showed, 'No match found' the worker said, "There is no one at this university by the name of Randy Miller."

"Are you certain?" Doug quickly asked.

"I'm positive," the worker said.

"What about Benjamin Bell?" Kenny asked.

The worker typed again on the computer. Again the message, 'No match found' came up. "He's not here either."

"Thanks," Alex said. "We're sorry to trouble you."

"No problem," the worker said.

Alex and the group turned and walked away. When they stepped into the hallway Cindy asked, "What now?"

Alex pulled out her cell phone from her purse and said, "I'm going to call Randy's mom. Perhaps she can tell me where to find him." Alex then dialed the number. A woman's voice answered the phone on the third ring. "Hello, Ms. Miller."

"I'm sorry, but you must've called the wrong number," the woman said.

"I'm sorry, Ma'am, to have bothered you," Alex said. Alex then put her phone back into her purse. "Well, that number doesn't belong to Randy's mom in this reality."

"So what now?" Cindy asked.

"I think Doug and I should talk to Randy's mom in person," Alex said.

"You can't be serious," Doug quickly said.

"Randy is the only person who can return us to our reality, so we have to find him," Alex said.

"Doug, I think Alex is right," Kenny said. "You and Alex are the only two who know where his mom lives... unless Randy's mom doesn't live in the same place."

"Doug, since I'm a woman in this reality, it might be better if you came with me, but if you don't want to, I'll go alone," Alex said.

"And how are you going to get there?" Doug asked.

Gerald Pruett

"Neither one of us can afford a plane trip to St. Louis."

"Doug, let me check my bank account and make sure I still have the same amount of money in this reality. And if I do, I'll give you and Alex the money to go to St. Louis," Brandy said.

"Brandy, are you sure about that?" Alex asked.

"I'm positive," Brandy said. "If our only chance to correct reality is to find Randy then helping you get to Randy is no problem for me."

"Okay, thanks," Alex said before gesturing towards her purse. "So check your bank book."

"Let's go to my dorm. I'll check my bank account from the Internet," Brandy said. Brandy turned and walked away. Everyone walked along side her.

A few minutes later, Brandy was logging onto her laptop while Alex and the others were standing nearby.

Once Brandy logged onto the Internet, Brandy saw a message from Ben. When a curious expression crept across Brandy's face, Alex asked, "Brandy, what is it?"

"Ben sent me a message." While everyone was gathering around Brandy's laptop, Brandy opened the message and read it aloud, "Brandy, I'm hoping what happened to me has happened to you as well, otherwise you will see this e-mail as a prank. Fifteen minutes ago, I was at Harvard while studying with you, Kenny, Cindy and Alex. I don't know what happened; I blacked out and when I woke up, I was at a tire and auto shop while wearing the shop's uniform. According to the people who know me, I didn't get the scholarship and I took a job here. If you understand what I'm talking about then please respond; otherwise, I'm sorry to have bothered you."

"Well, we know what happened to Ben," Kenny said.

"Brandy, reply to Ben first, so he knows that he's not alone," Alex suggested.

"I was thinking the same thing," Brandy said before

27

clicking on the reply icon. She then typed out a message explaining what had happened. After sending her message, she checked her bank account. "Good news. Every cent I had is still there and not a penny more. Now while I'm on the computer, I'll book you two a flight to St. Louis. When do you two want to leave?"

"The sooner the better," Alex said.

"Okay, I'll book you and Doug on the first available flight," Brandy said before logging onto the site to book a flight. After a short time Brandy was looking over the flight schedules. "And the first available flight to St. Louis is at 3:00 P.M."

"Book it," Doug said.

"Okay, I'll book it and both of your tickets will be waiting at the airport when you get there," Brandy said before pressing a few buttons.

"Oh, Brandy, our last name in this reality is Larson," Alex said. "So book the flight using that last name."

"Okay," Brandy said.

"Why is your last name Larson?" Cindy asked.

"We haven't found that out yet, but I am working on knowing why," Alex said.

Doug pointed to the computer clock while saying, "Alex, we need to get going if we're going to make it to the airport by three."

"Brandy, thanks a lot for doing this," Alex said.

"You can thank me by finding Randy," Brandy said.

"I'll do my best," Alex said. "Oh; before Doug and I leave, I should give you the number to my cell phone." Brandy got out her cell phone and put in Alex's number. Brandy then gave everyone her number. "Bye, everyone."

"Bye," everyone said.

"And good luck," Cindy added.

Alex and Doug left Brandy's dorm.

Minutes later, as Alex and Doug were walking up to Alex's Jeep liberty, Doug said, "I'll let you drive this time."

"Fine," Alex said. Alex walked up to the driver's door. "We still need to find your Jeep at some point."

"As long as we have yours, we should be all right," Doug said before he and Alex climbed into the Jeep.

Several minutes later, as Alex and Doug waited at the airport for their flight, Alex read more of the diary. Alex was only able to read for a few minutes before she and Doug had to board the plane. After getting comfortable on the plane Alex again pulled out the diary to read.

Chapter Three

Minutes after Alex and Doug's plane landed they were walking into Lambert Airport. Melissa, Avery's sister and a worker at the airport saw them and briskly walked towards them.

When Melissa was a short distance away, she called out, "Alex! Doug!"

Alex and Doug stopped and turned around. As Melissa walked up to them, they gazed at Melissa as if she was a stranger.

Alex read her name tag before saying, "Hi... Melissa Hartman."

Melissa gave Alex a curious look while asking, "Are you okay?"

"Of course, Melissa. Why would you ask me if I'm okay?"

Melissa continued to give Alex a curious look while asking, "Since when have I become Melissa and not Aunt Melissa?"

Alex thought for a second before saying, "Oh that. I figured since I'm twenty-one now and was legally an adult, it would be okay to call you Melissa. But now as I say it, it really doesn't sound right, so I'll go back to Aunt Melissa."

"I prefer that you call me Aunt Melissa anyway. So why are you two here and not at Harvard where you two belong?"

Alex was trying to think of an answer when Doug said, "A friend of ours is turning twenty-one today and he really wants us here for his party. He even bought our plane tickets."

"Do your parents know that you two are here?" Melissa asked.

"It was really a last minute thing, so we didn't get the chance to say anything to them," Alex said.

"Our tickets are round trip, so we were only going to stay long enough to make an appearance; stay for a short time and then catch the next flight back to Boston," Doug added. "So I was thinking that telling our parents would be a waste of time anyway."

"Your parents are going to want to know that you two are in town."

"Since we aren't going to be here long enough to visit them, could you turn a blind eye to our visit?" Doug asked.

"No, sir!" Melissa quickly told him. "I want you or Alex to call your parents right this instant and let them know that you two are in town."

Alex pulled out her phone from her purse and said, "I'll call mom."

"Good," Melissa told her.

After calling her mom's cell phone, the phone went to voicemail. Alex left the message, "Mom, call me after you get this message. Doug and I are in St. Louis. We just got off the plane. We came home to wish a friend 'Happy Birthday', and then we're returning to Harvard. Bye." Alex hung up before facing Melissa again. "Mom's phone went straight to voicemail, and as you witnessed, I left a message explaining everything."

Melissa gave Alex a skeptical look before saying, "Just to be safe, call your dad."

"Fine," Alex said before dialing Avery's office. Within a few rings Tiffany answered the phone. "Tiffany, is my dad busy?"

"He's again with a patient," Tiffany said.

"Well, tell my dad that Doug and I are in St. Louis. We just got off the plane. We came home to wish a friend 'Happy Birthday', and then we're returning to Harvard."

"Okay, I'll give him the message, but he's going to flip when he gets it," Tiffany said.

"Okay thanks," Alex said.

"Is there anything else?" Tiffany asked.

"That's it for… " Alex was able to get out.

"Alex, I want to talk to Tiffany," Melissa interrupted with.

"Tiffany, Aunt Melissa is with me and she wants to talk to you." Alex then held out the phone for Melissa to take.

After taking the phone Melissa asked, "Tiffany, are you there?"

"I'm here. What's going on?"

"I'm not quite sure myself, but make sure my brother gets Alex's message," Melissa said.

"I will," Tiffany said.

"Bye." After Melissa hung up the phone she handed the phone back to Alex.

As Alex was putting her phone away, Doug asked, "So are we free to go and wish our friend 'Happy Birthday'?"

"Go," Melissa said.

Alex and Doug waved bye to Melissa before walking away. Melissa returned the wave and then skeptically watched as Alex and Doug walked away.

Alex and Doug walked up to the cab stop and stepped up to the first available cab. After getting in they told the cab driver the address.

Minutes later, the cab driver was pulling up in front of a house on Victoria Place. Once Doug paid the cab driver he and Alex got out.

As the cab driver was driving away Alex watched for a moment before saying, "Maybe we should have told him to wait."

Doug looked towards the cab before saying, "It's too late now." He and Alex then turned and walked towards the house.

Once Doug and Alex stepped up to the door, Doug pressed the doorbell.

After Randy's mother, Phyllis, opened the door, she saw Doug first and then Alex. As she looked at Doug again she asked, "Yes? May I help you?"

"Hi, Ms. Miller, you may not remember me, but my sister Alex and I are friends of Randy's."

Phyllis leaned against the doorjamb before asking, "You two know Randy?"

"We do," Doug said. "Is he here by any chance?"

"How is it that you two know him?" Phyllis asked.

Doug gestured towards Alex while saying, "Alex and I met Randy in first grade. All **three** of us had several classes together since then too."

"And what are your names **again**?"

"I'm Douglas Larson and **this** is my sister, Alexandra. Ms. Miller, it's very important that we talk to Randy."

"Well, I'm afraid you are three years too late," Phyllis said.

"What do you mean?" Alex quickly asked.

"A day after his high school graduation, he packed a bag with a few days worth of clean clothes and left. I haven't heard from him since."

"Did he say where he was going?" Doug asked.

"He never told me that he was leaving, but the last discussion Randy and I had before he disappeared was about him finding his dad. I thought I'd talked him out of it, but I'm sure that is what he left to do."

"Do you know where Randy's dad is?" Doug asked.

"No, I don't. I haven't seen or heard of Randy's dad since I told him that I was pregnant," Phyllis said.

Before Doug was able to ask another question, Alex said, "Thanks for the information, Ms. Miller. Doug and I should be on our way. Goodnight."

"Goodnight," Phyllis said before re-entering the house and shutting the door.

As Alex and Doug were slowly walking away, Doug said, "If you allowed me to ask a few more questions, I might've been able to get a clue to where he's at."

"Doug, I have a clue to where he's at."

"Where?" Doug quickly asked.

While the two were leisurely walking away from Phyllis's house, Alex said, "Two weeks before graduation, Randy told me that he had met someone who knew his father. Randy was told that his father lived in Mexico City, Mexico. I was the one who talked him out of going to Mexico. Chances are we never met in this reality, so I wasn't here to talk him out of it. In fact, the day I talked him out of going to Mexico was the same day he started doing research on alternate realities."

An amused grin came across Doug's face before he accused jokingly, "Oh, so our predicament is actually all your fault for talking Randy out of going to Mexico to find his dad."

Alex gave Doug a smirk before saying, "I'm so glad that you are enjoying this." Before anything else was said, Alex's phone rang. She glanced at the number before nervously answering the phone with, "Mom, hi. What's up?"

"Alex, where are you and your brother right now?" Beverly angrily asked.

"We are on a street named Victoria Place. I was about ready to call for a cab..."

"I'll come and get you two, so what is the address to the closest house to you?"

"Mom, we could be arrested for stalking if we wait here for you," Alex said while looking at Doug. "So why don't Doug and I wait for you at a restaurant?"

"What restaurant?!" Once Alex told Beverly the name of the closest fast food restaurant Beverly replied, "Okay, you two wait there and I'll be there as soon as I can. Bye."

"Bye," Alex said before cringing.

As Alex went to put her phone away, Doug said, "From what I heard from your side of the conversation that went better than I thought it would."

"I think she's saving it for when she sees us in person." Alex then gestured in the direction of the restaurant. "Well, we better get there before mom does."

While walking to the restaurant, Doug asked, "So how do we find Randy if he is in Mexico?"

"I think we'll have to go to there," Alex answered.

"I was scared that you were going to suggest that."

"Well, we have to find Randy, and the possibility of him being in Mexico City is the only lead we have."

"Well, before we do something drastic, like going to Mexico, I want to discuss it with Kenny, Brandy, Cindy and Ben first."

"Doug, this is not our reality and we need to do what is necessary to find Randy."

"We don't know for certain that Randy is even in Mexico City, and that is why I want to discuss it with the others."

"Fine, we can discuss it with the others and after we discuss it, I'm going to Mexico with or without you."

Doug sighed before asking, "And how are you going to get to Mexico? You certainly don't have the gas money to drive there."

"I'll figure something out," Alex assured him. Doug just shook his head in disbelief.

After getting to the restaurant, Alex and Doug each bought a soda. They sat at a table for fifteen minutes before Beverly walked in. Alex's back was to the entrance and when Doug saw Beverly, he gestured and said, "Mom's here."

When Alex and Doug walked up to Beverly, Beverly told them in an unhappy tone, "Let's go."

Before taking a step, Doug said, "Mom, I can..."

"Save it until we get home," Beverly sternly told him.

"Yes, Ma'am," Doug said before he, Alex and Beverly walked towards the exit.

No one talked during the ride home and they continued to remain quiet as everyone entered a two-story house. Alex walked in first followed by Doug and then Beverly. As they walked into the living room Alex and Doug saw Avery and Michelle watching TV. Michelle was Alex and Doug's sixteen-year-old sister and when they saw Michelle, they gazed at her as if they were seeing her for the first time.

Avery turned off the TV and as he was standing up, he said, "Michelle, your mom and I need to talk to Alex and Doug alone, so I need you to go to your room and do your homework."

"My homework's done."

"Then listen to your music CD's," Avery quickly told her.

Michelle said while standing, "Fine." As Michelle was walking towards the door, she looked at Alex and Doug. "I'm not sure if I want to hear this anyway."

After Michelle left the room, Avery gestured towards the couch while saying, "Sit down you two." Alex and Doug sat down. Alex placed her purse on the coffee table. "You two are going to blow any chances of graduating Harvard by skipping classes and taking plane trips to St. Louis."

"Whose idea was it for Doug and I to go to Harvard?" Alex asked.

"I suggested it, and you and Doug jumped on the suggestion," Avery shot back. "Any more smart remarks from either of you?"

Alex timidly said, "That wasn't meant to be a smart remark."

"Alex, you want to go to medical school like your mother and I did, but you'll blow that by skipping classes," Avery said. "So why are you here?"

"Didn't you get the message that I left with Tiffany?" Alex nervously asked.

"Your mother and I both got the same message, but your Aunt Melissa had a hunch and ran a check on who paid for the tickets, so we all know that the message you left was bogus. Oh and speaking of a message, why were you asking about a man name Nicholas Christopher O'Brien?"

When Doug saw Alex searching her thoughts for an excuse, he blurted out, "Alex and I have our reasons to believe that Nicholas Christopher O'Brien is our real dad."

"Who told you that?" Beverly demanded to know.

"Does it matter how we found out?" Doug questioned. "The fact is you two have been lying to us about who our father is."

Avery proclaimed loud enough for Michelle to hear, "Hey! I'm your father! I was in the hospital delivery room the day you and Alex were born! I contributed greatly for your education and your care providing! And I..."

Alex quickly stood up and interrupted with, "Dad, I don't think Doug meant for that to sound the way it did. We know you're our dad, but if Nicholas O'Brien is our biological dad then we have the right to know that. That's the reason why we're in St. Louis. We came back to find the truth about Nicholas O'Brien and we didn't ask either one of you because we didn't think you would tell us."

"Well, you two can stop looking for Nicholas O'Brien because you two will never find him," Beverly told Alex and

Doug.

"Why won't we?" Alex quickly asked.

Beverly took a breath before saying, "Alex; Doug, Nicholas was your biological dad; however, a month before I found out that I was pregnant with you two, he died."

"How did he die?" Doug asked.

"He was injured on the job and was taken to the hospital," Beverly began. "Within minutes after getting to the hospital he was given an injection that he was severely allergic to. Complications set in and he died from his allergies. To my surprise he had taken out a will and a life insurance policy on himself two months before and named me the sole beneficiary. The money I received was enough to help me stay in medical school. I met Avery two days before I found out I was pregnant with you two." Beverly looked at Avery with a heartfelt gaze. "Avery found out that I was pregnant at the same time when the doctor gave me the news, and he stuck by me without hesitation. Avery may not have been the one who got me pregnant with you two, but he is your dad."

"Doug and I have the right to know this," Alex said. "So why was this kept from us?"

Doug gave Alex a curious look as Beverly gestured towards Avery while saying, "This man is your dad. When you and Doug were born he and I agreed on that us being your parents was the only thing that mattered."

"No offense, Mom, but that wasn't your right or dad's right to decide that," Alex said.

"Alex, you know the truth now," Avery said. "So tell me, does knowing the truth change anything? Does it change who you are? Does it change the way you feel about me?"

"It doesn't change the way I feel about you, but it does change who I am. I mean, I have a heritage that I didn't know about, and you and mom tried to keep it from Doug and me.

That alone is wrong. A person needs to know where his or her ancestors came from."

"Alex, perhaps what your mom and I did wasn't the right thing to do," Avery began. "Up until now I thought it was the right thing, but now you actually have me second guessing myself on what would've been the right thing. Anyway, regardless of what the right thing was, we did it to give you and Doug two living parents who love you."

"Dad, even if you and mom had told Doug and me the truth ten years ago, we still would've had two living parents," Alex said. "Dad, we love you." Alex looked at Doug. "Right, Doug."

Doug gave Alex a slightly skeptical look before saying, "Of course." Doug then stood up. "Dad; Mom, since everything is out then perhaps Alex and I should be heading back to Boston."

Avery looked at his watch before saying, "A plane back to Boston doesn't leave for another five hours."

"I had chicken out to thaw for dinner, but that obviously won't be enough," Beverly said. "So how about we order a pizza?"

"Pizza's fine for me," Alex said.

"Same here," Doug added as Alex's phone rang.

Alex gestured towards her purse and said, "I should get that." Beverly just nodded. After Alex got the phone from her purse she looked at who was calling. "Trudy, hi. What's up?"

"Where are you?" Trudy quickly asked.

"I'm actually at home and standing in my living room."

"Your home is in St. Louis and you cannot be in St. Louis right now."

"Why can't I?"

"Because you have a date with my brother Miles in two hours, that's why you can't be."

"Trudy, I completely forgot about that," Alex said while trying to sound sincere.

"Alex, you have been asking me to fix you up with my brother since he and his girlfriend broke up three weeks ago, and when I do, you bail."

"I wasn't bailing I swear. Something personal and very important to me had come up."

"Well, you are the one who is going to call and explain things to Miles."

"Fine, I'll call. What is his number?"

"Alex, his number is stored on your phone."

"Yes, I forgot that too," Alex said while trying to sound convincing. "I'll talk to you later. Bye."

"Bye," Alex heard Trudy saying just before she hung up.

As Alex was scrolling through her phone numbers, Beverly asked, "What's going on?"

"Oh, uh, Trudy was just reminding me about a date I was supposed to have had tonight. Since I'm here, I have to reschedule my date." Alex gestured towards the hallway before she continued to say, "Well, I'm going to make this call in... in my room."

"Of course," Beverly said.

As Alex was walking out of the living room, she mumbled, "If I can find my room that is."

Alex walked upstairs and as she was looking around Michelle came out of her bedroom. She noticed right away that Alex was looking around as if she was lost and when Alex looked at her, Michelle asked, "Are you okay?"

"Don't I look okay?" Alex nervously asked.

"You seem... confused," Michelle answered as she stood by her door. "Even when you and Doug walked into the living room earlier, you acted as if you were seeing me for the first time."

Alex thought for a moment before saying, "Actually, I am confused. When you saw me I was thinking about how I am twenty-one years old, and... and I'm confused about the direction of where my life is going."

"What are you talking about?" Michelle quickly asked. "You had your life mapped out since you were seventeen. You'll go to Harvard and then you'll go to medical school to become a doctor like mom and dad."

"Most likely that is what I'll do, but I have been thinking, 'Is being a doctor is what I really want to do with my life.' What if my life was supposed to have been different?"

Michelle gave Alex a curious stare before asking, "Did you have a near-death experience or something? You're acting a bit strange."

"Not exactly a near-death experience, but very recently... in fact, it was this morning that I had this very vivid and intense dream. In this dream Mom was Mom. Doug was Doug, but someone else was Dad. Also in this dream, you weren't born."

"I now know why you gave me a strange look earlier."

"This is going to sound a little bizarre, but I still feel as if I'm in some kind of dream. So can you point out my bedroom to me?"

Michelle gave Alex a curious look. She then slightly laughed before saying, "You had me going there for a second."

Alex gestured to a bedroom door before saying as if only to make a joke out of it, "Oh, so my bedroom is still this one." In the same joking manner she gestured towards another room. "Or is it this one like it was in my dream?" Alex pointed to even another door. "Or perhaps it's this one?"

Michelle gestured towards a closet and said, "Try that one."

Alex opened up the door and looked in before playfully

saying, "This bedroom is very cramped. There's not even enough room for a bed. You wouldn't want to switch rooms with me, would you?"

Michelle grinned before gesturing towards Alex's bedroom and saying, "That's your bedroom."

Alex cautiously walked up to the door before saying, "You tricked me into thinking that the closet was my bedroom. So how do I know that this isn't a bathroom?"

"Well, I guess you'll have to just look and see," Michelle playfully said.

Alex opened the door and saw that it was a bedroom. The wall was painted in a rose color. She then jokingly said, "This isn't my bedroom. I remember the walls being a different color."

Alex was caught off guard when Michelle said, "Yeah, Dad painted your room a week after you went back to Harvard."

"Okay, I guess this is my room then."

Before Alex was able to walk into her bedroom, Michelle said, "Alex, thanks."

Alex gave Michelle a curious look before asking, "For what?"

"For treating me like someone you can joke around with. You never did that with me before."

Alex grinned before saying, "You're welcome." Alex then held up her phone. "Well I actually need to make a phone call. I'll see you in a few minutes."

Michelle grinned and nodded. As Michelle was walking away, Alex walked into her bedroom and shut the door. She then looked over the room for a short time before she turned her attention to her phone and scrolled through the numbers for Miles' number. When she found it she dialed it.

Miles answered his phone on the second ring. "Alex, you caught me just before I got into the shower. What's up?"

"Miles, I'm afraid I'm going to have to postpone our date for another day."

"Is there anything wrong?"

"It's too long of a story to go into over the phone, but I'm actually in St. Louis right now and the first flight back to Boston doesn't leave for another five hours. I know I should have called you sooner about this, but things around me got a little weird."

"I was actually thinking that dating this soon after Maria and I had broken up was too soon anyway, so us canceling the date might be a good thing."

"I wasn't calling to cancel," Alex quickly said. "I just want to postpone."

"Alex, I wasn't really ready for this date, so if it's all the same to you, I'd just rather cancel."

"If that's what you want. Bye." Once Alex ended the phone call she looked into the mirror. "I'm sorry, Alexandra. I didn't mean to ruin things for you." Alex was then slightly startled when someone knocked on the door. Alex rolled her eyes before facing the door. "Come in."

Doug walked in and as he shut the door he asked, "How are things?"

"Things are a slight mess. I tried to postpone the date with Miles, but I think Miles took it as a sign to completely cancel the date."

Doug gave Alex a concerned look before stepping up to her and saying, "Repeat after me. My name is Alexander O'Brien and not Alexandra Larson."

"I know who I am," Alex quickly said.

"Are you sure?" Doug skeptically questioned.

"Yes, I'm sure," Alex insisted.

"I'm not as certain as you are. In fact, it seems to me that you're confusing yourself with Alexandra."

"I'm not confusing myself with anyone," Alex quickly said. "Alex and Doug Larson are innocent bystanders and I just feel responsible for ruining their lives."

"Randy is responsible and as soon as we can find him, the sooner we can straighten this mess out."

"Randy being in Mexico is the only clue we have, but what if that clue doesn't pan out? What are we going to do if we don't find Randy?"

"Even if it takes us a while we'll find him."

"Well, until we do we need to learn who Alex and Doug Larson are, so we can minimize ruining their lives."

"How are we supposed to do that?"

"Well, while we're home... so to speak, I can get Alexandra's diaries. I doubt Doug of this reality would have a diary or a journal, but you can search his room and his computer... if he has a computer that is."

"I guess it wouldn't hurt to get to know the person I'm supposed to be. I'll go check out the room now." When Alex just nodded Doug turned and walked out.

Alex stood looking over the room for a few seconds before she walked over to the closet and opened it. There were very few clothes hanging in the closet. A few pairs of high-heel shoes were in the floor. A medium size box was on the shelf.

When Alex saw the box, she said, "Okay, Alexandra, let's see what you have here."

Alex took the box and placed it on the bed. She then opened it and looked in.

Inside the box were trivial items such as pictures of her and a guy she didn't recognize; three good size stuffed animals; several movie stubs and a few souvenirs from Disney Land and Six Flags.

"Okay, Alexandra, where are your diaries?" Alex's attention was then drawn to the door again when someone knocked. "Come in."

Beverly opened the door and walked in. When she saw that the box was on the bed and opened, she said, "There's a sight I didn't think I'd see for a while."

Alex gave Beverly a confuse look before asking, "What do you mean?"

"You told me that you never wanted to see those items from Seth again. You even tried to throw that box away, but I talked you out of it. And now you're looking at the items."

Alex gazed into the box while saying, "I'm just trying to remember things. Memories that were once vivid to me are no longer as clear." She then turned towards Beverly. "In fact, I want to get my diaries and re-read them."

Beverly gave Alex a concerned look while saying, "You are a little too young to be having memory problems."

"Oh, it's not that," Alex quickly said. "It's just that memories like when I got these items from Seth just seem a bit distant. This may sound a bit strange, but I just want to remember things as if they had happened yesterday. That's why I want to re-read my diaries."

"Okay, before I drive you and Doug to the airport, we will pack up your diaries and you can take them with you."

Alex gave Beverly a smile before saying, "Thanks for understanding."

"Well, I'm going to leave you to your memories. The pizza should be here in about twenty minutes."

Alex nodded while saying, "Okay."

Beverly grinned before she turned and walked out.

Alex took out a movie stub and stuck it in her pocket. She then put the box back on the shelf and left the room.

Chapter Four

At a coffee shop near Harvard, Kenny, Brandy and Cindy were sitting at the back table with their drinks. Brandy was on the phone while talking to Ben. When she hung up she said, "Well, Ben is leaving Atlanta and he'll be here as soon as he can."

"Which will be a waste of time for Ben to come here if Alex and Doug don't find Randy," Kenny said.

"Let's hope Randy is able to be found in this reality," Cindy said.

"Why wouldn't he be found in this reality?" Brandy asked.

"Last year, in our own reality I made a family tree and apparently so did the Cindy of this reality. Like me, Cindy of this reality still had the file on her flash disc, and earlier when I accessed the file, my baby brother Cory wasn't on the family tree; however, I did see that my mom had two younger brothers and no sisters. In our reality, my mom is the only child."

"I ran into similar situations earlier," Kenny said. "I called a friend's house and when his mom answered I asked to talk to my friend. In this reality my friend died at the age of two. I got an ear full before she slammed the phone down."

"I must be a boring person," Brandy said.

"Why would you say that?" Kenny asked.

"Earlier I scrolled through the school transcripts belonging to the Brandy of this reality and they're exactly the same in our reality. I placed a few phone calls to friends and old boyfriends. All of that is the same. I even have the same roommate. Me and the Brandy of this reality are so much alike that if it weren't for the lives around me being different, I wouldn't have known that I jumped into a whole new reality."

"If we can't get back to our own reality, perhaps you're the lucky one," Cindy said.

"Brandy, if it helps you to know this, my college life is pretty much the same in this reality as it was in our reality," Kenny said.

"Ditto," Cindy said.

"What I'm curious to know is how the 'We' of this reality are adjusting to our reality?" Brandy asked.

"They are probably completely confused and disoriented," Cindy said.

"Chances are they don't even have a clue as to how their reality got switched," Kenny said.

In the reality Alpha 0.0.0.0.0.0.0, at a hospital near Harvard University, Alexander O'Brien was heavily sedated and strapped to a bed.

Doug, Randy, Kenny, Brandy, Benjamin and Cindy were also at the hospital, and each one was held in a separate quarantine room.

Beverly and Nicholas O'Brien along with Phyllis Miller stepped out of a cab in front of the hospital and walked straight to the nurse's station. The waiting area was in view from the nurse's station. As the three stepped up, the nurse asked, "May I help you?"

"Yes, I'm Nicholas O'Brien and this is my wife Beverly and a neighbor of ours Phyllis Miller. Dr. Theodore Simon called my house and Phyllis' house and told us that it was urgent to get here as soon as possible. Dr. Simon also told us to ask for him when we arrived."

The nurse picked up the phone's handset while saying, "One moment please." She then dialed the phone. There was a short delay before she spoke again. "Dr. Simon; Nicholas and Beverly O'Brien and Phyllis Miller are standing in front of me and they're requesting to speak to you."

"Tell them to wait there and I'll be right down," Dr. Simon said.

"Yes, Doctor," the nurse said before hanging up. "Mr. and Mrs. O'Brien; Ms. Miller, Dr. Simon will be right down." She then gestured towards the chairs. "So you three can have a seat while you wait."

Beverly nodded while saying, "Thank you."

Beverly, Nicholas and Phyllis walked over to the waiting area and sat down. They sat quietly for ten minutes before Phyllis saw a doctor stepping up to the nurse's station.

When Phyllis saw the nurse pointing in her direction, she said, "I believe Dr. Simon is coming."

Beverly, Nicholas and Phyllis stood up once they saw Dr. Simon walking their way. When Dr. Simon stepped up, Dr. Simon introduced himself with a handshake for each of them while starting with Nicholas.

"I'm Nicholas," he said before pointing out the others. "This is my wife Beverly and Randy's mother, Phyllis. Phyllis is also a friend of ours."

Once the handshakes were done, Phyllis said, "Dr. Simon, I understand that our sons are here somewhere, but no one will tell us more than that."

"Please come with me and I will explain on the way." As everyone walked towards the elevator Dr. Simon continued to say, "Alexander, Douglas and Randy along with four others Kenny Johnson, Brandy Harrison, Cindy Hartford and Benjamin Bell had all passed out in Harvard's library. This greatly concerned the librarian and he called nine-one-one. By the time the paramedics got there all seven of them were awake and very disoriented. Alexander was the worst of the seven. He was delirious and had to be sedated."

"In what way was he delirious?" Beverly asked.

As they stepped up to the elevators, Dr. Simon pressed the call button before saying, "According to the paramedics and the police, he was raving about that he was a she, and somehow she fell into the twilight zone and became a he."

"Alex woke up thinking that he was once a she?" Nicholas asked.

"He did, but that's just half of it," Dr. Simon said.

"What's the other half?" Beverly asked.

"Douglas also shares Alexander's delusion and the other five have delusions of their own."

"What are Randy's delusions?" Phyllis asked.

"The only thing we can get out of Randy is that he doesn't know how he got to Harvard and that he doesn't know any of the others. The others also claim they don't know Randy."

"Alex and Randy have been best friends since the first grade," Beverly said.

The door to the elevator opened and everyone stepped in. As Dr. Simon pressed the button for the correct floor, he said, "Well, we had video taped Douglas, Randy and the other four, and you can see for yourselves the extent of their delusions."

As the door was closing Nicholas asked, "Do you know what caused them to faint and what is causing their delusions?"

"We are still looking into that," Dr. Simon said. "We did test them for drugs and they all tested clean, so the possibility of drugs is out."

"Could there be something in the air?" Phyllis asked.

"There was nothing toxic in their system either, so something in the air is not likely."

"So what is going to happen to them?" Beverly asked.

"I would like to keep them in the hospital for seventy-two hours for observation. We can discuss my recommendation once that time is up. Mrs. O'Brien…"

"You can call me Beverly."

"Okay, I will. Beverly, are you a doctor in St. Louis?"

"No, but I did attend two years of medical school. I got pregnant with Alex and Doug, and I had to drop out. I didn't have the money to finish medical school after they were born."

"According to Douglas, you are a surgeon at a hospital and that you are married to a doctor named Avery Larson."

"Where am I supposed to be?" Nicholas asked.

"Douglas claims that he doesn't know who you are," Dr. Simon said.

"So in his delusions I was replaced by a fictional character," Nicholas said.

"Dr. Avery Larson is not a fictional character," Dr. Simon said. "He has a private practice in St. Louis. I would also like to get him out here and see what his role is in Douglas' delusion."

"If you think that would help then by all means do it," Beverly said.

The elevator stopped and everyone exited.

In the reality Alpha 0.0.0.1.0.0.0 at 11:55 P.M., Alex sat on her bed at Harvard and was writing out the events of the day along with writing a detailed explanation of what happened. After writing for several minutes she put the diary up and went to bed.

Friday, October 22 at 8:30 A.M., Alex, with no makeup on, was casually eating breakfast in Harvard's lunchroom while reading one of her diaries. Her plate was more than half full with her breakfast. Her purse and book bag were on the table beside her.

Miles was carrying his food tray towards the tables and saw Alex sitting at one of them. As he stepped up to her, he said, "Alex, hi."

Alex looked up and stared at Miles as if he was a stranger before saying, "Oh hi." Alex turned her attention back to the diary.

Miles gave Alex a confused look for a second before saying, "Oh I get it. You're giving me the cold shoulder treatment."

Alex looked up and replied, "I'm sorry, I was reading. What was that you said?"

"I get it, Alex. You're mad at me for not rescheduling our date."

Alex looked at Miles while trying to figure out who he was. It suddenly dawned on her who she was talking to. "Miles. Uh, I'm not mad at all, but I am reading here."

"Alex. Maria and I dated for four years and I just can't move on after being broken up for only three weeks."

"You don't have to explain, Miles. It's fine. Now if you don't mind, I am trying to read."

Miles looked at the book that Alex was reading before saying, "What you're reading looks like a diary."

"It's one of my diaries from a few years ago. I'm trying to remember certain details. Now if you don't mind, I would like to be left alone."

"You say you're not mad, but you're not inviting me to eat breakfast with you either. If that is not giving me the cold shoulder then I don't know what is."

"Miles, I don't want any company this morning. Not yours; not anyone's. And I swear I wasn't mad at you, but now I'm starting to be."

"Okay, Alex. If you want to be left alone then I'll certainly do that," Miles said before turning and walking away.

Alex watched Miles for a second before turning her attention back to her diary.

Miles walked over to a table that was several tables from

Alex and as he was taking his seat, Trudy walked into the room and saw him by himself. She then saw Alex at a nearby table.

Trudy walked over to Miles and said, "I understand that last night was a bust, but the least you can do is talk to Alex."

"I tried. She doesn't want anything to do with me."

"That doesn't sound like Alex."

Miles gestured towards Alex while saying, "Well go talk to her and see for yourself."

"Okay, I will," Trudy said before turning and walking towards Alex. Without saying a word, Trudy sat down in a seat across from Alex.

Alex looked up from her diary and when she saw who it was she said, "Trudy, I really want to be left alone right now if you don't mind."

"Actually, I do mind. You have been acting weird since yesterday and I'm worried about you."

"I know I have been acting a bit out of character, but..."

"A bit out of character?" Trudy quickly echoed. "That's an understatement. You're not even wearing makeup and that alone is out of character for you."

"Trudy, please just give me some space, and I'm sure I'll be back to my normal self in no time."

"Alex, we have been friends since our freshman year. I'll admit we weren't close friends right away, but I think... or at least I thought that we were becoming close friends. I know I think of you as a close friend, and if there's anything troubling you, you can always come to me."

"Thanks, Trudy, but what is going on with my life right now, I really need to solve it on my own. Now if you don't mind, I'm trying to read."

Trudy looked at what Alex was reading before asking, "Isn't that one of your diaries?"

"It is. I'm trying to refresh my memory from a few years

ago and I can't read with distractions. That is why I would like to be left alone."

As Trudy stood up she said, "All right, but the only important memory that you need to remember is what happened on February 3, 2010."

Trudy noticed that Alex was acting uncomfortable before she replied, "Yeah; yeah, I doubt that I will ever forget that day."

Trudy gave Alex a perplex look for a second before saying, "Well, I'm going to join Miles. Hey, don't you have a history class in twenty minutes."

"I do. I'm going to read for another ten minutes before I go."

"I just thought I would remind you. I'll see you later." Trudy then turned and walked away.

Seconds later, as Trudy was taking a seat next to Miles, Miles asked, "So is she giving me the cold shoulder treatment as I suspect?"

"I don't think that's her problem. I think she is having memory problems."

"Why do you think that?"

"As a joke, I mentioned a bogus date as being an important date to remember and she tried to play it off as if she knew what I was referring to."

"Perhaps she was going along with your joke."

"I don't think so," Trudy said before standing up again. "Hey, I'm going to the library and research what would cause a person as young as Alex to lose her memory."

As Trudy was leaving, Miles said, "Bye."

Trudy just waved as she walked away.

Minutes later, Alex dumped half of her breakfast in the trashcan before leaving for her classroom. A short time later, she and Kenny were approaching their classroom at the same time.

Before Alex was able to step into the classroom, Kenny asked, "So what happened last night in St. Louis? Were you and Doug able to find Randy?"

"Things could have gone better last night, and no, we couldn't find Randy. Doug and I have a clue as to where he might be though. We'll go over everything when the group is together."

"Where do you think he might be?"

"I'm thinking he is in Mexico City, Mexico."

"Why do you think that?"

"Three years ago in our reality I talked him out of going there to search for his dad. I think he went there in this reality."

Kenny said sarcastically, "That's just great. How are we going to get to him if he's in Mexico City?"

"All of us or at least one of us will have to go there and bring him back."

"You can't be serious!"

"He is the only person who can straighten this crossed reality mess out. So it's either go to Mexico and find Randy or we live in this reality for the remainder of our lives. In either case, we'll have to worry about that later." Alex gestured towards the classroom as she continued to say, "This is my class and it's getting ready to start."

"It's my class too," Kenny said before gesturing towards the door. "Ladies first." Alex grinned, shook her head and rolled her eyes all at the same time before walking into the classroom. Kenny followed her in. "Oh, uh, Ben arrived last night. He checked into a motel."

"That's good," Alex said as she and Kenny were walking up to two empty seats that were next to each other.

Soon after Alex and Kenny sat down and got settled in their seats Kenny saw Doug walking into the classroom. Kenny gestured towards Doug while saying, "It seams that you and Doug took the same courses in this reality also."

Alex stared at Doug while saying, "So it seems."

Doug saw Alex and Kenny and walked towards them. As Doug stepped up, he said, "I spoke with Brandy and Cindy. All of us are to meet Ben at the Little Bucks Bar and Grill at eleven o'clock."

"Okay, I'll be there," Kenny said.

"Ditto," Alex said.

"Well, I better take a seat," Doug said before turning and walking towards an empty seat.

An hour later, Alex, Doug and Kenny were leaving the classroom. Trudy was waiting in the hall outside the classroom while holding papers. When she saw Alex, she stepped up to her and asked, "Alex, can I speak to you in private?"

Alex gave Trudy a curious look. She then turned towards Doug and said, "Doug, I'll catch up to you and Kenny in an hour."

"All right," Doug said before he and Kenny walked away.

As Alex and Trudy were casually walking in the opposite direction, Trudy said, "I believe I know why you are reading your old diaries and why you aren't acting like yourself."

Alex gave Trudy a curious look before asking, "You do?"

"You're having memory problems, and I have done some research as to what could cause it," Trudy said before she held up the papers. "Here is what I found."

Alex continued to give Trudy a curious look while asking, "Where did you get the idea that I'm having memory problems?"

"Alex, February 3, 2010 was an ordinary day," Trudy pointed out. "There's nothing special to remember about that day. I said what I did as a joke and you acted as if you were hiding the fact that you couldn't remember what took place on that day."

"Okay, I'll admit that I thought I had forgotten something when you mentioned that day, but I don't have memory problems."

"Okay, then you won't have any problems with answering a few of my questions."

"Trudy, I'm not going to play twenty questions with you."

"If you're not having memory problems then these will be easy questions."

"Trudy, I'm not answering any questions. In fact, I'm going to end this discussion and walk away." Alex then turned and walked in the opposite direction.

Trudy watched Alex for a second before yelling after her, "Admitting that there is a problem is the first step at getting help."

Alex just waved as she continued to walk away.

Trudy turned and went straight to the soccer field. She watched Miles for twenty minutes as he was practicing at stopping the soccer ball from entering the goal.

Miles knew that Trudy was watching and when he took a break he walked over to her.

When Miles stepped up, Trudy said, "You look like a natural goalie. I think the coach was right to put you in that position."

"Since you don't care too much about sports, I doubt that you came here to talk about me being a goalie."

"I came here to get your help."

"Help with what?"

"Alex will confide in you if you talk to her."

"Confide in me about what?"

"Alex is having memory problems, but she denies it. If anyone can get her to admit to it, it's you."

"With what happened earlier, you think she'll confine in

me?"

"I know Alex. She had a crush on you for a while now, so I'm thinking…"

"Wait a second," Miles quickly interrupted with. "How long has Alex had a crush on me?"

"I promised Alex that I wouldn't tell you this, but she liked you even before she started dating Stephen Keith. Alex would never tell you this because you were with Maria."

"I can't believe Alex liked me for that long and I didn't know."

"Well she did, and I think you're the only one who can get Alex to admit she has a problem with her memory."

"I'll be here for another thirty minutes. I'll try to talk to her after that."

"Thank you."

"Well, I just hope she doesn't blow me off the way she did this morning."

"I don't believe she will. So, are you ready for your first game as a goalie this evening?"

"I'll be ready," Miles said before gesturing towards the water cooler. "Well I'm going to get some water before my break is over." When Trudy nodded, Miles turned and walked away.

11:00 A.M. at Little Bucks Bar and Grill, Alex and Doug were walking in. Alex was noticing a 'help wanted' sign for a waiter or waitress at the moment when Doug saw Kenny, Cindy, Brandy and Ben at a back table.

Doug gestured to the table and said, "Alex, this way."

Without responding Alex turned away from the 'help wanted' sign and followed Doug to the table.

Alex took a seat next to Brandy, and after getting comfortable she saw that Brandy was giving her a curious look. Alex gave Brandy a confused look while uttering, "What?"

"Oh… uh, I was just noticing that you had makeup on yesterday, but you're not wearing any today," Brandy said.

"Yesterday I joined this reality after Alex had put on her makeup, and since I'm a guy in our reality, I don't know anything about putting on any makeup," Alex answered. "I probably look worse than a cheap whore if I would attempt to put some on."

"I could always teach you how to put on makeup."

Before Alex was able to answer, Doug said, "I don't mean to interrupt girl talk, but we have more important issues to discuss than Alex learning how to put on makeup."

Alex whispered to Brandy, "I'll consider it."

As Ben stirred his coffee, he asked, "Does anyone know where Randy is?"

"Alex and I have a clue to where he might be; however, that clue is a weak one," Doug said.

"What is the clue?" Cindy asked.

"Three years ago in our reality, and I'm thinking in this reality also, Randy was told that his long lost dad was in Mexico City, Mexico," Alex began. "In our reality I had talked him out of going to Mexico in search of his dad, but I think he did go there in this reality."

"Do we wait here and see if Randy will look for us?" Ben asked.

"Alex thinks we should go to Mexico and look for him," Doug said.

"And that would be a waste of time if he's not in Mexico," Cindy said.

"Well, we have to start looking somewhere, and Mexico is the only clue we have," Alex said.

"How do you propose that we get to Mexico?" Ben asked.

"I'm open to suggestions," Alex said.

"Since driving would take too long, we would have to

charter a plane," Brandy said.

"Where are we going to get the money to charter a plane?" Ben asked.

"We need to find out how much it will cost first, and then go from there," Brandy said.

"When we leave here we can search the internet for Charter companies," Kenny said.

Alex saw a waitress approaching and as she stared at the waitress she said, "Meanwhile I'm going to get something to eat."

Everyone turned and looked at the waitress as she stepped up. She pulled out her writing tablet and asked, "What can I get everyone?" One by one they gave the waitress their food and drink order. After the last one was done, the waitress put her tablet away. "I'll be back with your drink order." The waitress then turned and walked away.

As the waitress walked away, Doug asked, "Alex, have you learned anything interesting while reading Alexandra's diaries?"

"I've been learning quite a bit from the diaries actually. One important thing I learned is that Alexandra was a very unpleasant person to be around in high school."

"Why do you say that?" Doug asked.

"I have been reading about when Seth and Alexandra dated back in high school, and Alexandra took Seth for granted," Alex began. "She would cancel dates so she could go to parties with certain friends. Seth finally dumped Alexandra when he caught her at a party after telling him that she was sick."

"Was Alexandra always like that?" Cindy asked.

"Actually, she became like that after becoming friends to four girls in her high school sophomore year. Losing Seth as her boyfriend actually woke Alexandra up a little on how she was treating people. She dumped those four friends and tried to make amends with her old friends."

"At least Alexandra realized at what she was doing was wrong," Kenny said.

"Well, unfortunately most of her unpleasantness took place in her senior year, so she wasn't able to make amends with all of her old friends before everyone went off to college. There was one person in particular she wanted to make an amends with, but she was unable to."

"Let me guess; that particular person is Seth," Cindy said.

"No, actually the person is a girl named Jennifer," Alex corrected. "Jennifer and Alexandra had been friends since kindergarten. Alexandra became hateful towards Jennifer in the beginning of their junior year and before Alexandra started making amends to people Jennifer moved away."

"And I doubt that Jennifer would've let Alexandra know as to where she had moved to," Brandy said.

"Exactly," Alex said. "I found pictures of Alexandra and Jennifer together in Alexandra's wallet so I know what Jennifer looks like if I ever see her."

"That's good," Cindy said.

"It is," Alex agreed. "Anyway, let's talk about something else." Cindy grinned before she started a new topic.

The group had a casual conversation before and after the food arrived. Alex was only able to eat half of what she had ordered before getting full and pushing her plate away. After everyone was done eating, the group paid for the meal and went back to campus.

The group was walking towards the entrance of the dormitory when Miles saw Alex. As Miles was stepping up to the group he looked into the faces of the others before saying, "Alex, I would like to talk to you."

Alex looked at her group while saying, "Hey, guys, I'll catch up with everyone after I speak to Miles."

"All right," Doug said.

As the group walked away Alex looked at Miles and asked, "So what do you want to talk to me about?"

Miles glanced at the departing group before focusing on Alex and saying, "Trudy came to me and expressed her concerns about you..."

"Stop right there," Alex quickly interrupted with. "If this is about me having memory problems then I'm leaving right now."

"Alex, you have to admit that your memory hasn't been reliable for the past twenty-four hours."

"There is an explanation for that," Alex quickly said. Miles gave her an inquisitive look. "But I can't tell you what it is."

"Why can't you?" Miles quickly questioned.

"Miles, I'm going to rejoin my friends, so I'll talk to you later."

Before Alex had the chance to walk away, Miles asked, "Since when have you and your brother been hanging out with those four people?"

Alex gave Miles a curious look before asking, "Why are you concerned about that?"

"I'm not concerned about it. It's just that... I've never seen you even talking to any of those four people before. And that one guy I've never even seen before."

"Most likely you're referring to Benjamin, and we all do know each other. Now if you'll excuse me, I'm going to rejoin them."

"Alex, why won't you talk to me?" Miles quickly asked.

"Because you want to discuss topics that I won't discuss with you or Trudy," Alex said before turning. While walking away she said, "Bye, Miles."

Miles watched Alex for a second before he turned and went to the lunchroom.

Trudy and three women were sitting at a table eating when Miles stepped up to the table. When Trudy noticed him stepping up she asked, "What's up?"

Miles gestured towards an empty table while asking, "Can we sit at that table over there?"

Trudy looked at her group and said, "I'll see everyone later."

"See you," the three said.

Trudy got up with her food tray and followed Miles to the table. As Trudy and Miles were taking their seats, Trudy asked, "What's going on?"

Once Miles was seated, he faced Trudy while saying, "I briefly talked to Alex and she definitely won't confide in me as to what is going on with her. Whatever is going on with her, I have a feeling that it's not her memory like you suspect."

"Why don't you think it's her memory?"

"When I was talking to Alex, the vibe I picked up from her felt as if I was talking to a complete stranger."

Trudy grinned and asked, "You think Alex was replaced by an imposter?"

"Okay, I know it sounds ridiculous, but when I talked to her within just those few minutes, it just felt as if I wasn't talking to the same Alex who you and I know. She and Doug are even hanging out with four people who they normally don't hang out with. Three of them I've seen around campus, but I've never seen the fourth one before."

"Well, I still think that her problem is her memory, and I feel that we both need to confront her about it at the same time."

"Alex will just walk away again like she did before."

"Then we won't give her a chance to."

"How will we do that?"

"You and I will wait in my dorm. Alex has to return

sometime and when she does we won't let her leave until she admits that she has a problem."

"When do you want us to do this?"

"We can start now and we will wait all night if we have to."

"Trudy, both of us have classes."

"I have two classes this afternoon and I'll skip them if I have to. I want you to skip whatever classes you have."

"Well, I have a game at seven that I can't miss, so I can only stay for a few hours."

"Fine; I just hope Alex will return before you have to leave." Trudy then stood up. "Well, we might as well go wait for her now." Miles stood up and walked alongside Trudy as they walked away from the table.

Chapter Five

In Brandy's dorm, Brandy was talking on the phone and inquiring about charter planes to Mexico City. Alex, Doug, Kenny, Cindy and Ben were listening to Brandy's side of the conversation.

When Brandy hung up, Cindy asked, "So how much for a round-trip charter plane to Mexico City?"

"It cost six times more money than what I have in the bank," Brandy said.

"Where are we going to get the rest of the money?" Cindy asked.

"All of us will have to get jobs," Kenny said. "Also the time it takes to earn the money will give Randy the time to come to Harvard; if he's coming that is."

"We don't even know who's hiring," Cindy said.

"I saw a 'help wanted' sign for a waiter or a waitress at Little Bucks," Alex said. "I can apply for that position."

"Do you know anything about waiting tables?" Kenny asked.

"Actually I do," Alex said. "I worked as a waiter for four years back in St. Louis."

"You can't put that down on your job application though," Doug pointed out.

"I can still fill out the job application," Alex said.

"Alex, before you fill out any job applications and go on any interviews, you need to put on some makeup," Brandy strongly suggested.

"Fine," Alex agreed. "I'll go back to my dorm, see what Alexandra has for nice clothes, put an outfit on and then come back here for you to help me with my makeup."

"Alex, put on a dress, and not slacks and a blouse," Cindy said.

"I'll see what Alexandra has," Alex said. She then turned and walked out.

Minutes later, as Alex walked into her dorm room, Trudy and Miles got up from their seats and gave her a serious stare.

Alex, with a confused expression across her face, looked back and forth from Trudy to Miles just before Trudy said, "Good, you're here."

Alex continued to give Trudy a confused look while asking, "What's going on?"

"This is an intervention," Trudy said.

Alex continued to give Trudy a confused look while asking, "Excuse me?"

"Alex, you have a memory problem and I'm not going to let you leave this dorm until you admit to it," Trudy said.

"Trudy; Miles, I appreciate your concern over my welfare, but there's nothing wrong with me," Alex insisted. "And I really don't have time for this. I'm going to my room, change clothes and leave."

"You're not leaving this dorm, and when you do leave it, it will be to see a doctor about your memory loss," Trudy said.

"You think you'll be able to stop me from leaving?" Alex asked.

Trudy crossed her arms while saying, "There's no way that you'll be able to get passed Miles and me, so you might as well start admitting that you have a problem so you can get help."

"I can let out a bloodcurdling scream and when people come to investigate, I'll leave then."

"You would scream?" Miles asked.

Alex nodded as Trudy said in a convincing tone, "Scream as much and as loud as you want. No one will pay any attention to it. They'll just think it's paranoid Betty seeing her shadow again."

Alex thought for a brief moment before saying, "I doubt that my scream would sound anything like paranoid Betty."

"Alex, paranoid Betty is a forty-year-old woman who is presently living next door to my parents, and if you weren't having memory problems like you claim then you would have remembered that," Trudy pointed out.

"How can I convince you and Miles that I don't have memory problems along with getting you to stop testing me like you are?"

"Actually, I'm the only one who thinks that you have memory problems. Miles thinks that you are an imposter."

Alex slightly chuckled before questioning, "Me, an imposter? You two can check my DNA and run my fingerprints. I'm Alex. Now if you two will excuse me, I'm going to my room, change my clothes and then I'm going to go to Little Bucks Bar and Grill to apply for a job."

"You're going to apply for a job at where Stephen Keith works?" Trudy asked.

"Nice try," Alex quickly said. "But I'm not falling for your memory test this time."

"Alex, Trudy wasn't testing you this time," Miles said. "Stephen is a cook there."

"So far, you're zero for three," Trudy said. "So is Miles right or am I right? Are you having memory problems?"

Alex stared at Trudy as if she was scared to even say anything else. After a long pause she sighed before she finally said, "I swear that I don't have any memory problems, and I'm not an imposter… exactly."

"What do you mean by 'exactly'?" Miles asked.

"You or Trudy won't believe me, so it would be a waste of time to even say anything," Alex told him.

"Let us be the judge of what we'll believe," Trudy said.

"Okay," Alex said. "Have either of you ever heard of the multiple realities theory?"

"Of course, but what does that have to do with anything?" Miles asked.

"A friend of mine, Randy Miller, was obsessed with proving that theory, and yesterday he did; except there was one flaw in his thinking."

"What was his flaw?" Miles asked.

"He thought that a wormhole would open up after he activated a remote that he designed, and whoever wanted to visit an alternate reality would jump in, but apparently it doesn't work that way."

"How does it work then?" Miles asked.

Alex cringed before saying, "I am Alex, but I'm not the Alex from this reality." Trudy and Miles gave Alex a concerned look as Alex continued to say, "After Randy activated his remote to create a wormhole, I and the Alex of this reality switched bodies. Miles; Doug and the four who were with me earlier had also switched bodies, and they are friends of mine from my reality."

"You can't be serious," Trudy said.

"I told you that you wouldn't believe me, but I'm telling you the truth," Alex said. "When Alex of this reality passed out yesterday that was when we switched bodies. I don't have certain memories because in my reality my life took a totally different path."

Trudy gave Alex a skeptical look as Miles said, "Trudy, I'm not sure why, but I believe her. So, Alex, which one of those two men is Randy?"

"Neither. We don't know for sure where Randy is, but we

do have a clue that he is in Mexico City, Mexico. And to correct this cross reality mix up, finding Randy is our only hope."

"Why do you believe he's in Mexico?" Miles asked.

"Three years ago in my reality Randy was told that his long lost dad was there and I talked him out of going there to look for him," Alex said. "The Alex from this reality never met Randy, so I believe no one was around to talk him out of going."

"Why did you go to St. Louis last night?" Miles asked.

"Randy is also from St. Louis. I went to his house and talked to his mom. His mom was the one who gave me the clue that Randy is in Mexico."

"Alex, can I talk to you in private for a second?" Trudy asked.

"Let's go to my bedroom," Alex said. "You can help me pick out an outfit."

"Okay," Trudy said.

Alex stepped into her room followed by Trudy. Once the door was shut behind Trudy, Alex asked, "So what do you want to talk to me about?"

"I'm still partially skeptical of you being from an alternate reality…"

"Trudy, that's actually understandable. I would be skeptical too if I was in your shoes."

"Speaking of shoes that you are in; yesterday after you came to you practically went hysterical. You were actually shocked to be a woman."

"Yeah," Alex nervously said while fidgeting. "I was really hoping that you would have forgotten that part."

"So in the other reality, were you a guy?"

"I was. In my reality my name is Alexander. Just put green eyes and red hair on Doug and that would be pretty close to what I had looked like."

"Interesting."

"Trudy, I'm no good about picking out women's clothes to go look for a job, so I was wondering if you can help me."

"Don't you need to go to Mexico and look for Randy?"

"My friends and I don't have any money to get to Mexico and the only way to get money is for us to get jobs. Besides, Randy could be on his way here to find us. The time that it will take for us to collect the money will actually give Randy the chance to get here."

"Okay, I understand your reasoning for wanting a job, but the Alex from this reality and Stephen once dated."

"I actually knew that part from reading the diaries."

"And you still want to apply for a job there?"

"That's the only place I know that's hiring. Besides, I know who Stephen is, so I think I can handle it."

"Okay; well let's see what clothes you have." Just as Alex and Trudy began browsing through the clothes, Trudy said, "Alex, you actually do look good without any makeup, but while applying for a job, you may want to put some on. I can help you."

"I actually have someone who is going to help me with that, but thanks for the offer."

"You're welcome. Oh and in case you don't know you do have a class in two hours."

"I actually did know, but thanks for reminding me."

"No problem."

Alex and Trudy looked at a few dresses before Alex agreed to wear a blue one.

After Alex put on the dress, she saw Trudy holding up a pair of high-heeled shoes that matched the dress. Alex looked at Trudy as if she had lost her mind before saying, "I hope you don't plan on me wearing those."

"What's wrong with these shoes?"

"You mean besides the fact that I will fall and break my neck in them?"

"Ah, I see your point, but unfortunately, Alex of this reality was big on wearing high-heeled shoes, so besides her one pair of tennis shoes, high-heeled shoes are all you have."

"Nice," Alex sarcastically said. "Any suggestions?"

"Yeah, put these shoes on and walk around the room and let's hope you're a natural at wearing them."

"I guess it's better to learn in front of you rather than trying to wear them in front of the other people," Alex said while reaching out for the shoes.

After Alex put on the shoes she walked around the room to get comfortable at wearing them. Once she felt as though she wouldn't fall, she left the bedroom.

Miles was sitting on the couch and when he saw Alex stepping in, he stood up and exclaimed, "Wow! You look amazing."

Alex grinned before saying, "Thanks. Well, I better get going. Oh, Trudy, before I go, do you know where Doug's Jeep is parked?"

Trudy amusingly grinned before saying, "I do."

After Alex was told where to find Doug's Jeep, she left for Brandy's dorm.

Thirty minutes later, Alex approached the counter at Little Bucks. Eric, the man working behind the counter, asked as she stepped up, "What can I get you?"

Stephen looked out from the kitchen and saw Alex. He strained to hear as Alex said, "I saw the 'help wanted' sign and I want to apply for the job."

"Okay," Eric said before reaching underneath the counter for an application and a pen. As he handed the items to Alex he continued to say, "Sit down at one of the tables and fill it out.

Victor will most likely interview you after you finish."

"Okay, thanks," Alex said before turning and walking towards the first table. After Alex took her seat and was preparing to fill out the application, she saw Stephen walking up.

As Stephen stepped up he demanded to know, "What do you think you're doing?"

"How am I doing? I'm doing fine. How are you doing?"

"That's not what I asked and you know it."

"Actually what you asked is really none of your business, but if you must know I think I'm going to apply for the waitress position."

"Isn't serving customers beneath you?"

"I'm not the same person you knew several weeks ago. Now if you'll excuse me, I have an application to fill out."

"I would say good luck with getting the job, but you're going to need a miracle more than luck after I talk with Victor."

"I'm flattered that you are scared to be around me..."

"What do you mean I'm scared to be around you?" Stephen interrupted with.

"Obviously you still have feelings for me if you're planning to sabotage me from getting the job, but I'm not interested at getting back together with you."

"You're flattering yourself."

"Then why would it bother you by me applying for a job here? I'm willing to forget the past and move on. How about you? Unless you still have feelings for me that you're too scared for me to see."

"Go ahead and apply here, and instead of me trying to stop you from working here, I'm going to put in a good word for you."

Alex grinned before saying, "Thanks..." A slightly worried

expression came across her face. "I think."

Becky entered the restaurant and saw Stephen as he was walking away from Alex. She then walked directly to Alex's table and sat down across from her.

Alex looked up from trying to fill out the application. She gazed at Becky as if Becky was a stranger before she asked, "May I help you?"

Becky stared at the application while saying, "You're filling out a Little Bucks job application."

"I can't get anything passed you," Alex sarcastically said.

"If you're here to try to win Stephen back it's not going to work." Alex gave Becky a curious look as Becky continued to say, "He's with me now."

It dawned on Alex of who she was talking to and mumbled, "Oh, Becky."

Becky didn't quite hear Alex and asked, "What was that?"

"Becky, I'm only here to get a job, and I would still be applying for this job even if Stephen wasn't working here."

"And you expect me to believe that?"

"I'm pretty sure I stopped caring about what you believe a month ago."

"Stephen and I are talking marriage, so you don't have a chance you know."

"And I'm happy for you and all of the little Keiths who'll be running around in a few years, but I'm only here to work."

"Oh Stephen and I discussed that. Neither one of us want any kids."

Alex gave Becky a curious look before asking, "Did Stephen tell you that he didn't want any kids?"

Becky slightly hissed, "I just said he did!"

"When Stephen and I first started dating he told me different. Oh well, he must have changed his mind about the six kids he told me that he wanted to have."

Becky nervously said, "No-no; Stephen and I discussed this thoroughly. You wanted three or four kids, and that was what frightened him while he was dating you. That was one of the many reasons that he broke up with you and started dating me."

"All right, whatever you say, but that's not how I remember it. Of course my memory hasn't been reliable lately, so you're probably right. Well, in any case I wish you and Stephen the best of luck. Now if you'll excuse me, I want to finish filling out this application."

Becky stood up and as she briskly walked towards the counter, Alex had a big grinned on her face.

Becky stepped up to Eric and demanded, "Let Stephen know I'm here and I want to see him ASAP."

Eric gave Becky a curious look before saying, "I'll tell him." Eric then turned and walked into the kitchen.

When Eric stepped out of the kitchen followed by Stephen, Becky gave Stephen a serious look while demanding to know, "Did you lie to me about not wanting any kids?!"

Eric's attention was focused on Becky and Stephen. Stephen gave Becky a perplex look while asking, "What are you talking about?"

"I just had an eye opening conversation with Alex, and…"

"Whoa-whoa, stop right there. You and Alex were talking?"

"We were and according to her, you want six kids." When Stephen busted out laughing Becky demanded to know, "What's so funny?"

"Becky, Alex manipulated you. You confronting me about having kids was exactly what Alex wanted you to do and you played right into her hands."

Becky shot Alex a fiery look before saying, "It seems that I underestimate how manipulative Alex could be." Becky turned back towards Stephen. "I'm not comfortable with the idea of Alex working here."

"Alex is applying for the waitress position, so she'll be out here while I'll be in the kitchen. We won't be around each other."

"I'm still not comfortable with the idea."

Stephen saw Alex getting up from her seat and Becky turned to see who Stephen was looking at.

Alex saw Stephen, Becky and Eric staring at her and as she stepped up to Eric, she held out the job application for Eric to take.

As Eric was taking the job application, he said, "Just have a seat and Victor will be with you shortly."

As Eric was walking away, Alex turned towards Becky and said, "Becky, you were right."

"Excuse me?"

"After you left the table, I remembered that it wasn't Stephen who wanted all those kids. I wonder if Trudy is right and I should see a doctor about my memory."

"Alex, there's nothing wrong with your memory," Stephen said.

"According to Trudy there is and she has been concerned about me all day. In fact, I can't even remember when you and I were together intimately. Were we…"

"Alex, stop!" Stephen demanded.

Alex looked at Becky and said, "Oh, Becky, I'm sorry. That was very insensitive of me to bring up hot intimate moments between me and your current boyfriend."

"And yet you are still doing it," Becky said.

"You're right, I'm sorry. I…"

"Alex, you're not sorry," Stephen quickly interrupted with. "You manipulated this whole conversation like you have always done."

Alex gestured towards the table and said, "I think I had better go back to the table and wait for Victor." As Alex turned to walk away she tried to keep from smiling.

Alex only took three steps when Becky told Stephen, "I am not comfortable at all with Alex working here."

"Becky, Alex is a master at manipulation, and she'll say and do anything she can to get under your skin. Just ignore her."

"Oh the problem is, if Alex gets the job, can you ignore her?" Becky quickly asked.

Stephen took hold of Becky's hand before saying, "Becky, I'm with you. If Alex gets the job, I promise I will go out of my way to avoid her."

"Fine, but I'm going to be visiting a lot when Alex is working."

Stephen gave Becky a pleasant grin before giving her a passionate kiss.

Alex was sitting down and saw Stephen and Becky kissing. Her attention was then drawn to Victor as he left the kitchen area.

When Victor stepped up to the table, he asked, "Are you Ms. Larson?"

"Yes, but you can call me Alex."

As Victor was taking a seat across from Alex he said, "Okay, I will, and you can call me Victor." He then started the interview.

During the interview, Victor was impressed with Alex's responses. The interview took twenty minutes and when Victor was done, he offered Alex the job.

After Alex accepted the job, Victor asked, "Can you work tomorrow?"

"I can start tonight if you want."

"We have a full crew tonight, but we are short a person for

tomorrow's evening shift. The shift starts at 5:00 P.M. and you will work till close."

"I'll be here, and thanks again."

As Victor was standing up, he said, "You're welcome." He then stuck out his hand to shakes hands.

Alex stood up before shaking Victor's hand and saying, "Well, I better get back to campus. I have a class that's going to start in about thirty minutes."

"I'll see you tomorrow then. Bye," Victor said before turning to walk away.

Alex noticed Becky walking up as Victor was walking away. When Becky stepped up she said, "I want to get something clear. While you're here, you are to stay in front and not to go into kitchen."

"I'm sorry, but didn't I just get hired by Victor and not by Rebecca Steward?"

Becky showed a distasteful grin before saying, "Joke all you want, but you're to stay away from Stephen."

"Okay, one, I'm not interested in your boyfriend. Two, are you frightened by me so much that you can't trust the fact that Stephen would rather be with you."

"I'm just telling you to stay away."

"Becky, you won Stephen over a month ago… or before. Just go and enjoy your victory. I'm just here because I need the money."

"So you're no longer mad at me?" Becky questioned.

"With Stephen and me working here, most likely we'll be seeing a lot more of each other than what we did in the past month, so all I'm asking for is a cease fire."

"Fine. You got your cease fire… and if I see you trying to rekindle something with Stephen then it's off."

"Sure, Becky," Alex said before she started to turn away from Becky, but hesitated. Alex faced Becky again before asking, "Becky, why is Stephen working here anyway?"

"What do you mean?"

"I'm surprised Stephen has time to work here while being a quarterback."

Becky gave Alex a curious look before saying, "Stephen's football career ended last year when he was sacked. He broke his leg in two places."

"Oh, right," Alex said while pretending to recall the event. "As I said earlier, my memory hasn't been reliable lately." Alex then turned and walked away.

Becky curiously watched Alex as Alex walked away.

Ten minutes later, Alex was walking towards the dormitory. Trudy saw Alex and caught up with her. As Trudy walked beside Alex she asked, "So, did you get the job?"

"I got it. I start tomorrow. Oh and I also met Becky at Little Bucks."

In an excited manner, Trudy said, "Oh my God, you must tell me what happened."

"Becky was acting as if my only reason to be there was to steal Stephen back, and that I was wasting my time. She said that she and Stephen were going to marry and live out their lives child free and happy. I then made a ripple in her happy future when I made a convincing comment about how I thought that Stephen wanted six kids. Becky practically rushed to Stephen to find out if what I said was true. As Stephen was smoothing that ripple I walked up to them and made another one. I told Becky how my memory hasn't been reliable lately. I then asked Stephen to refresh my memory on the hot intimate moments that we had together. I manipulated the whole conversation and I doubt that Becky will be able to have an intimate moment with Stephen without thinking of me or the thought of getting pregnant for a while."

"Oh my God. I would love to have been there to see the

look on her face."

"Trudy, was the Alex of this reality manipulative?"

"When she wanted to be, she was very manipulative, but in spite of her many vices, Alex was a good hearted person."

"From what I read of her diaries, I actually agree with you. I was only curious of her being manipulative because in my reality, I wasn't as manipulative, but it seems to come easy to me now."

"So you're picking up her characteristics?"

"I think I might be."

"Well, it has been proven that women and men use different parts of their brain, so that can be one of the reasons that you are picking up her characteristics."

"That's sounds reasonable, I guess," Alex said as Trudy was noticing how gracefully Alex was walking.

"It seems as though you learned to walk in high-heels pretty quickly also," Trudy pointed out.

"I did have trouble walking in them at first, but then I got the hang of it," Alex said as they were approaching the building. "It's not even bothering my feet as much as I thought it would."

"With all the high-heels that are in the closet that's a good thing," Trudy said while stepping up to the door.

"Definitely," Alex agreed before opening the door. "Well, I'm going to change back into my blue jeans and a shirt."

As Alex and Trudy were walking in, Trudy said, "Alex, if you're okay with wearing high-heels, you should probably wear those black boots that Alex has."

"Why should I do that?" Alex asked while they were heading for the stairs.

"That was what Alex wore more than ninety percent of the time, and if people start seeing you in tennis shoes all the time, they're going to start getting curious in the way that Miles and

I did," Trudy said while they were reaching the stairs. Trudy gestured for Alex to go first.

"Thanks for the hint," Alex said just before the two ascended the stairs.

"No problem."

After reaching their floor Alex saw Trudy in deep thought. Alex then broke Trudy's thought by asking, "Are you okay?"

"Oh yeah I'm fine," Trudy said as she and Alex were walking towards the dorm room. "There was one other thing I wanted to ask you or tell you, but… oh wait. I do remember. Miles has a soccer game tonight, and I was going to go and cheer him on. Since you're not working tonight you should come with me."

"Miles plays soccer?"

"He does; he's the goalie."

"It sounds like fun. I'll be there. Oh, when does it start and where is it?"

"The game starts at seven, and it's a home game, so it will be here. Oh and we will be walking on grass and dirt, so wear tennis shoes to that."

"Definitely," Alex agreed with a grin.

Chapter Six

After Alex and Trudy walked into their dorm room, Alex went directly to her bedroom and changed into blue jeans, a nice shirt and the black pair of high-heeled boots. Alex put her purse over her shoulder before grabbing her book bag and leaving her dorm room.

Minutes later, as Alex was walking through the hall towards her classroom, she saw Doug and Cindy walking down the hall and she went to catch up to them.

Doug noticed Alex walking towards him while wearing high-heels. When Alex stepped up Doug stared at the boots while saying, "Nice shoes."

Alex grinned while saying, "They're actually boots, but thanks."

"I didn't say that to be nice," Doug confessed. "I'm actually curious to know why you're wearing high-heels when you don't have to."

"The Alex of this reality wore high-heels and Trudy suggested that for me to act like Alex of this reality, I should do the same."

Cindy worriedly asked, "Your roommate knows about you?"

"Yes, she knows about each one of us and she's cool with the whole situation."

"Alex, why would you tell Trudy about us?" Doug demanded.

"It was either take a chance on telling her and Miles or be

dragged to the doctor by them to have my memory checked," Alex pointed out.

"Whoa, wait a minute!" Doug uttered. "Miles knows too?"

"They were together and they're cool with it."

"Doug, even if Trudy and Miles do know about us, who is going to believe them even if they say anything to anyone?" Cindy asked.

"That's a good point," Doug said.

"Alex, who's Miles anyway?" Cindy asked.

"He's Trudy's brother," Alex said.

Doug made a praying motion while saying, "Alex, please don't say anything to anyone else."

"I don't see that as a problem," Alex said. "With Trudy coaching me and telling me the stuff that Alex didn't write in her diaries, I should be fine without anyone else getting overly curious about me. Anyway, I wanted to tell you two that I got the job. I start tomorrow afternoon."

"That's good," Cindy said. "I was checking the paper earlier and I saw a job that I'm qualified for. As soon as I get a ride there I'm going to apply for it."

"Oh, speaking of rides; Doug, Trudy told me where your Jeep Liberty is parked," Alex said just before she told Doug where he could find his vehicle. She then gestured down the hall and continued to say, "Well, I better get to class."

"Before you go, what are you doing this evening?" Cindy asked.

"At seven o'clock, I'm going with Trudy to watch a soccer game. What do you have planned?"

"O'Shannon's didn't burn down in this reality and all of us were planning to go there tonight," Cindy said. "Most likely we will be there until it closes, so after the soccer game you and Trudy should meet us there."

"Okay, I'll be there, and I will invite Trudy to join us,"

Alex said before waving bye. "Well, I'll see everyone later."

Doug and Cindy just waved to Alex. As Alex was walking away Doug asked Cindy, "Since I know where my Jeep is, do you want me to give you a ride so you can apply for that job?"

"Sure," Cindy answered. "I'm not going to turn down a ride." She and Doug then walked towards an exit.

6:40 P.M. at the soccer field, the bleachers were more than half full and were filling up fast. A large number of people were walking in front of the bleachers. Alex and Trudy had stopped at the concession stand before they continued towards the bleachers. Alex bought nachos, a hotdog and a drink. Trudy bought a hotdog, a bag of chip and a drink.

A short time later, Alex and Trudy were making themselves comfortable in a section of the bleachers that was six rolls from the field and next to an aisle that was closest to one of the goals. There was a large gap between Trudy and the next person sitting on the same bench.

Just after Alex took a bite of her hotdog, she spotted Kenny and Ben in the crowd who were walking around in front of the bleachers. Alex quickly swallowed the bite that she took before calling out, "Kenny! Ben! Up here!"

As Kenny and Ben turned to look, Trudy asked, "Are they the ones from your reality?"

Kenny and Ben saw Alex and as they were making their way towards her, Alex said, "Yeah." Alex then pointed them out. "That one is Kenny and the other one is Benjamin; everyone calls him Ben though."

"I've seen Kenny around campus, but I had never seen Ben before."

"In my reality Ben won a scholarship to Harvard, but in this reality he didn't win that scholarship."

"Interesting," Trudy said just before taking a bite of chip.

As Kenny and Ben were stepping up to Alex and Trudy,

Kenny said, "Doug told us that you'd be here."

"Yep, I'm here," Alex said before gesturing towards Trudy. "This is my roommate Trudy."

"Hi," Trudy, Kenny and Ben said.

"So are you two here to watch the game?" Alex asked the two new arrivals.

"Yeah, when Doug mentioned this was where you were, we thought we'd come here and join you... as long as it's okay with you and Trudy," Ben said.

"There's plenty of room beside me," Trudy said.

"Have a seat," Alex added.

Kenny and Ben squeezed passed Alex and Trudy. Ben sat next to Trudy as Kenny sat next to Ben.

Just after Kenny and Ben sat down, everyone's attention was drawn to the field as the players were taking the field.

Kenny then turned towards Alex and asked, "Hey, Alex, why are you and Trudy so close to one of the goals? The better seats are around midfield."

"Trudy's brother Miles is the goalie and he'll be on this end of the field when the game starts," Alex said.

"When the teams swap sides after the first half ends, Alex and I were going to move to the other end," Trudy added.

"Trudy, I'm glad I'm not in your brother's shoes," Kenny said.

"Why do you say that?" Trudy asked.

"Harvard is the underdog by three goals," Kenny pointed out.

"This is Miles' first game as a goalie, so maybe he can prevent those three goals," Trudy said.

"Actually, I hope Miles does prevent those goals," Kenny said. "I bet someone twenty bucks that Harvard will win before I found out that Harvard was the underdog."

Before anything else was said, an announcement came over

the speaker, "Please rise for our national anthem." Everyone who was sitting stood up and faced the flag. The people who were walking stopped and faced the flag. Except for a few people clearing their throats, everyone was quiet as one of the students sang the national anthem.

A few miles away, Doug, Brandy and Cindy walked into the O'Shannon's Pub. The counter bar was near the entrance with eight customers sitting at the bar, randomly spaced. Three rows of four tables were arranged orderly just a few feet from the barstools. Two groups of three people were sitting at two of the tables. A room with three pool tables and two dartboards was sectioned off only by a wide entranceway. A few tables with chairs were setting against the wall not far from the pool tables. One of the pool tables was being used by two pools-shooters. A second table was being used by four pool-shooters. Three dart players were playing on one of the dartboards.

When Doug, Brandy and Cindy walked up to the bar, the bartender asked to see their ID. Once the bartender was satisfied of their age, he took their drink order. When they got their drinks they carried them to a table next to the pool table that wasn't being used. After setting their drinks down, they walked up to where the pool sticks were kept and browsed through them. Doug and Cindy each found a stick that they felt comfortable with and went back to the pool table.

When Brandy picked up a pool stick and was testing its weight, a man in his late twenties stepped up and said, "Brandy, hey." Brandy turned to look at the man while holding the pool stick. "You walked in here without saying 'hi' to me."

At first she didn't recognized him, but then it dawned on her of who he was. She then spoke as if she was scared to say anything, "Devin; you... you're here. Hi."

Devin gave Brandy a confused look before saying, "I'm always hanging out here. You know that."

"Yes, of course," Brandy nervously said. "How are you?"

Devin continued to give Brandy a confuse look before saying, "I'm good. I'm here shooting pool with my brother Scott. Maxine will be here in a few minutes…"

"Maxine?" Brandy quickly uttered. "Your wife Maxine? She's coming here?"

The confused expression across Devin's face had deepened as he said, "She is."

"So how is Maxine?"

"She's fine," Devin answered. "Are you okay though?"

"Don't I seem okay?" Brandy quickly asked.

"Truthfully, you seem to be a bit nervous to be around me."

Brandy timidly echoed, "Me nervous? Me not nervous… I mean, I'm not nervous."

"Brandy, I drank too much last Saturday and I don't remember all what I did, so did I offend you last week in someway?"

"No; not at all," Brandy nervously said before she slightly held up the pool stick. "Well, I got my pool stick and I better get back to my friends."

Before Brandy had a chance to leave, Devin said, "When Maxine gets here perhaps we can join you three."

"Err, sure," Brandy politely said with a matching tone and grin. "That would be good, I guess… but there are supposed to be four or more who will be joining us in about two hours or so." Brandy then gestured towards Doug and Cindy. "Well, I'll be over there."

Devin glanced in Scott's direction before saying, "I think it's my turn to shoot anyway. You and Cindy don't be strangers."

"We won't," Brandy said before walking away from Devin.

As Brandy was stepping up to Doug and Cindy, Cindy asked Brandy barely loud enough for Doug to hear, "Hey, who's that?"

Doug stepped closer to hear as Brandy said, "Think back to our first month at Harvard. Who did we hang out with a lot in this place for that month?"

Cindy thought for a moment before asking, "Is that Devin?"

"That is Devin," Brandy confirmed.

"Who's Devin?" Doug asked.

"He's a local and a frequent customer to this bar," Brandy said.

"In our reality, Brandy and I hung out with Devin and Devin's wife Maxine for three... maybe four weekends; I'm not sure which," Cindy began. "Anyway the Monday following the last weekend we spent with them, Brandy and I saw an article in the paper that Devin was arrested for killing Maxine and Maxine's lover when Devin caught them together. He was convicted and sentenced to twenty years in prison."

"In this reality Maxine is still alive," Brandy added. "Devin just told me that Maxine will be here in a few minutes."

"I wonder if Maxine didn't cheat in this reality or just didn't get caught," Doug wondered aloud.

"Brandy, wasn't the man's name who Maxine had cheated with printed in the paper?" Cindy asked.

Brandy slightly shrugged before saying, "It might have been, but I can't remember what it was though."

"I believe it was Douglas something," Cindy said before gesturing towards Doug. "I think that because I met Doug a few days later and I remember thinking that Doug had the same name as Maxine's lover."

"It wasn't Douglas Shultz by any chance, was it?" Doug asked.

"That's exactly who it was," Brandy said. "You must have read the article."

"I didn't read the article," Doug said. "Douglas Shultz was my and Alex's trigonometry instructor our first semester at Harvard. After the fourth week into the semester all of the students of Mr. Shultz were reassigned to different classes. I went to Mrs. Wyse's class."

"Doug, that was when you and I met," Cindy said. "You joined my study group that same week."

"So Maxine's and Mr. Shultz's deaths were the reason Cindy and I know you and Alex," Brandy commented. "I find it interesting that if one event was different, it changes several other events."

"That is interesting," Doug agreed. "Anyway, are you two ready to play?"

"I'm ready," Cindy said. "Rack 'em up."

As Doug walked up to the pool table he pulled quarters from his pocket.

At the soccer field, Harvard was trailing by one goal. As the Harvard's team was maneuvering the ball towards the goal for the tying point, Harvard's spectators were on their feet and cheering in anticipation of a goal. When the Harvard's players kicked for a goal, the spectators' anticipation for the tying point was crushed when the goalie stopped the ball. Everyone sat down. As the opposing players were maneuvering the ball towards Miles, Alex watched with a fixed focus on Miles as he was preparing himself to stop the goal. As the opposing team kicked for a goal, Miles was right there to prevent it. Trudy noticed that Alex was the loudest one cheering.

Trudy tapped Alex's arm and when Alex looked, Trudy said, "Wow, you're really getting in the game."

Alex grinned before saying with some enthusiasm, "I have gone to soccer games before, but for some reason I'm really getting into this one. Miles is a great goalie."

Trudy wasn't sure what to think when she saw Alex

looking at Miles for a few seconds before she turned to look at the Harvard's team as the team was maneuvering the ball back towards the other goal. Trudy shook it off and when she turned to watch the players, she looked in time to see Harvard tie the game. The Harvard's spectators stood up and cheered.

As the spectators were taking their seats again, Trudy again noticed Alex looking at Miles before focusing on the players in the field; however, she didn't say anything about it.

At O'Shannon's Pub, Doug was taking his shot on the pool table as Maxine escorted her blind sister Mary into the pub. Maxine saw Brandy, Cindy and Doug at one of the pool tables and after Mary sat down, Maxine told Mary, "I'll be back in a second. Brandy and Cindy are playing pool with Doug and I'm going to say 'hi' to them."

Before Maxine was able to walk away, Mary told her, "Tell them to come over and say 'hi' to me."

"Okay," Maxine said before she walked towards Brandy and Cindy.

Once she stepped up to Brandy and Cindy, she started a casual conversation.

Doug shot in four balls, one after the other, to win the game. When he stepped up to Brandy, Cindy and Maxine, Maxine looked at him before asking, "So where are Richard, Carl and Toby?"

Doug thought for a moment before saying, "I'm not sure, but I think they'll be here at some point."

"It's strange," Maxine began. "I didn't know that you three were friends. Of course I knew that you, Brandy, were friends with Cindy and vice versa, but as to how often that I see you three in here, I didn't think that you two were friends with Doug."

"We're friends now," Brandy said.

Maxine grinned before saying, "That's good. Well, I'm

going back over and sit with Mary. You three should join us."

"Sure, we'd love to," Brandy said.

Doug gave Brandy a curious look just before telling Maxine, "We will be there in a second."

"All right," Maxine said before turning and walking away.

Doug noticed Devin and Scott joining Mary at the table and when Maxine stepped out of earshot, Doug said, "Brandy, I don't know those four people."

"Well, Maxine knows the Doug from this reality," Brandy said.

"And I think Alex has the right idea too," Cindy added. "We need to do what the us of this reality would do, and the us of this reality would most likely join them."

"Okay; fine," Doug said in a defeated tone. "We'll join them."

Doug, Brandy and Cindy put their pool sticks up, and after picking up their drinks from the table they walked towards Maxine's table. As they stepped up, Maxine said, "Mary; Brandy, Cindy and Doug are joining us."

While staring forward with a pleasant grin on her face, Mary said, "Doug, it's been a while since I came in here while you were here."

As Brandy, Cindy and Doug were taking their seats, Doug said, "Yeah, I guess it has been a while."

Everyone at the table noticed that Mary's facial expression had changed from a pleasant one to a perplex one just before Mary asked, "So how have you been?"

"I've been good," Doug said. "How have you been?"

"I'm good, but you're not as good as you are claiming," Mary said.

As everyone gave Mary a confused look Doug asked, "Why do you think that?"

"Something about you is different," Mary said. "I can sense

it when you speak. Did something dramatic happen to you recently?"

"No; my life is the same as it has been," Doug said.

"Now I sense in your voice that you are lying to me," Mary said. "I thought you learned when we first met that you can't lie to me."

"Okay, you're right," Doug confessed. "Something has happened to me recently, but it's not anything that I'm willing to discuss."

"Fair enough, but whatever you went through, you came out of it as a different person," Mary said. "So, Brandy; Cindy, how have you two been?"

Brandy and Cindy were slightly scared to even answer and after a slight hesitation, Brandy was the first one to say, "I'm doing okay. My life is basically the same as it has always been."

Mary showed a curious expression on her face before asking, "Cindy, how are you doing?"

"I'm doing good," Cindy answered. "Oh and you look good."

"Something is different about you too, Cindy," Mary said. "In fact, I sense something different about all three of you, but with varying degrees."

"Cindy and I along with four others had also gone through the same experience that Doug had gone through, and like Doug said, what we went through is not anything we want to discuss," Brandy said.

"Again that's fair," Mary said. "Out of curiosity, do I know the other four?"

"You might know two of them," Doug said. "My sister, Alex and a friend of ours named Kenny."

"Mary doesn't know Alex and I had the unfortunate pleasure of meeting her once," Maxine said.

Doug gave Maxine a concerned look just before asking, "Can you refresh my memory of what Alex did when you two met?"

Mary showed a curious expression on her face over Doug's request as Maxine answered, "As I said, I only met Alex once, but the impression I got of her was that she was very opinionated, critical and a bit of a snob."

"What did Alex do for you to think all of that?" Cindy asked.

"I remember her complaining about the décor of the bar, along with telling me her opinion about people working minimum wage jobs. When I told her that I had a minimum wage job, her response was something like, 'Oh, I'm sure you're doing the best you can with what you have. So you shouldn't feel bad about yourself.' When she said that, I completely lost my cool."

"How long ago did you meet Alex?" Brandy asked.

"It was just before Christmas about two years ago," Maxine said. "I met Doug and Alex at the same time."

"Alex is not the same person who she was two years ago," Brandy said. "In fact, she'll be here in an hour or so, and you'll see for yourself that Alex is not the same person."

"Thanks for the warning," Maxine said.

"I remember Alex saying just before she left the bar that she was never coming back in here again," Devin said. "So that alone is a change right there."

"I hate to be like this, but let's talk about something other than Alex," Maxine requested.

"So have anyone seen any good movies lately?" Cindy asked. She then as an afterthought looked at Mary and cringed for asking what she did.

At the soccer game, Harvard's spectators were disappointed when their team lost by a goal after going into overtime. As the players were leaving the field Alex, Trudy, Kenny and Ben walked up to Miles.

Miles saw them and as they stepped up he said, "Hey, I'll meet you guys at O'Shannon's as soon as I can. Right now my teammates and I get the joy of listening to the coach telling us what we did wrong."

"I thought you guys played good," Alex said. "The other team was just better."

Miles sarcastically said, "Thanks, Alex. That was just what I wanted to hear."

"Sorry," Alex timidly said. "That actually came out wrong."

Miles gestured in the direction of his teammates while saying, "Well, I better go or the coach will chew my head off for not going in with the others."

"See you at O'Shannon's," Alex said.

"Bye," Miles said.

"Bye," Trudy, Kenny and Ben said.

As Miles was walking away, Trudy continued to say, "Well, I want to change clothes before I go anywhere."

"I actually want to do the same," Alex said. "Kenny; Ben, we'll meet you two at O'Shannon's."

"All right; let's go, Ben," Kenny said. Ben nodded before he and Kenny walked away.

When Alex and Trudy walked into their dorm room, they both changed into nice clothes. Alex again put on her black high-heeled boots.

Fifteen minutes later, Alex and Trudy were walking into the slightly crowded O'Shannon's behind two couples and another woman. Alex stopped near the entrance and looked over the room. Almost instantly Alex noticed that a person was setting up a karaoke machine in the back corner.

Trudy saw Doug and the others, and as she pointed towards

them she said, "Alex, everyone is over there."

Alex turned to look before saying, "I see them." She and Trudy then walked towards them.

When Alex and Trudy stepped up to their group, Alex noticed Devin, Scott, Maxine and Mary sitting among her friends. Alex then noticed that Maxine was giving her a harsh stare. She ignored the look and said, "Hi... everyone. Brandy; Cindy and others who don't know my roommate, this is Trudy."

"Hi, everyone," Trudy said.

Doug was standing up as Maxine said, "Trudy, since I doubt Alex remembers me, I'll introduce myself and the ones I'm with." Alex gave Maxine a perplexed look. "My name is Maxine..."

As Maxine was pointing out the others who were in her group, Doug grabbed Alex's arm before whispering, "We need to talk."

"Okay, but what's that woman's problem?" Alex demanded.

"That's what I want to talk to you about so come with me," Doug whispered.

"Fine," Alex said.

Once Doug and Alex were out of hearing distance from the group Doug said, "Apparently the Alex of this reality had only been to O'Shannon's once in her life, and that was about two years ago."

"I know that part. Trudy had already told me that I... or she would frequent a place called Diamonds. Apparently Becky, Trudy and the Alex of this reality were the first three customers through the doorway when Diamonds made its grand opening about two years ago."

"Well, here's the part that you might not know. The only time that Alex of this reality was here, she left a bad and lasting impression on Maxine. Maxine was the lady with the problem."

"Okay, what did Alex do?"

"According to Maxine, she was opinionated, critical and a bit of a snob."

"Great," Alex sarcastically said. "So what was Alex opinionated about?"

"Apparently minimum wage jobs are degrading to Alex, and at the time when Alex met Maxine, Maxine worked for minimum wage. Alex made a patronizing comment about it."

"Well, the comment that Stephen said at Little Bucks makes better sense to me now. Well, we better join the others."

Before Alex had a chance to walk away, Doug said, "Do me a favor and don't bring any of this up."

Alex grinned while saying, "Okay, I won't. I'll be on my best behavior."

"Thank you."

"Oh, and since you pulled me away while Maxine was introducing everyone I don't know who's who."

Doug told Alex who was who before walking back towards the table. As Alex and Doug were returning to the table, the waitress was just walking away.

Alex hung her purse on an empty seat next to Trudy and as she was sitting down, Trudy whispered, "Alex, according to Ben and Kenny you drink beer so I ordered you that."

"Thanks," Alex whispered back. "That was what I wanted. What did Alex drink though?"

"She did drink beer at times, but her common drink is actually wine coolers," Trudy whispered.

"So people won't think that I'm out of character if I drink beer?" Alex questioned.

"Not at all; however, I don't know how you normally drink your drink, but Alex drinks hers from a glass."

Before Alex was able to respond Mary said, "Alex, I met everyone at the table, but for you. Tell me a little bit about yourself."

Alex thought for a second before saying, "I'm Doug's sister. I'm in pre-med at Harvard, and there's not really too much more to tell."

"Perhaps you can tell us what brings you back to O'Shannon's," Maxine prompted.

"I'm just meeting my brother and friends here to have a good time," Alex said.

"The décor of the bar doesn't bother you?" Maxine asked.

Alex gave Maxine a curious look before asking, "Should it?"

"The last time that I saw you in here, you didn't like the décor," Maxine pointed out. "I'm just wondering if you still feel that way."

Alex looked around for moment before saying, "O'Shannon's pub is much like other neighborhood bars, so the décor is okay."

"So you decided that the décor of this place is okay after visiting other bars," Maxine said.

Before Alex was able to respond Devin asked, "Maxine, what are you doing?"

"I'm just curious to know if Alex still has the same opinions about things as she did two years ago," Maxine answered.

"Maxine, I see nothing wrong with the décor of this place," Alex said.

Mary took hold of Maxine's arm before saying, "Maxine, you're purposely trying to bait Alex, and Alex just came here to be with her friends and have fun. Alex doesn't even remember the talk that you and she had two years ago."

Alex gave Mary a perplexed look as Maxine asked, "Is that

true? You don't remember the discussion about it?"

"To be honest; no, I don't remember it," Alex said.

"I bet you don't even remember meeting me," Maxine said.

"I have met a lot of people in my life, and I'll admit that I can't remember all of them," Alex began. "Please forgive me, but you are one of those people who I had met and don't remember."

Mary showed a perplex expression on her face as Maxine said, "That's typical of a snob."

"Maxine, I'm not going to take offense to that or defend myself," Alex said.

"That's because you know it's true," Maxine said.

"Maxine, it's time for us to leave," Devin said.

"It's okay," Alex said. "Maxine is entitled to her opinions, and it's obvious that Maxine had these strong opinions of me with only meeting me once..."

Mary interrupted Alex by saying, "Alex, I'm not sure what's going on, but I do know that you have never met Maxine before today. That is also true with Doug."

"Mary, what are you talking about?" Maxine quickly asked.

"Maxine, you have never met Alex or Doug before," Mary said.

Alex, Doug, Trudy, Kenny, Brandy, Cindy and Ben looked at Mary as if she was about to tell their secret. Devin, Scott and Maxine looked at Mary as if she had lost her mind just before Maxine said, "Mary, I have never known of you being wrong about anything, but you are wrong about this. I've known Doug for a while now."

"I can't explain it, but I know what I'm saying is true," Mary said.

"Are you saying that Doug and Alex are imposters?" Scott asked jokingly.

Marry thought for a second before saying, "No, they're not imposters, but I also know that Alex and Doug have never met me, Maxine, Devin or Scott before today. That was why I felt Doug as being different to me earlier. I mistook the feeling as a change in his life."

The waitress was returning with Trudy's and Alex's drinks as Devin said, "Mary, what you are saying doesn't even make sense."

"I know it doesn't, but I also know I'm right," Mary said.

"Mary, I think it's time for me to take you home," Maxine said.

"I think it's time for the four of us to go," Devin added.

Devin, Maxine and Scott were standing up as the waitress stepped up to the table. Maxine was helping Mary up as the waitress was giving Trudy and Alex their drinks along with an empty glass for each of them.

Before anyone could step away from the table, the waitress asked Devin, "Are you four leaving?"

"We are," Devin confirmed.

"Well, drive safely," the waitress said.

"Thank you," Devin said.

Before Mary was led away, she said, "It was nice meeting everyone."

"It was interesting in meeting you," Trudy said.

As Maxine, Mary, Devin and Scott were walking away, the waitress turned towards Doug and his friends before asking, "Does anyone want anything else?"

"We're good," everyone responded.

The waitress collected the empty beer bottles and glasses that were left behind and walked away.

When the waitress was out of earshot, Trudy said, "You guys almost got discovered by a blind psychic."

"Yeah, that wasn't good," Brandy said.

"Doug, why didn't you call and warn me about Mary?" Alex practically demanded to know.

"Since Mary never met the Alex of this reality before, I didn't think she would get a feeling of you like she did," Doug said.

"Well, she did, and it was lucky that Maxine distrusted Mary's psychic feeling," Alex said.

"If I run into another psychic I'll warn you about him or her first," Doug said.

As Alex was pouring her beer into the glass she said, "Well, hopefully we won't run into anymore psychics." Once Alex's glass was filled a second later, she put the bottle down and took a drink from the glass.

As Alex was putting her glass back down the karaoke DJ announced over the microphone, "Good evening ladies and gentlemen. I'm Dominic and I'm your karaoke DJ for tonight. There are fifteen songbooks around the room on various tables so pick out the songs you want to sing and bring them to me. Until then I will sing a few songs that I have selected. Oh and I'm not a good singer so the faster you guys and gals bring me your song selections the faster you won't have to listen to me sing." Dominic then began his first song.

Trudy tapped Alex on the arm before saying, "You actually have a good singing voice so you should get up and sing."

Before Alex responded she saw Doug grinning. She instantly gave Doug an inquisitive look before asking, "What?"

Doug smiled before saying, "I'm just thinking about Trudy's suggestion. I would love to hear you sing. It will be interesting to hear."

"I will sing," Alex said with a smirk. She then stood up and looked around for a book. Within seconds she spotted one on an empty table. She walked over to it, picked it up and carried it back to her table. After sitting down, she slowly flipped through the pages for a song.

After searching through a few pages, Alex found a song that she liked and as she was writing it down Miles walked up behind her to peek at what she was writing.

Miles was looking over Alex's shoulder for a few seconds when Alex looked up and saw who it was. She then grinned before saying, "Oh hi. I see you made it."

"I'm just glad I made it in time to hear you sing," Miles said. "Oh and you picked a nice song too."

"Thanks." As Alex was picking up the slip of paper with her selected song, she continued to say, "Well, I guess I'll take it up to the DJ."

Before Alex was able to stand up, Miles said, "I'll take it up for you."

Alex held out the slip of paper for Miles to take while saying, "Okay, thanks."

As Miles took the paper he said, "No problem." Miles then turned and walked towards the DJ.

Doug reached out his hand towards Alex while saying, "Alex, let me have the book. Tonight I think I'll give singing a shot too." Alex gave Doug a grin before handing him the book.

As the evening progressed several topics were brought up and discussed in a lengthy conversation. Everyone at Alex's table got to sing two, three or four songs along with several other people in the bar. A few times during the night Trudy and then later Brandy noticed when an attractive man would walk by the table, Alex would stare at him as if she was attracted to him. Neither Brandy nor Trudy said anything to Alex about it. Also during the night, Trudy had warned Alex about drinking too much, but Alex failed to take it seriously.

Everyone stayed until the bar closed. Miles was pacing himself and was relatively sober compared to anyone else in the bar.

Once the bar was about to close and the bright lights were turned on, the workers shouted out, "Let's go people! It's time to go!"

As Alex and her group were standing up Miles asked, "Who all drove here?"

Alex, Doug and Ben said, "I drove here."

"I don't believe you three are in any shape to drive," Miles said. "I drive a van and it will fit all of us. I'll bring you three back tomorrow to get your vehicles after everyone has sobered up."

Alex motioned for Miles to go and said in her completely drunken speech, "Lead the way."

Trudy saw Alex's purse hanging on the chair and before Alex had a chance to walk away from the table, Trudy gestured towards the purse while saying, "Alex, don't forget your purse."

"I can't forget that," Alex agreed before picking up the purse and putting it over her shoulder. Everyone then left the bar.

Chapter Seven

Saturday, October 23 at 9:10 A.M., Richard was studying in the common room of his and Doug's dorm room when Doug left his bedroom.

Richard looked at Doug before asking, "Where did you go last night, dude?"

"A few of us went to O'Shannon's pub."

"And you didn't even think to invite me?"

"It was a spur of the moment decision to even go, and I misplaced my phone, so I couldn't call you."

"Dude, check your jacket. You wore it three days ago and it was the last time I saw you with it."

"Ooh, I didn't even think to check there. Thanks for the hint."

As Doug was turning towards the bedroom, Richard said, "No problem, dude."

Doug walked back into his bedroom and shut the door behind him. After he walked up to the closet, he checked the pockets of his winter coat. When he didn't find the phone, he checked the pockets of a lighter jacket and found it in the right pocket. He looked at the phone and saw that it was set on vibrate. He also noticed that there were ten missed calls and a few text messages. Doug checked to see who had called. When he saw Elizabeth (Liz) Wrights' name among the missed calls he grinned and hit the button to call her back

Liz was running on a treadmill at a moderately crowded fitness club when her phone rang. She stopped running and looked to see who was calling before answering with, "You have a lot of nerve calling me after standing me up."

"It wasn't like that, Liz," Doug said.

Liz said in an unpleasant tone, "I tried calling you Thursday evening and twice last night, so tell me. What was more important than answering my calls or keeping our date?"

"Well, about not answering your phone calls, I just found my phone after misplacing it for two days. As for missing our date, wasn't our date for tonight?" He then cringed for making his last statement.

"Our date was for last night, and you were to pick me up at my grandparents' house at seven o'clock."

"Liz, I'm so sorry that I went brain dead about our date last night, and please let me make it up to you tonight."

Doug noticed a short silence before Liz said, "You can pick me up at my grandparents' house at noon. We can have lunch and if you don't show up this time, don't bother calling me again."

"I'll be there," Doug assured her. Liz hung up without saying another word. Doug then clipped the phone to his pants and left his room.

When Richard saw that Doug had his phone, he said, "Good, dude, you found it."

"I did, and I also discovered that I missed my date with Liz last night."

"That explains the phone call from her I got last night."

"Liz called you?"

"She called me about eight last night and was asking me where you were. She was all agitated and when I told her that I didn't know where you were, she hung up without saying so much as a 'goodbye'. I didn't know you had a date with her or I would have reminded you about it yesterday."

"I have a lunch date with her, so everything's fine," Doug

said before gesturing for the door. "Well, I'm going to talk to Alex."

"Later, Dude."

Doug politely nodded before he turned and left the dorm.

Trudy, while carrying clean clothes and her shower items, left her dorm room. Before she was able to walk into the women's bathroom, she heard someone calling out for her. When she stopped and looked she saw Doug hurrying towards her.

As Doug stepped up Trudy asked, "So how do you feel this morning?"

"I feel fine. Is Alex in the dorm room?"

"Alex is still in bed. I told her to take it easy on those drinks last night, but she wouldn't listen."

"I'll go and get her up. We need to get with Miles so he can drive us to our vehicles anyway."

As Trudy reached into her pocket she said, "I doubt you'll be able to wake her up while knocking." She pulled out her door key and held it out for Doug to take. "So here's my key. Just have Alex bring it to me while I'm in the showers."

Doug took the key while saying, "Will do."

As Doug turned and walked towards the dorm room, Trudy continued towards the showers.

Alex had the covers pulled up to her neck and when Doug entered the bedroom he shook her awake.

Alex opened her eyes in a squinted fashion. When she saw who it was she faced away and closed her eyes, before saying, "I'm sleeping. Go away."

In a normal voice Doug said, "Alex, we have to..."

Alex uttered without facing Doug, "Shshsh, stop the yelling. My head is pounding."

"I'm not yelling."

"Then whisper it. Better still, tell me when I'm up."

Doug said in a quieter voice, "You need to get up now, so we can get our vehicles."

Alex asked without facing Doug, "What's your hurry?"

"I want to prepare for my date with Elizabeth Wright."

Alex faced Doug and opened her eyes. Her covers were still pulled up to her shoulders as she asked in a slightly disbelieving tone, "You have a date with Liz?"

"Apparently I had a date with her last night that I didn't know about. She agreed to have lunch with me today."

"You've been trying to get a date with Liz for nearly a year, and in this reality you get one," Alex pointed out.

"And I don't want to blow this chance to date her. That's why I want to get my Jeep. I need to prepare for my date now and I doubt Miles will agree to take us to our vehicles at different times."

"Okay, I'm up," Alex said before she slightly raised the covers and noticed that she was nude. She quickly covered up again while saying, "No, I'm not up."

Doug gave Alex a confused look before asking, "Why aren't you?"

"I don't have any clothes on and I'm not getting up while you're standing there."

Doug grinned before questioning playfully, "What's the big deal? We're siblings."

Alex uttered sternly and somewhat loudly, "Doug, get out!" She then quickly covered her forehead with her right hand and cringed from her searing headache. "Okay, that was too loud."

After seeing Alex's reaction, Doug questioned, "Since when do you get headaches from hangovers?"

"Apparently Alexandra gets bad hangovers. Trudy did warn me against drinking as much as I did."

"Oh, that reminds me. I have Trudy's door key and she wants you to return it to her."

"Why can't you return it?"

"I would, but she went to take a shower and the women in there would act like you and tell me to leave."

"Speaking of leaving, will you please leave so I can get up and get dressed?"

"Fine, I'll wait for you in the common room," Doug said before turning and walking away.

Alex waited for the door to shut completely before she got out of bed.

Doug sat on the couch in the common room for a short time when Alex stepped out of her room while dressed in the clothes that she had on the previous night. She was carrying clean clothes and her bathing items.

Doug gave Alex a curious look as Alex said, "I'm going to take a shower, and while I'm doing that you should find Miles and Ben."

"All right," Doug said while standing up. "Just don't take forever in the showers."

"I won't," Alex said while following Doug to the door.

Thirty minutes later, Trudy helped Alex put on makeup.

11:00 A.M., Miles was driving Alex, Doug and Ben to O'Shannon's pub. As always, Miles had his radio playing. Ben was in the front seat. Alex and Doug were in seats directly behind the front seats. As Miles was approaching a twenty-four-hour diner, Miles gestured towards the diner while asking, "Is anyone interested in grabbing some lunch?"

"I just ate, so no for me," Ben said.

"I have a lunch date, so I'm out," Doug said.

"I'm actually hungry, so I'll go with you after you drop Doug and Ben off," Alex said.

"I'll drop you off too, Alex, and you can meet me at the diner," Miles said.

"All right; that's fine," Alex said.

Five minutes later, Miles dropped off Alex, Doug and Ben near their vehicles. After Alex got into her Jeep, she followed Miles back to the diner.

One-third of the tables were empty along with a half of the stools at the counter. When Alex and Miles walked in, Alex immediately saw Maxine waiting tables. She quickly stopped and faced Miles before saying, "I can't eat here."

Miles gave Alex a curious look before asking, "Why not?"

Alex gestured towards Maxine and whispered, "That waitress' name is Maxine and she doesn't like me... well, actually she doesn't like the Alex of this reality, but she thinks I'm her."

Maxine saw Alex and Miles talking near the entrance. She walked up to them before saying, "Well, I'll be. Alex, I never expected to see you in here."

"You don't have to worry about me because we're not staying."

"I was about ready to re-evaluate my opinion of you, but if you're leaving, my opinion of you stands," Maxine said.

"I was planning to leave because I didn't think you wanted me in here," Alex said.

"So are you telling me that the quality of food that is served in a diner like this and the type of service you would get are not beneath you?" Maxine questioned.

"Not at all," Alex assured her. "I like the food that is served in a greasy spoon."

"There are a few tables that are open and I'd be more than welcome to be your waitress... unless you have a problem with being here."

"Not at all," Alex quickly said. "Miles, I changed my mind. We're eating here."

Miles wasn't sure how to react and slightly hesitated to say, "Sure. No problem."

Alex saw an empty table to where a person sitting at that particular table could see the activities of the cook and Maxine. She pointed to it while saying, "Miles, let's sit there."

Before Miles had time to respond Alex was walking towards a seat. Miles and Maxine just followed. Alex hung her purse on the back of the seat and as she was sitting down Miles said, "This table will be good."

As Miles was taking a seat Maxine asked, "Do you two need to look over the menu first?"

"Am I able to get breakfast still?" Alex asked.

"Breakfast is served twenty-four hours a day," Maxine said.

"Then I know what I want," Alex said. "Miles, what about you?"

Miles slightly grinned before saying, "I'm ready to order too. You go first."

Maxine pulled out her ordering tablet just as Alex was saying, "Okay, I'll have bacon and scrambled eggs with potatoes and toast."

"Anything to drink?" Maxine asked.

"Yeah, I'll take an orange juice now and a glass of milk when the meal arrives."

Maxine wrote down Alex's order and then turned towards Miles while asking, "What can I get you?"

"Breakfast actually sounds good," Miles began. "So I'll have ham and eggs over easy with potatoes and toast. I'll also take orange juice now and a glass of milk."

Maxine put her tablet away before saying, "I'll be back with your OJ's."

Miles saw the serious look that Alex was giving Maxine as Maxine was walking away. After a moment of noticing it, Miles asked, "Why are you letting Maxine get to you?"

Alex looked at Miles before she defensively asked, "Who

says I'm letting her get to me?"

"Oh, so you're not eating here while Maxine is waiting tables in order to prove a point to her."

"Okay, fine; I am," Alex admitted, "but I'm not a snob like Maxine thinks I am."

"You may not be, but the Alex from this reality is to a small degree... possibly even more than a small degree. Anyway, you can either accept the reputation that you inherited or you can drive yourself ragged while trying to change people's opinions of you."

"Well at the moment, I'm only looking to change one person's opinion of me," Alex said while gesturing towards Maxine. "I'll worry about the other people's opinions later."

Miles just grinned and shook his head before asking, "So, in your reality, did you have plans to become a surgeon also?"

"I had plans to go into the scientific field, but with my current situation, I'm actually rethinking that plan. Attending medical school and becoming a surgeon does sound like something I would like to shoot for though, so I'm thinking about switching majors to that when I return to my own reality. What are your plans?"

"I'm in my fourth year of college, and I'm still undecided on a major, but I'm leaning towards law. I have even been taking courses to prepare for law school."

Alex saw Maxine returning with the drinks as she was saying, "Well you better decide something definite before next September."

Miles turned to see who Alex was looking at.

Maxine stepped up and placed the drinks on the table. After she was done putting the drinks down she said, "It will be a few minutes on your food order."

"Thank you," Alex said.

Maxine gave Alex an astounded look for a second before

she turned and walked away.

Before the meal arrived and while eating the meal, Alex and Miles enjoyed a casual conversation.

Miles was done eating first and when Maxine saw Miles pushing his crumb-filled plate away, she walked up to the table. As she stepped up she saw that Alex still had about half of her food left. She then asked, "How are you two doing?"

Alex saw that Miles was giving her an inquisitive look before she answered, "I'm fine." Alex then pushed her plate away. "In fact, I'm done also."

Maxine looked at Alex's plate again before asking, "Was there anything wrong with the food?"

It took a second before it dawned on Alex as to why Maxine had asked that. She then quickly and politely said, "Oh no. The food was great. I just wasn't as hungry as I thought I was."

"Perhaps we can get the check," Miles said.

"Sure, I'll be back in a minute," Maxine said before she turned and walked away.

Once Maxine was out of earshot, Alex asked, "So how much tip should we leave?"

Miles gave Alex a curious look before saying, "Leave as much as you want."

"I normally would, but in this case I don't want to tip not enough to where Maxine thinks that I'm cheap... or something like that," Alex began. "And I don't want to tip too much to where she thinks that I'm trying to give her charity."

"You're over analyzing the situation, Alex," Miles pointed out. "Just tip her what you normally would and if she's bothered by that then that's her problem."

Alex nodded while saying, "You're right." Alex saw Maxine returning. She grabbed her purse and as she was pulling out her wallet Maxine stepped up with the check.

Before Alex was able to get any money from her wallet Miles took the check and said, "Put your wallet away, I'll get this."

"Well how much was my part?"

Miles pulled out a twenty-dollar bill while saying, "Don't worry about it." Miles handed the check back to the waitress along with the twenty-dollar bill.

As Maxine was giving Miles his change, Alex said, "I never expected you to pay for mine."

"Alex, I want to."

"Well, thanks."

"You're welcome."

"Have a nice day," Maxine said.

"Thanks, you too," Alex said. Maxine just nodded and walked away. Alex laid three dollars on the table before looking at Miles. "Well, I'm leaving the tip."

"Okay," Miles said with a grin before putting his change away. "So what are your plans for today?"

"I have to be at Little Bucks at five or before to start my shift. Between now and then I'll be studying; unless something comes up."

"What is the possibility of you putting your studies on hold to go see a movie with me?"

Alex gave Miles a curious look before asking, "Are you asking me out?"

"Yeah, I guess I am."

"Miles, I'm not Alexandra," Alex pointed out.

"Well, I know you're not Alexandra from this reality. In fact, I'm more attracted to you than the Alexandra from this reality."

Alex again gave Miles a curious look before asking, "Trudy didn't tell you about me, did she?"

"What didn't she tell me?"

110

Alex shook her head before answering, "It's not important. Miles, I'll go to the movies with you, but we can't date."

"Oh I get it. You're dating someone and you would feel as though you would be cheating."

"It's not that."

"Then what is it?"

Alex thought for a second before saying, "Miles, in days, weeks or even months, I'll be returning to my reality, and for us to date... well, it just wouldn't be right."

"Alex, there's a possibility that this is your reality now."

"Okay, that is a possibility, but I have to try to get back to my reality. It's not fair to the other Alex if I don't try. So are we good with just remaining friends?"

Miles grinned before asking, "Would you hold it against me if I try to change your mind?"

Alex slightly grinned before saying, "You'll be wasting your time."

"Honestly, I can't think of a better way to waste my time."

"Okay... well, I think we should go find out what's playing."

"I'm ready," Miles said before standing up followed by Alex. Alex zipped her purse before putting it over her shoulder.

As they were walking into the parking lot, Miles told her, "We should take one vehicle."

"Which do you want to take?"

"I don't mind driving; as long as you don't have a problem with it."

"I'm fine with you driving."

"My van it is then," Miles said with a grin before he and Alex walked towards the van.

Miles and Alex walked up to the passenger's side of Miles' van. Mile unlocked the door with the remote and then opened it for Alex to get in. Once Alex was inside, Miles shut the door.

As Alex was putting her seatbelt on, Miles walked to the drivers' side.

Minutes later, Miles was buying two tickets to see a horror film. The movie didn't start for another hour so they went to play video games.

2:00 P.M., Doug and Liz were walking through the corridors of the mall. When Liz noticed the bored expression on Doug's face she nudged him before saying, "I know shopping with me at the mall wasn't your idea of a fun date, but today is the only day I have time to get my sister a wedding gift before she gets married next weekend. I also have to buy a dress and a pair of shoes."

Doug took a deep breath before saying, "Oh, I'm okay with being here with you."

"If you can say that while not looking bored to death, it would be more convincing."

Doug said in a more cheerful voice, "I'll admit that shopping at the mall is not in my top-ten list of fun things to do, but spending time with you no matter where we are is number one."

Liz stared delightfully into Doug's eyes before saying, "Okay, I accept that response."

Just after Liz's response, Doug saw an intimate moment and leaned towards her to give her a kiss. Liz allowed the kiss and the kiss lasted for a few seconds.

In the theater's parking lot, after the show, Alex and Miles were walking towards Miles' van. As they walked Miles put his hand on Alex's far shoulder.

Alex looked at Miles and said, "Miles, remove your hand."

Miles removed his hand before asking, "So what do you have planned for the next two and half hours before work?"

"I haven't done any type of studying for two days, and I really need to."

"You have tomorrow to study."

"Miles, playing video games and watching the movie were fun, but I should study for Monday's class."

"Are you sure I can't talk you into going somewhere with me?"

Alex gave Miles a curious look before asking, "Where?"

"Do you know Chris Swan?" Miles asked. Alex just shook her head. "Well, he's the person I replaced as a goalie. Right now he's hooked up to a machine at the hospital and hoping that a kidney donor can be found soon. He asked me to come by sometime today, and I'm not going there alone. Trudy had already told me that she won't go with me, and I don't know who else to ask."

"Is there a reason that you won't go alone?"

"Will you go with me without me telling you the reason?"

Alex again gave Miles a curious look before asking, "Why don't you want to tell me?"

"Since I'm an adult, it's a bit embarrassing to say."

Alex grinned before asking, "Who better to tell an embarrassing secret to other than a person who won't be around in a few weeks or so to tell it?"

"Fine, I'll tell you," Miles said. "I'm terrified of hospitals. I avoid them when I can and I will never walk into one alone."

As Alex and Miles were approaching the van, Alex asked, "Is there a reason why you're terrified of hospitals?"

As Miles and Alex were walking up to the passenger's side of the van, he said, "When I was seven my mom, Trudy and I were involved in a serious car accident." Miles unlocked and opened the door; however, Alex just stood outside the van to finish listening to what Miles had to say. "We where all sent to the hospital, and I was put in a room by myself. I was alone for what I thought was an extremely long time, so I left the room. I overheard a doctor telling another doctor about a woman who was involved in an accident and was taken to the basement. I thought the doctor was talking about my mom and so I went to find her. But what I found in the basement were dead bodies. One of the bodies... a woman's body, looked as though it was something out of a slasher movie. She was completely cut in half just below the shoulders. Her arms were severed off just above the elbow and they were lying beside the body. Seeing what I did traumatized me. Since then, I'm terrified to walk into a hospital."

Alex said in a sympathetic tone, "Miles, I'll go with you."

Mile grinned before saying, "Thank you."

"You're welcome," Alex said before turning and climbing into the van. Once Alex was in, Miles shut the door. As Alex was putting on her seatbelt, Miles walked around to the drivers' side.

Miles was quiet after driving away and Alex noticed within the first few minutes as to how quiet he was. She then broke the silence by talking about musical groups that she liked.

As Alex and Miles were approaching the entrance to the hospital, Alex noticed that Miles was pale. Sweat was forming up at his forehead and his body was slightly trembling.

Alex put her hand on Miles' back and asked, "Are you okay?"

Miles asked in a nervous and trembling voice, "Don't I look okay?"

"You're talking as though you just came in out of freezing weather and as pale as your face is right now, you look as though you should be admitted here."

"It has been a while since the last time I was in a hospital, so I guess I'm more frightened to be here than I thought."

As they were entering the hospital, Alex asked, "Are you this way with doctor's offices too?"

"I'm fine to be in a doctor's office or a small clinic. It's just hospitals that frighten me. Well, we should find a help desk to find out what room Chris is in."

Alex pointed to a male nurse standing at a nurse's station and said, "Let me ask him."

As Alex and Miles walked up to the nurse, the nurse asked, "May I help you?"

"Can you tell us what room Chris Swan is in?" Alex asked.

The nurse pressed a combination of keys on the computer's keyboard. Once the information popped up, he told them the room number and then explained how to find the room.

"Thanks," Alex said.

"No problem."

She and Miles walked in the direction of the nearest elevator. Miles pressed the button as they stepped up and the door opened immediately.

They stepped onto the elevator and after Miles pressed the button for the proper floor, Alex asked, "Did the Alex of this reality know Chris Swan?"

"She did. Trudy dated Chris last year and it was a hostile break up. That's why Trudy wouldn't come with me to see him."

"That's good to know before I meet Chris." Alex was quiet for a second. She then asked, "Oh, how does Chris feel about Alex?"

"He likes Alex."

"So Alex didn't completely alienate herself from everyone around her?"

Miles grinned and said, "No, not everyone. To be fair to Alex, I really don't think she means to alienate herself. Her standards are just set too high and I really think that she doesn't realize as to how she treats people."

"From what I read from her diary, I agree with you."

In Chris' room, Chris' mother Linda and older brother

Chad were visiting. The TV was turned off. Chad was in the middle of telling Chris about a movie that he watched the previous night. He stopped talking and turned to face Miles as Miles walked in followed by Alex.

Chris and Linda also turned and looked at Alex and Miles. Miles was still slightly pale. Chris then gestured and said, "Mom; Chad, meet Miles and Alex. Miles; Alex, meet my mom Linda and my brother Chad."

Chad stepped up to Miles and held out his hand to shake hands. As Miles shook Chad's hand, Chad said, "Nice to meet you."

"Likewise," Miles said.

Chad turned and held out his hand to shake Alex's hand. As Alex went to shake Chad's hand Chad kissed Alex's hand before saying, "It's nice to meet you as well."

Alex nervously grinned and said in an uncertain tone, "It's nice to meet you."

Linda walked up also and greeted Miles and then Alex.

When the introductions were finished Chris feebly said, "Alex, I never expected to see you."

"Oh sure. When I heard that Miles was coming, I just tagged along so I can say 'hi' and see how you're feeling."

Chris grinned and said, "I never knew you could lie in a compassionate manner, but thanks for trying."

"Why do you think that I'm lying?"

"You never cared for me much and I knew that."

"I wasn't mean to you, was I?"

"Well, no, you weren't mean or rude to me, but you would barely speak to me when we were in the same room."

"Well, I'm talking to you now."

"So, Chris, how are you feeling?" Miles asked.

"I'm as good as a person can be for being hooked up to a machine. You don't look so hot though."

"I'm fine. Being in a hospital just reminds me of a memory I'd rather forget."

"What happened?" Chris asked.

Miles glanced at Alex before saying, "I'd rather not say."

Alex tapped Miles' shoulder and said just above a whisper, "I'm going to search for a restroom." When Alex saw the worried look that Miles was giving her she added, "I shouldn't be gone long."

"Okay."

Before Alex was able to walk out, Linda said, "Alex, I'll show you to the ladies' room."

"Okay; thanks."

After Alex and Linda left the room, Chris asked, "So what's going on with you and Alex?"

"Presently there's nothing going on, but I'm hoping I can change that."

"You might not know this, but Alex has a crush on you, so you shouldn't have any problems being with her."

"Alex is going through a situation right now, and she has already mentioned that she will not get involved with me because of it. But as I told her, I'm going to see if I can change that."

"You should make romantic gestures, like sending her flowers or surprising her with something romantic," Chad suggested.

"That actually isn't a bad suggestion," Miles said.

"Alice, my fiancée is coming up from New York, and tomorrow I was going to show her all the fun sites in Boston," Chad said. "You and Alex are welcome to join us."

"I'll talk to her about it."

As Chad reached for his wallet he said, "I'll give you one of my business cards. It has my cell phone number on it and you can call me tomorrow so we can meet."

"Okay." Just as Miles was taking the card he looked at Chris and said, "And this is probably an inappropriate discussion to have in front of you."

"I'm fine, Miles," Chris said. "You and Alex should go and see the sites of Boston with Chad and Alice. Last year Trudy and I spent an entire day going to every site that was open and we had a great time. Speaking of Trudy, is she still mad at me?"

"Saying that she's mad at you is putting it mildly."

"I really messed up with Trudy. Before I die, I really would like it if she would forgive me."

"If mom heard you talking about dying she would give you an ear full," Chad said.

"Mom doesn't want to face facts."

"There's always a chance that a donor will be found," Miles said.

"I won't be holding my breath," Chris said.

"We need to change the subject before mom gets back," Chad said.

"Miles, I want you to tell Trudy that I would like to see her," Chris said.

"I told her once already, but I'll tell her again." Miles gestured towards the television. "So have you seen anything good on TV?"

"Just sitcoms and reruns."

Miles started a conversation about a particular sitcom that came out the previously September. Alex and Linda were gone for eight minutes before they walked back into the room and joined their conversation.

Alex and Miles visited for an hour, before leaving the hospital. Miles drove Alex back to her Jeep and they talked casually the entire way.

Chapter Eight

4:50 P.M., Alex walked into Little Bucks to start her shift. After walking in, she was introduced to another waitress named Sylvia. Sylvia was also to begin her shift at 5:00 P.M. Stephen was in the kitchen. Becky was nowhere to be seen.

As the evening progressed, Victor watched Alex as she waited tables in a manner that impressed him. Alex was also averaging slightly more tips than Sylvia.

At 7:30 P.M., Little Bucks was busy with the dinner crowd. Alex was at the table closest to the entrance and was writing down the three men's food and drink order. She paused and looked up from what she was writing as Doug and Liz walked in. Alex slightly grinned at the sight of Doug and Liz being together. She then refocused her attention back to the men's food order.

Once Alex was done writing down the food order, she said, "I'll be right back with your drinks." After Alex turned away from the men she looked over the room for a second. When she saw what table Doug and Liz were sitting at, she walked up to them.

Alex saw Sylvia walking towards the table as she was saying, "Hi, Liz." Liz just politely waved. "Doug, Sylvia is coming to take your order. The table you sat down at is one of her tables."

"That's no problem," Doug said.

"Well, I have a food order to turn in." When Doug nodded, Alex turned and walked away.

As Alex and Sylvia were about to pass each other, Sylvia asked accusingly, "You weren't thinking about stealing one of my tables were you?"

Alex stopped walking and said defensively, "The two who are sitting at your table is my brother and a friend of his, so before you start accusing me of something you need to know your facts."

"Oh, I'm sorry. I thought..."

"You should be sorry because I'm not the person you think I am." Alex didn't wait for a reply and continued towards the kitchen.

When she walked into the kitchen she walked up to Stephen and held out the ticket for him to take. John, the second cook just watched.

As Stephen took the order he said, "We are getting backed up here, so it will be about five to ten minutes longer before these orders can be filled."

"I'll let the customers know." Alex never attempted to walk away and looked at Stephen as if she was searching her thoughts for the proper words to say something.

Stephen gave Alex a curious look before asking, "What?"

"Are you saying something to Sylvia about me?"

"Like what?"

"Doug and his date Liz sat down at Sylvia's table a few minutes ago. I walked up to the table to tell my brother 'hi' and when Sylvia stepped up, she accused me of attempting to steal her table. Now I would like to know why she had the idea that I would steal her table."

"Sylvia didn't get the idea from me." Alex gave Stephen a skeptical glare. "Alex; Sylvia doesn't even know that I knew you before today... I swear."

"Did Becky say something to her?"

"I honestly doubt it. Alex, three weeks ago Sylvia was

working at a different restaurant, so perhaps she was used to the other waitresses there stealing her tables."

"Okay, that sounds reasonable. Well, I better get back out there." Alex then turned and walked out.

As Stephen was putting the ticket on the holder John said, "Alex doesn't seem to be the unreasonable person who you told me she was."

"I can't put my finger on it, but she does seem to be different."

At the bar, Alex waited for Bryon the bartender to finish drawing the drinks. A couple of minutes later, Alex returned to the table with the tray of drinks. As she was taking the drinks off the tray and handing them to the three customers, she said, "It will be approximately fifteen minutes for your food order."

One of the men gave Alex a wink before saying, "We're not in a hurry."

Alex grinned nervously before asking, "Can I get anyone, anything else?"

The man who winked slapped Alex on her butt while saying, "We're fine for now."

Alex said in a tone as if she was holding her cool, "Okay, well, I'll be back in a little bit to check up on you." Alex turned and walked away while carrying the empty tray. She walked up to another one of her tables with five customers and as she collected the empty glasses she asked, "Can I get anyone anything else?"

They each said one at a time, "You can bring me another drink."

"I'll be back."

As Alex was walking up to the bar for their drinks, Doug recognized a woman who entered Little Bucks. The woman's name was Bonnie in Doug's reality; however, in the present reality her name was Catherine. "Liz, I'm going to talk to Alex for a minute."

Liz nodded while saying, "Okay."

Alex's back was turned towards Doug as Doug walked up to her and tapped her on her shoulder.

Alex turned to look and when she saw who it was, she asked, "What's going on?"

"Your fiancée just walked in."

Alex gave Doug a confused look and asked, "What are you talking about?"

"Bonnie just walked in." Alex turned to look as Doug continued to whisper, "We have only been in this reality for two days and you have already forgotten about your fiancée in our reality."

Alex stared at Catherine while saying, "So much has happened these past two days, Bonnie never even entered my mind."

Bryon got Alex's attention as he said, "Here are your drinks, Alex."

Alex faced Bryon before saying, "Thanks." Alex picked up the tray of drinks before facing Doug again and whispering, "Well, in this reality, Bonnie would be nothing more than a friend to me... if she's even that."

"I just thought you might want to know that she's here."

"I do; thanks." Alex then walked away with the tray of drinks.

Doug stayed at the bar and bought a scratch-off lottery ticket.

Before Alex was able to get to the table with the drinks, Catherine stepped up to Alex and said in a slightly amused tone, "Alex, don't tell me that you're working here."

Alex stopped walking and said, "Hey, Bonnie. And yes; I am working here."

"Bonnie? Why did you call me Bonnie?"

Catherine saw Alex thinking of a response before she answered with, "Oh my god. I can't believe I called you by that name. Bonnie is this woman who came in earlier who caused a slight scene. I guess my mind is still on her."

"Ah; well you better serve your drinks. I'll find a seat at the bar."

Alex nodded before continuing towards the table with the drinks. Catherine stepped up to Doug and tapped him on the shoulder.

Doug was checking to see if he was a winner, and before Doug had a chance to see who tapped him, Bryon said, "Hi, Catherine. Can I get you your usual?"

Doug looked at Catherine as she answered, "That would be good; thanks." She then saw the confused look that Doug was giving her. "What's wrong, Doug?"

As Doug crumbled the lottery ticket, he said, "Oh, nothing. So Catherine what brings you here?"

As Doug tossed the crumbled ticket onto the bar, Catherine said, "This place is my hangout. Of course I'm not usually here before ten, but Becky wanted me to meet her here around eight for some reason."

"You're friends with Becky?"

"Of course I'm friends with Becky. What kind of question was that?"

"I just thought you were friends with Alex."

"Just because Alex and Becky are not on good terms doesn't mean I have to choose one of them to be friends with over the other. I'm remaining friends to both of them."

"Of course. I didn't mean anything by that."

"You know this anyway, so why were you questioning me about it?"

"I just went temporarily brain dead."

Catherine slightly laughed before saying, "Okay that was

too easy of a set up, so I'm not going to comment on that statement."

Doug slightly laughed before saying, "Yeah, I guess I did set myself up with my last statement." Doug then gestured towards Liz. "Well, I better get back to my date."

Catherine looked in Liz's direction and said, "So you did get a second date with Liz."

Doug gave Catherine a slightly surprised look before grinning and saying, "Of course. Well, I'll see you around." When Catherine nodded, Doug walked away.

Alex, while holding an empty drink tray, had walked up to Liz and was talking to her before Doug walked up. Before Doug took his seat he whispered in Alex's ear, "Bonnie's name in this reality is Catherine, and I'm willing to bet that she is the Catherine Weis who you read about from your diary."

As Doug was taking his seat, Alex said, "Thanks for the information."

"No problem. Oh and, uh, Becky will be here in thirty minutes."

"Okay; now thanks for the warning." Liz gave Alex a confused look while Doug just grinned. "Well, I better get back to work."

"See you around," Liz said. Alex nodded before walking away. "So, Doug, what were you and Alex going on about?"

"Oh, uh… well, most likely you know that Alex and Becky don't get a long," Doug said. Liz just nodded. "Okay, well, Becky will be here shortly and I was just telling Alex that so she can prepare for the unpleasantness."

Liz gave Doug a skeptical stare before saying in an uncertain tone, "Okay."

Alex walked up to a table that was seating an adult couple and two pre-teenaged boys. The family paused from eating when Alex asked, "Can I get anyone anything else?"

"We're good for now; thanks," the man said.

"You're welcome," Alex said before she turned and walked towards the bar.

Catherine was sitting at the bar next to where Alex and Sylvia would be served by Bryon. After Alex stepped up, Catherine asked, "So, Alex, how long have you been working here?"

"This is my first night," Alex said while picking up a watered down soda with little ice.

Alex was taking a drink when Catherine asked, "So why did you take a job here?"

Alex swallowed the mouth full of soda that she had and as she was putting her drink back down on the bar, she said, "I need the money."

"Why don't you just ask your parents for it?"

"I can't do that."

"Why not?"

"It's a personal matter that I can't involve my parents or anyone else."

"You can at least tell me about it, can't you?"

"Sorry, Catherine, I won't involve you either."

"Alex, we're friends."

"And that's the reason that I'm not involving you."

"It's not anything illegal, is it?"

"No; of course not," Alex quickly answered. "It's just a very personal matter to me that's all."

"All right, I won't ask again, but if you ever decide to share, I'll be around to listen."

Alex grinned before saying, "Thanks." She then gestured towards the tables. "Well, I better see if anyone wants anything."

As Alex was walking away while carrying an empty tray, a man with a vase of assorted flowers walked in. Alex saw the man with the flowers coming towards her and didn't think anything about it as she and the man passed each other.

The man with the flowers walked up to the bar. When Bryon faced the man the man asked, "Is there an Alexandra Larson working here?"

Catherine turned to look as Bryon pointed towards Alex and said, "Yeah, she is the red head who is waiting tables. You can wait here. She'll be back in a minute or two."

Catherine saw a card attached to the flowers.

Five minutes later, Alex walked back up to the bar with dirty glasses on her tray. Alex saw that Catherine was smiling at her as she walked up. She then gave Catherine a curious look before asking, "Why do you look like the cat that ate the canary?"

"In two seconds you will be smiling too."

"What are you talking about?"

Catherine pointed to the man with the flowers before saying, "That man is here to see you."

As Alex faced the man the man asked, "Are you Alexandra Larson?"

Alex looked at the flowers and said cautiously, "Yeah, that's me."

The man held out the flowers for Alex to take and said, "These flowers are for you."

Alex slightly held up the tray of dirty glasses while saying, "Just one second." Alex put the tray on the bar and told Bryon, "I need five beers."

"Okay," Bryon said.

Alex turned towards the man with the flowers and as she took the flowers the man said, "Have a nice evening, Ms. Larson."

"Thank you; you too," Alex said before the man could walk away.

As Alex was setting the flowers on the bar, Catherine said, "Read the card." Alex smelled the flowers before picking up the card. After she opened the card she began silently reading it. "Read it aloud." Alex looked at Catherine for a second before reading what was on the card, which was a short romantic poem that brought a pleasant grin across Catherine's face as well as Alex's. "So who sent you the flowers?"

Alex looked at all sides of the card before saying, "I don't know. It's not signed."

Catherine smiled before saying, "You have a secret admirer. That's so romantic."

Bryon put the last of the five beers on the tray before saying, "Alex, here are the beers you ordered."

"Okay, thanks."

"And I'm going to put your flowers behind the bar and out of the way of serving drinks," Bryon said.

"That's fine."

As Alex picked up the tray of drinks, Catherine asked, "So who do you think your secret admirer is?"

"I can't think of anyone who would send me flowers," Alex said before walking away with the drinks.

Alex was gone for a few minutes from the bar and when she returned with some dirty glasses, a guest check and the money, Catherine gestured towards an attractive man who was sitting at the other end of the bar while saying, "I would love to get flowers from that guy." Alex looked at the man who Catherine was talking about. "Don't you think he's handsome?"

Alex quickly said without thinking, "Oh, yeah; he's very handsome." Alex suddenly realized of what she had said and mouthed out the words to herself, "Oh, yeah; he's very handsome?" Alex then slightly cringed in disbelief.

Alex stepped up to the bar and as she was putting down the tray, Catherine said, "Well, unfortunately he's married."

Alex handed Bryon the guest check and the money before facing Catherine and asking, "You know who he is?"

"I don't know his name, but I've seen him in here before with his wife."

Bryon placed the change on Alex's tray and said, "His name is Gary and he's married to my sister Jessica. So you two can leer in another direction."

"I wasn't the one leering," Alex insisted.

"Come on, Alex," Bryon said. "I saw how you were watching Gary when he walked in forty minutes ago."

"I was just watching him to see where he was going to sit," Alex quickly retorted. She then picked up the change and walked away.

Catherine looked at Bryon before saying, "Okay, someone is very defensive."

"Actually she seemed to have been more embarrassed than defensive," Bryon said as Stephen was stepping out from the kitchen.

Before Catherine was able to respond, Stephen stepped up to Bryon and said, "Hey let Alex know that one of her food orders is done."

"Will do," Bryon said.

"Hey, Stephen," Catherine said.

"Hi, Catherine," Stephen said before turning and walking away.

Catherine faced Bryon again before saying, "I've seen Jessica in here many times, and I didn't know she was your sister."

"The subject never came up before," Bryon said. He then stepped away to wait on another customer at the bar.

Alex was gone for a couple of minutes and when she was returning to the bar, Bryon saw her stepping up. "Hey, Alex, one of your orders is up."

"Okay, thanks."

Before Alex was able to walk away, Catherine asked, "Alex, getting back to your secret admirer; is there someone who you hope that the flowers are from?"

Alex grinned long enough for Catherine to see it. She then tried to keep a straight face while saying, "Not at all."

"There is a guy," Catherine said.

"I swear there's not."

"If you didn't grin before you answered I might've believed you."

"I have food to serve, so I can't stand here debating this," Alex said before turning and walking away.

Catherine watched Bryon as he stepped up and said, "I think you're right about Alex liking someone."

"I wonder if the guy who sent Alex the flowers is the same guy who Alex likes."

"Good question," Bryon said before Sylvia stepped up to order a few drinks.

Four minutes later, Alex was serving food to the three men near the entrance. When she put the last plate down, she asked, "Is anyone ready for another drink?"

One of the men gestured for Alex to wait before gulping down the little that he had in his glass. He then held it out for Alex to take while saying, "I'll take another one."

As Alex took the glass and placed it on the tray the other two men also said, "I'll take another drink."

Alex slightly grinned and said, "I'll be back in a couple of minutes with your drinks."

Bryon was waiting on a customer at the other end of the bar as Alex was walking towards the bar.

When Catherine saw Alex stepping up Catherine asked, "So, Alex, who's the guy who you like?"

"Catherine, I'm not interested in anyone, honest," Alex said before putting the tray on the bar.

"Then, if what you say is true, I know this guy who would be perfect for you."

"I can get my own dates, thank you very much."

"Oh, I know you can, but I met this guy last night, and I was thinking that he would be a great date for you."

"Catherine, I'm not interested in being fixed up on a date."

"This guy is a real catch."

"If he's a catch then why don't you date him?"

Catherine said sarcastically, "I'm dating Dale."

Alex thought for a second before asking, "You're dating Dale Hathaway?"

"Yeah. You know this, so why do you look shocked?"

"It's not that I'm shocked." Bryon was walking up as Alex continued to say, "I just think that you can do better than Dale."

"Alex, you told me that you would stop putting Dale down."

"You're right. You date whoever you want and I'll date whoever I want, and I don't want any blind dates."

"Okay, Alex. You made your point."

Alex saw Bryon pointing at her before telling him, "I need three beers."

As the evening progressed, and when Alex was at the bar, Alex and Catherine casually talked. When Becky came in she sat next to Catherine. Becky would talk to Alex in a civil manner as she, Alex and Catherine talked. Doug and Liz stayed long enough to eat and then left. When the kitchen closed for the night Stephen joined Becky at the bar.

Little Bucks closed at 1:00 A.M., however, Alex, Sylvia and Bryon stayed thirty minutes longer to clean up. When Alex left the bar she took her flowers.

Sunday, October 24 at 8:00 A.M., Trudy walked out of her

bedroom and noticed the flowers along with the card on the coffee table. She picked up the card and read it. A grin came across her face before she said above a whisper, "Someone has a crush on Alex." Trudy put the card back, grabbed her purse and walked out.

Ten minutes later, Trudy was joining Miles with her breakfast in the lunchroom; however, Miles was just finishing his meal. Once Trudy had sat down, Miles asked, "So where's Alex?"

"She's still sleeping," Trudy said before taking a bite.

"I should go and wake her up."

Trudy swallowed the bite before saying, "I doubt she's been sleeping all that long, so she might get mad at you if you wake her."

"I'll take my chances. Can I get your key?"

Trudy pulled out her key from her purse and as she was handing it to Miles she said, "Don't say I didn't warn you."

Miles stood up and said, "I won't." He then picked up his tray.

"And bring back my key."

Miles just waved as he walked away. Before leaving the lunchroom he dumped the trash into the trash bin and placed his tray on top of the bin to be collected by the worker. Five minutes later, he was gently shaking Alex to wake up.

When Alex saw who was shaking her awake she asked, "Why are you in my room?"

"Chad invited you and me to see the sites of Boston with him and his fiancée and I was hoping that I can talk you into it."

Alex gave Miles a curious look while asking, "When did he invite us?"

"At the hospital yesterday, just after you and Linda left to go to the restroom."

131

"And you waited until now to tell me this?"

"I had planned to tell you about it after we left the hospital and it slipped my mind. I thought about it again after I woke up this morning. So can I talk you into going?"

"What time is it?"

"It's about 8:20 A.M."

"I should shoot you for waking me up this early on a Sunday."

"Lucky for me, security doesn't allow guns on campus." Alex just gave him a smirk. "So how about it?"

"I have to be at work at 4:00 P.M."

"No problem. We'll be back in plenty of time."

"Fine, I'll go with you, but I want to be back around 3:00 P.M. to take a shower."

"Again, no problem."

"Wait in the common room and I'll be right out once I'm dressed."

Miles just nodded and walked out.

Miles was sitting on the couch for ten minutes before Alex walked out. Miles stood up and gestured towards the flowers before asking, "So does Trudy have someone special in her life?"

Alex gave Miles a curious look before saying, "Actually someone sent those to me last night while I was at work. I was actually thinking that you might have sent them to me."

"So does that mean that you would accept flowers from me if I sent them to you?"

"Nothing can come from it, so you would be wasting your time if you did."

"Well, it's a good thing I didn't waste my time then, isn't it?"

Alex gave Miles a curious look before asking, "Are you being honest with me and you didn't send me those flowers?"

"You sound disappointed."

"No, it's not that I'm disappointed. It's just that… if you didn't send them then I have no idea who did."

"It sounds as though you have a secret admirer."

Alex gave Miles a skeptical look for a second before saying, "Yeah… I guess I do."

Miles stepped closer to the door before asking, "Are you ready to go?"

"I have to use the restroom before we leave the dormitory."

Miles opened the door before saying, "Ladies first." Alex slightly grinned and walked out. Miles walked out behind Alex with a big grin on his face. "Oh, I have Trudy's key and she wants it back."

"Where is she?"

"In the lunchroom."

"Okay, after I use the restroom, we'll go by the lunchroom."

"So whose vehicle are we taking?"

"This is your idea of going so we're taking your van."

"That's fine with me," Miles said before taking Chad's business card out of his back pocket along with taking his cell phone off his belt. "Well, I better call Chad to find out where he and Alice are going to be." Alex gave Miles a nod before he dialed his phone.

Minutes later, after Alex had used the restroom along with returning Trudy's key, Alex and Miles left campus in Miles' van.

As Miles was driving in the direction of a fast food restaurant that served breakfast, Alex pointed towards it while saying, "I want to go through the drive through and get something that will hold me over till lunch."

"Okay," Miles said before turning on his blinker to get over.

Chapter Nine

After Miles parked his van next to Alice's car in the parking lot at the Museum of Fine Art, he and Alex got out of the van and walked up to Chad and Alice.

After the introductions between Alex, Miles and Alice were done, Alice said, "The museum doesn't open till ten."

"I think the only thing that is open right now is the national parks; like the Charleston Navy Yard and the Bunker Hill Monument," Alex said.

"One of those places would be a good place to start," Chad said.

"Chad, I have plenty of room in my van if you and Alice would want to ride with us," Miles said. "I also know where the sites are."

Alice looked at Chad while saying, "That's fine with me."

"Okay," Chad said.

Alex got back into the passenger seat while Chad and Alice got into the seats directly behind Alex and Miles.

Just after Miles drove off the parking lot, Alice said, "So Alex; Miles, I hear that you two go to Harvard."

"That's right," Alex said.

"Where are you two from?" Alice asked.

"I'm from St. Louis," Alex said.

"I'm not from any city in particular, but the last city before coming to Harvard was Wichita, Kansas," Miles said.

Alex looked at Miles before asking, "You and Trudy moved around a lot?"

"My dad is a one-star general in the air force and so my parents, my sister and I traveled from base to base," Miles said. "The longest place that we lived at was two years."

"So you and Trudy must have grown up in a disciplined environment," Alex said.

"Actually, my dad might have been an officer in the air force, but my mom made sure that when he was home that his rank came off before entering the house."

Alex chuckled before saying, "So in other words, your mom out ranked your dad at home."

"No," Miles quickly said. "My parents talked and decided things as partners."

"That's good," Alex said.

"So, Miles, where have you lived?" Alice asked.

Miles listed a long list of cities and one was in Germany.

"Oh, can you speak German?" Alice asked.

"I can." Miles then said in German, "Alex is a gorgeous woman."

Alex gave Miles a curious look as Alice asked, "What did you say?"

"Since I heard my name mentioned, I want to know what you said too," Alex said.

Miles glanced at Alex while saying, "I said that you are a gorgeous woman and you are."

Alex gave Miles a stunned look as Alice said, "Ah, that's sweet that you tell your girlfriend that. Chad tells me I'm pretty all the time too."

"Except Miles and I aren't dating," Alex said. "We're just friends."

"It sounds as though Miles wants to be more than friends and you two do make a lovely couple," Alice said.

"Alice, I think we should stay out of Alex and Miles' personal matters," Chad said.

"Chad, Alice didn't say anything wrong," Alex said. "I actually know that Miles wants to be more than friends, but I won't date anyone until I straighten out some things in my life."

Miles looked at Alex while saying, "We'll see."

Alex grinned before saying, "I'm telling you, you're wasting your time."

Miles grinned before repeating, "We'll see."

"Okay, time to change the subject," Alex said. "So, Alice, where are you from?"

"I'm from Long Island, New York," Alice said. "Chad and his family are also from there."

"Why does Chris remain in Boston?" Alex asked.

"Chris is still attending Harvard," Chad said. "My mom and the people at Harvard worked out something to where Chris doesn't have to attend classes, but he does have to turn in his homework. That is where I come in. I go to his classes to get his assignments and I turn in his completed ones."

"How long has Chris been in the hospital?" Alex asked.

"Ten days," Chad said.

"Keeping him in Harvard and paying his medical expense must be costing your parents a fortune," Alex said.

"Well, my dad is a president at a fortune-five-hundred company," Chad said. "It may be draining my parents' finances, but they'll survive."

"So do you work for your dad?" Alex asked.

"No," Chad said. "I'm actually a computer game designer. I have my laptop at the hotel that we're at and I work from there when I'm not with Chris."

"That's fascinating," Alex said. "Alice, what do you do?"

"I actually do work for Chad's dad," Alice said. "In fact, I'm his dad's secretary."

"That is also how we met," Chad added. "My dad didn't

like the idea of me dating his secretary, but he calmed down when we became serious."

"We actually hid the fact that we were dating from him for the first five months which I thought was romantic," Alice said. "Then we got caught kissing in the parking lot of the company."

"You can probably imagine the choice words that my dad had for me when he found out," Chad added.

"Oh yeah, I can imagine," Alex said.

"So, Miles, what was it like to grow up on an air force base?" Alice asked.

In a long and detailed story, Miles described the experiences he had while living on each base.

As the morning slowly passed, Alex, Miles, Chad and Alice had visited three museums. At one point Miles and Chad were telling jokes. Alex and Alice just listened. Alice also noticed as to how Alex was enjoying herself around Miles.

At 1:30 P.M., Alex, Miles, Chad and Alice entered a pizza parlor for lunch that had a dining room and a jukebox. After the pizza and the drinks were ordered Chad and Alice excused themselves and left the table.

When Chad and Alice stepped away, Miles asked, "So, Alex, are you having a good time?"

Alex nodded before saying, "I am. I've been to these museums before, but for some reason I'm enjoying them more today."

Miles grinned and said, "I'm also enjoying myself and by seeing the sites with you, today is a perfect day."

Alex gave Miles a smirk before saying, "You're really full of it."

"I'm serious. I've seen these sites before also, but I didn't enjoy myself as I am today, and I do believe it's because you are with me."

Alex gave Miles a delightful stare for a brief moment. She then broke the stare and as she was standing up she said, "I'm going to use the restroom."

Miles just watched Alex as she walked away.

As Alex walked into the restroom, Alice was washing her hands. Alice looked at Alex before asking, "Why do you deny your feelings for Miles?"

"What do you mean?" Alex quickly asked.

Alice pulled out a paper towel and as she dried her hands she said, "I see how you look at Miles. You're romantically interested in him. He's definitely interested in you, so you should go for it."

Alex said in an unconvincing tone, "I'm not romantically interested in Miles."

"Yeah... you don't sound convincing."

As Alice was throwing the paper towel away Alex tried to sound more convincing while saying, "Miles is just a friend and that is the only way I see him. So the only feelings I have for him is of a brother image."

Alice grinned before questioning, "Are you trying to convince me or yourself?"

"I'm serious. I'm not interested in him."

As Alice walked towards the exit she said, "Okay. Whatever you say."

As Alice was opening the door to step out, Alex said, "I'm serious." Alice just waved as she walked out. When the door shut behind Alice, Alex looked into the mirror. "I am serious. I'm a heterosexual so I can't be attracted to Miles. I can't be." Alex thought for a second as she stared at her reflection. "Oh god I think I'm losing my identity and becoming a woman." Alex turned towards a stall. "I have to do something to speed up at getting back to my own reality before I lose my identity completely." Alex stepped into the stall.

At the table, Miles, Chad and Alice were having a pleasant conversation as the waitress stepped up to the table with the drinks. Alex was walking towards the table and saw the waitress as she was walking away.

After Alex took her seat, she said in a distant tone, "Miles, I'm sorry to be a party-pooper, but I just remembered something that I really have to do. So if you don't mind, can you take me back to Harvard? Of course I mean after we eat."

Miles gave Alex a confused look before saying, "Okay, after we eat, I'll take you back to Harvard."

"Thank you," Alex said in the same distant tone before she picked up her soda and took a drink.

"Miles, perhaps you should take us to our car before you take Alex back to Harvard," Chad said.

"Is that okay, Alex?" Miles asked.

Alex swallowed the drink that she took before saying, "Of course, it's okay." She then put her soda down and stood up. "It's too quiet in here. I'm going to play the jukebox."

As Alex was walking away, Chad said, "Okay, Alex suddenly turned into an iceberg."

"She did act a bit strange," Miles said before standing up. "I'm going to see what's up."

Alex was looking through the songs when Miles stepped up to Alex and tapped her on the shoulder. Alex glanced at Miles and then turned back towards the jukebox before asking in a distant tone, "What do you want?"

"Did I do something to get you mad at me?"

"I'm not mad at you."

"Then why all of a sudden that you turned cold towards me?"

Alex looked at Miles before saying, "I'm not..." Alex cut off what she was about to say.

"Alex, you had talked to and listened to me all morning.

Earlier you even smiled and laughed at my stupid jokes. You were enjoying yourself and now all of a sudden you're acting as if you're not having fun at all."

"I told you earlier that I was having a good time."

"Then what is it, Alex?"

Alex stared into Miles' eyes while saying, "I am not Alexandra. I do not belong here. I told you this yesterday."

"It doesn't matter how you got here; you're here now. Shouldn't that be the only thing that matters?"

Alex pressed the top play list button before saying, "I do not belong here and as soon as I'm able to, I'm going home." Alex then turned and walked back to the table. Miles took a troubled breath before following behind Alex.

As the minutes slowly passed, Alex remained quiet and just listened to the others as they talked. Alice would ask Alex questions while trying to get her into the conversation; however, Alex remained short with her responses.

After the pizza came, Miles, Chad and Alice continued with the discussion as they ate. Alex ate two slices of pizza before placing a few dollars on the table and saying, "I'm going outside for some fresh air."

Alice saw a heartbroken expression on Miles' face as Miles watched Alex leave. Alice then told Miles, "Alex is very much interested in you."

"Well, if that's true then she has a funny way of showing it," Miles said.

"She's just scared to open up around you," Alice said. "Just be patient and give her, her space. Just don't give up on her."

Miles, Chad and Alice finished eating, paid for the meal and left. Alex was again quiet as Miles drove Chad and Alice to their car and she remained quiet as Miles was driving back to Harvard.

Miles got frustrated with the silence and asked, "Alex, will you talk to me?"

"I have nothing to talk about."

"Talk about anything. Talk about your favorite movie. Talk about the weather. Just please talk to me."

"Miles, I'm sorry, but I'm not in the mood for small talk."

"This silence between you and me is driving me nuts."

"Okay, fine; if you want to talk then let's talk," Alex said before taking a deep breath. "I need to raise more than five thousand dollars in addition to what we have already so my friends and I can charter a plane to Mexico City. Do you have any suggestions on how I can do that?"

"Alex, that's not what I meant."

"You told me that you want to talk about anything and that's the subject I want to talk about."

"I don't know where or how to raise that much money."

"If you can't help me get to Mexico City then there's really nothing for us to talk about," Alex said in an unpleasant tone.

"Okay, with the mood you're in right now, I'll deal with us not talking," Miles said before turning up the radio.

With a mournful expression across her face, Alex looked over at Miles before saying, "I'm sorry. I'm just very confused about things right now and I need to deal with my problems."

As Miles was turning down the radio a little he said, "I understand that, Alex, but you're not alone in this. I'll help you through it."

"Miles, thanks for wanting to be there for me. I really appreciate that, but you are actually the one person who can't help me."

"Why can't I help?"

"You just can't. I'm sorry."

"Okay. I guess I have to accept that," Miles said before turning up the radio again.

Alex looked at Miles for just a second before turning and

staring out her window.

Several minutes later, Alex grabbed clean clothes and went to take a shower. Miles searched for Trudy for a few minutes before finding her at the library.

Miles sat in a seat across from Trudy and when Trudy looked up Miles said, "I need your help."

"You need my help with what?"

"Alex is acting a bit strange and I was wondering if you can talk with her to find out why."

"What do you mean that she is acting strange?"

"I was with Alex, Chris Swan's brother Chad and Chad's fiancée for the past few hours. We were having fun... but then all of a sudden it was like a switch was flipped and she turned cold towards me."

"I'll talk with her to find out what's up. Why are you hanging out with Alex anyway?"

"I know Alex switched places with the Alex from our reality, but I feel something for this Alex. For the first time since Maria and I broke up, I feel that I can move on."

Trudy grinned before saying, "You're the one who sent Alex those flowers."

"Yes, but don't tell Alex that I'm the one. I don't want her to know right now."

"Okay, I won't tell her, but you really need to refocus your attention on dating someone else."

"Why?"

"It's not my place to say," Trudy said before standing and collecting her books. "I'll go and talk to Alex for you."

Minutes later, when Trudy walked into her dorm, Alex was in her room getting dressed in a nice pair of blue jeans, a sloppy T-shirt, tennis shoes and no makeup. Trudy heard Alex moving around in her room before she walked up and knocked on her door.

Alex opened the door and as she stood in the doorway she asked, "Hi; what's up?"

Trudy looked at what Alex was wearing before asking, "Are you planning to go out looking like that?"

"I'm planning to go to work looking like this. Why do you ask?"

"I thought you were going to maintain Alex's character, and put on makeup and wear what she would wear."

"I don't think I can do that anymore."

"Why can't you?"

"Trudy, I'm not a woman, and I'm uncomfortable at pretending to be one."

"Well, physically you are a woman."

"Yes," Alex uttered, while being snippy. "And I'm reminded of that fact every time I look into the mirror, so I really don't need you to remind me of it."

"Okay, you're not due to become moody for another week, so what's up with you?"

"I am a woman is what is up with me," Alex unpleasantly uttered.

"Okay, I'm not following you."

"I'm feeling like a woman." When Trudy made a gesture that she's still wasn't following Alex blurted out, "I'm feeling things for Miles that I shouldn't be feeling."

Trudy thought for a second and when it suddenly dawned on Trudy as to what Alex was meaning, she said, "Oh. That's uh… that's uh…"

As Trudy was having trouble at finding the words to finish the sentence, Alex said, "Yes; my thoughts exactly."

"Okay… well if you can't get back to your reality then that's actually not a bad thing."

"Trudy, I have only been here since Thursday and already I'm being assimilated as a woman. That is not good. And why didn't you tell Miles that I was a man in my reality?"

"Okay, if you want Miles to know then that is something you have to tell him. That is not my secret to tell."

"Well, he wants to date me and if I tell him now, I feel that I would lose him as a friend."

"If you are going to act cold towards him then what does it matter?"

"I just need to get a handle on the feelings that I'm having, and then I can be around him as a friend."

"Yeah... good luck with that."

Alex gave Trudy a confused look before asking, "What do you mean?"

"You have a romantic interest in Miles..."

"Okay, you don't have to keep telling me what I already know."

"And that's not going to change, unless you find someone else who you are more attracted to."

"I wonder if I should go out and find a woman to be with."

Trudy gave Alex a skeptical look while saying, "Yeah, I really don't see that happening."

"Why don't you?"

"I've seen how you were checking out hot guys Friday night."

"What are you talking about?"

"O'Shannon's Pub was packed Friday night with men and women, and the only half I saw you staring at the entire night were the men."

"I'm sure I stared at a few pretty women." Trudy just shook her head 'no'. Alex gave Trudy a curious look before asking, "Not even one?"

Trudy continued to shake her head while saying, "I'm afraid not."

"Okay, I have to get out of this reality and back to mine as soon as possible, before I completely lose myself."

"Meanwhile I think you need to maintain the image of Alexandra."

"Fine, I'll put on nicer clothes and some makeup."

"Alex wore perfume too, so it wouldn't hurt for you to put some on."

"Fine, I'll put on perfume too," Alex said before stepping out of the doorway while walking towards her closet. When Trudy followed, Alex asked, "I think I know, but what did you mean that I'm not due to become moody for another week?"

"Your menstrual cycle is almost exactly a week before mine and mine is about two weeks away."

As Alex was opening the closet, she said, "And I thought that was what you were referring to." Alex pulled out a nice blouse. "Perhaps you should tell me what I need to know about that now."

Trudy grinned before saying, "I was actually thinking the same thing."

As Alex was changing her shirt, Trudy was telling Alex what she needed to know and do when she has a menstrual cycle.

After Alex put on a nice blouse, her boots, makeup, and perfume she went to Brandy's dorm and knocked on her door. The hallway was slightly crowded with people walking in both directions.

Chloe, Brandy's roommate, opened the door and asked, "Yes, may I help you?"

"Yeah, I'm Alex…"

Chloe said with a slight attitude, "I know who you are, but what I don't know is what you want."

"I'm looking for Brandy."

"She's not here," Chloe utter, while being snippy.

"Do you know where she is?"

Chloe shook her head while saying, "No; I don't."

"Thanks, and I'm sorry for what I did to you in the past."

"You never did anything to me."

"Then why are you having an attitude towards me?"

"I've seen how you treat people and you never did anything to me because I stay clear of you. Brandy stays clear of you too so I can't imagine what you want with her."

"Well, if you see Brandy please let her know I'm looking for her."

"Yeah, I'll put it at the bottom of my to-do list."

"You stay clear of me because of how I treat people, but where I'm standing at the moment you're no better," Alex hissed before turning and walking away.

As Alex was walking away, Chloe blurted out, "That's where you're wrong."

Alex never responded to what Chloe had said. The people in the hallway stared at Chloe as if she had lost her mind. When Chloe saw that the people were looking at her, she stepped back into her dorm and closed the door.

Alex went straight to the library and looked around. Brandy wasn't there, but Cindy was. She walked up to Cindy and asked before Cindy had a chance to notice her presence, "Hey, have you seen Brandy?"

Cindy looked up and when she saw who it was, she said, "I saw her this morning. What's going on?"

Alex sat down before saying, "I'm thinking that at least one of us needs to go to Mexico City to look for Randy now and I want to be the one to do it."

"None of us has the money to go to Mexico City."

"Brandy has the money for one person to go."

"Alex, I really think that we should stick to the plan and that we all should go there together."

"And that will take weeks; possibly even months."

146

Cindy gave Alex a curious look before asking, "Why is that a problem for you all of a sudden?"

Alex stood up before saying, "I can't stay in this reality and be a woman."

Before Cindy was able to respond Alex walked away. Cindy then said barely above a whisper, "Nice talking to you too." Cindy then went back to her studies.

Alex was gone for five minutes when Cindy noticed Doug walking in. Cindy then left her book on the table and as she walked up to Doug she said, "Hey, Doug."

"Hi, Cindy, what's up?"

"Something weird is up with Alex and I think you need to talk to her about it."

Doug gave Cindy a curious look before asking, "What do you mean?"

"She was in here about five minutes ago looking for Brandy. I think she wants to borrow money from her so that she can go to Mexico City alone."

"Did she say why she wanted to go alone?"

"I think she is having a problem with being a woman in this reality."

"Okay, I'll talk with her to see what's up. Do you know where she went?" Cindy just shook her head. Doug took a breath before he continued to say, "She works tonight so if I can't find her soon then I'll check there when her shift starts."

"Okay. Well I'm going to get back to my studies."

"Okay, bye," Doug said before turning and walking away.

After a short search, Doug saw Trudy in the hallway of the dormitory and walked up to her.

Trudy saw a concerned expression on Doug's face and as Doug stepped up Trudy asked, "Is there a problem?"

"I just talked to Cindy and she's worried that Alex is not adjusting to this reality too well. Have you seen her? I want to talk to her about how she's adjusting."

"I saw her about fifteen minutes ago. She was getting ready for work."

"How did she seem when you saw her?"

"Doug, I know what's going on with Alex and her adjusting to this reality isn't the problem. Her problem is that she's adjusting to this reality too well and that's frightening the hell out of her."

"I don't understand."

"Doug, Alex is losing her male identity..."

"Wait!" Doug interrupted with. "You know that Alex was a man in our reality?"

"I do, and because she's a female in this reality, she's having female urges and desires."

"When you say female urges, you mean what exactly?"

Trudy grinned before saying, "I think you know what I mean."

"I think I do too, but tell me anyway."

"Alex finds men sexually attractive... my brother Miles for one in particular."

"And you said this is frightening her, which explains why she's in a hurry to get to Mexico City to look for Randy. Thanks, Trudy, for the information. I'm going to Little Bucks and wait for her there."

"Okay; bye."

"Bye," Doug said before he and Trudy went their respective ways.

Chapter Ten

3:50 P.M. at Little Bucks, Doug was sitting at the bar drinking a beer and talking to Bryon. A man and a woman sat at the other end of the bar and were engrossed in their own conversation to notice anything around them. The tables were empty. Stephen was the only cook for the day and he was in the kitchen cooking a meal for Doug.

When Alex walked in she saw Doug at the bar. She walked up to an empty barstool next to Doug and placed her purse on the bar before sitting down.

When Doug looked at her, she asked, "Is it Super Bowl Sunday?" Doug gave Alex a confused look. "You don't usually drink on Sundays."

Doug gave an 'Oh' look with a slight grin before saying, "Actually I'm here waiting on you. I want to talk to you."

"What about?"

Doug gestured towards a table and said, "Let's talk in private."

"This must be serious." Alex then stood up followed by Doug. Before Alex and Doug walked away, Alex said, "Bryon, I want a cola."

"You got it; it will be next to your purse."

Alex just nodded before she followed Doug to a table. After they sat down Alex asked, "So what's up?"

"You have Cindy worried about you. She thinks that you're having a really rough time adjusting to this reality."

Alex slightly bowed her head before saying, "I am... to an

extent."

"Yeah I know all about it."

Alex quickly looked up at Doug before asking, "What do you mean you know all about it?"

"I ran into Trudy just after talking with Cindy and Trudy filled me in on how you are having female urges."

Alex blurted out in a shock tone, "What? I can't believe Trudy told you that."

"She only told me because I expressed my concern for how well you are adapting to this reality. She didn't tell me to betray your trust."

"Okay, well, since you do know, you know why I have to get to Mexico City as soon as possible."

"Alex, Randy might be on his way here, so you shouldn't be in a hurry to get to Mexico."

"Doug, I'm losing my identity as a man, and I can't sit still and let it happen."

"Well, by you running off to Mexico by yourself is not going to help anything. Randy might not even be there. The idea of him being in Mexico is just a hunch that you have."

"Then what am I suppose to do?"

"Just keep your mind occupied on making money, and try to think of other ways to make money... make money honestly."

Alex grinned before saying, "You didn't have to add the last part to that sentence."

Doug grinned before saying, "Well, with how desperate you are to get to Mexico, I thought I should."

Alex gestured towards the bar while saying, "Well, it's almost four, so I better get to work."

As Alex and Doug were standing up, Doug said, "I'm going back to the bar also. I ordered a cheeseburger and fries just before you came in."

Alex and Doug walked back to the bar and sat down. As Alex picked up her glass of soda to take a drink, Doug and Byron started their discussion at the point of where they had left off. Before the conversation got too far Stephen came out from the kitchen with Doug's food.

After Stephen put the plate of food down in front of Doug, he looked at Alex and asked, "So, are you ready to work the dinner crowd solo tonight?"

Bryon stopped talking and listened to Alex and Stephen as Alex answered, "Of course. Why wouldn't I be ready?"

"It's infrequent, but sometimes this place gets packed on a Sunday. In fact, last Sunday this place was busier than usual. That's why Sylvia didn't want to work Sundays... especially by herself."

"Well, if we get busy today, I'll just brave the storm."

"Alex, I was watching you last night and you can handle the rush if we get busy," Bryon said.

Alex grinned before saying, "Thanks."

"Oh, Bryon, you would know this," Stephen began. "What's the story behind Francis Star?"

"Who's Francis Star?" Alex asked.

"He's a rooky jockey who is going to be riding the horse White Dasher tomorrow," Byron said. "This is both Francis' and White Dasher's first race, and I hear White Dasher is fast. I think that horse is going to be interesting to watch."

Doug saw Alex in deep thought. He put his hand on Alex's shoulder and asked, "Are you okay?"

Alex came out of her thoughts before questioning, "What?"

"Are you okay?" Doug repeated.

"Why are you asking me that?"

"You spaced out there for a minute."

"I was thinking about something, that's all."

"What were you thinking about?"

Instead of answering Doug's question, Alex said, "So tell me all the juicy detail between you and Liz."

"All right, you made your point." Alex just grinned as Doug continued to say, "I won't ask you about private matters."

"I knew you would understand," Alex said with a slight smirk. She then took a drink of her soda.

As Alex was putting her soda down a group of eight people walked into the bar. The group consisted of three men in their early to mid thirties; two women also in their early thirties; a ten-year-old boy; a seven-year-old girl and a nine-month-old boy. The baby was being pushed in a stroller. The group waited at the entrance to be seated.

Bryon gestured towards the customers while saying, "Alex, you're on."

Alex scooted her purse towards Bryon and said, "I need a ticket book, and put my purse behind the bar."

Bryon grabbed a ticket book for her. As he was handing the book to Alex he said, "Your purse will be where it was yesterday."

As Alex was taking the book, she said, "Thanks." She then turned and walked towards the customers.

When Alex stepped up to the customers she gazed at the baby as he slept. The girl noticed Alex looking at the baby and said, "That's my baby brother. His name is Alex."

Alex gave the girl a grin before saying, "Alex is my name too."

"Alex is a boy's name," the girl said with certainty in her voice.

"Well, my name is actually Alexandra, but the people who know me call me Alex." The girl just bashfully grinned. Alex then focused her attention on the adults. She gestured to a group of tables and said, "I'll pull three or more tables together so everyone can sit together."

"Sounds good," one of the men said.

The customers followed Alex to the tables. Before Alex was able to push the three tables together, the three men did it for her.

As the customers were taking their seats, Alex said, "Thanks." Each table had a menu-holder with menus. Alex pulled out five menus and placed them in front of the adults. "So can I get anyone something to drink while you are deciding what to eat?"

As Alex was taking the drink order three more customers walked through the door. Alex heard the three customers and glanced at them long enough to see where they were sitting.

As the minutes passed, the dinner crowed remained steady for the first hour and an half. Alex had no problem keeping up. Doug remained at the bar and talked to Byron. When Alex was able to find the time for a short break she joined in on their conversation.

By 6:00 P.M. the dinner crowd was more than normal for a Sunday as small groups were coming in only a few minutes apart from each other. Alex wasn't able to wait on each group immediately as they walked in, but she made sure that she acknowledged their presence and waited on them as quickly as she could. The customers saw as to how hard Alex was trying to keep up and not one person complained about the time that it took for him or her to be served.

Byron stayed busy at the bar as the customers waiting to be served went to him for their drinks. Doug helped Alex by collecting the dirty dishes and glasses from the tables after the customers had left.

It wasn't until 7:00 P.M. when all the customers were waited on and Alex was able to take a short break. Alex was sitting down for five minutes when Kenny, Ben, Brandy and

Cindy walked in.

Alex saw them as they walked in. She walked up to them and said, "I didn't expect to see you four."

"Cindy told me that you were looking for me earlier," Brandy said. "I figured I could eat and find out what you were wanting." Brandy gestured to the others. "They wanted to come eat here too."

"About the part I was wanting earlier; I had a small crisis. Doug and I talked it over though, so I'm now good on that." Alex gestured towards an empty table near the bar and continued to say, "As for you four coming here to eat, there's a table up front."

Kenny gestured while saying, "After you."

Doug saw Kenny and the others as they were taking their seats at the table and joined them. Alex took their drink order and then went to the bar to fill it. Once she returned with the drinks, Kenny, Ben, Brandy and Cindy placed their food order.

Before Alex had a chance to walk away, Kenny said, "Hey, Alex. You and Doug should rent your favorite movies and watch them again."

Alex gave Kenny a curious look before asking, "Why should we do that?"

"Brandy, Ben and I spent most of the day watching movies that we saw before, but in this reality one out of every three movies has a completely different ending. One of the movies we watched was completely different and even another one had a different person playing the lead role. It's almost like watching remakes of your favorite movies."

"Do you still have the movies?" Alex asked.

"Some of the movies were on regular TV, but we did rent and watched four movies," Brandy said. "Two of the four were different. Do you want to see them before I return them?"

"I do. I'll be here after midnight, but if you want, you can give the movies to Trudy. I'll watch them when I get off and give them back to you tomorrow."

"Okay," Brandy said.

"Actually, you can give them to me to watch while Alex is at work and I'll give them to Trudy," Doug said.

"That's fine with me." Alex gestured towards the kitchen as she continued to say, "I'll turn in your food order." Alex turned and walked away.

As Alex was walking away, Doug asked, "So which movies were different?"

Kenny and Brandy named off a short list of movies.

As the minutes passed, Kenny, Ben, Brandy and Cindy ate their food and left within thirty minutes. Doug left with them.

As the minutes turned into hours, Alex remained slightly busy as groups of customers came through the door in intervals to where Alex was only able to take a five or sometimes a ten-minute break between waiting on customers. It wasn't until 9:30 P.M. when the intervals between waiting on customers were fifteen minutes or longer. When Alex saw as to how slow it was becoming, she had Stephen fix her something to eat. However, she was only able to eat two-thirds of it before feeling bloated.

Alex was walking in her dorm around 12:20 A.M., and as she walked in she saw the two movies on the coffee table. Beside the movies was an envelope with her name written on it. Alex placed her purse down next to the movies and picked up the envelope. As Alex was opening the envelope Trudy came out from her bedroom.

Alex looked at Trudy and asked, "Did Doug leave the envelope along with the movies?"

"I found the envelope attached to the outside of the door around six. I don't know who left it there."

Alex pulled out the letter inside and read it. Once Alex was done reading it, she pleasantly grinned before saying, "It's another one of those romantic poems like I got yesterday with those flowers. I first thought Miles sent me the flowers, but when I asked him about it, he said he wasn't the one. So now I'm wondering who is sending me flowers and poems."

"Miles told you that the flowers weren't from him?"

Alex thought for a second before saying, "Actually, he never really said one way or the other, but his reaction was as though he wasn't the one to send me the flowers."

"Miles would kill me if he finds out I'm telling you this, but he was the one to send you the flowers. I don't know for certain, but most likely, he's also the one who sent you the poem that you have in your hand."

"I'm going to have to tell him the truth about myself, aren't I?"

"Or you can keep quiet and date him."

"You can't be serious."

"Alex, the odds are against you at switching back to your reality. So why don't you just embrace what is and date Miles. I know you like him."

"I'm sorry, but dating anyone isn't an option."

"Suit yourself."

"Well, I'm going to watch my movies."

As Alex was picking up the movies, Trudy asked, "You never seen those movies before?"

"I have, but according to Brandy and Kenny, these movies are different from what they are from my reality."

"In what way are they different?"

"I don't know. I'll find out when I watch them."

"Do you want some company?"

Alex grinned before saying, "Sure." Alex held up the movies; one in each hand. "So which one do you want to watch first?"

Gerald Pruett

"I've seen both of them, so it doesn't matter with me."

Alex indicated to the movie that she had in her right hand while saying, "Okay, let's go with this movie first."

Alex stepped up to the entertainment center and turned on the TV and DVD player. After putting in the movie, she went to the couch and sat down at the end of the couch. Trudy sat down at the opposite end.

The movie was the same for the first twenty minutes. When the plot suddenly shifted from what it was in Alex's reality, Alex said, "Okay, the movie just changed from what I know." Alex then described in what direction the movie went in her reality.

The movie was two hours long and when it came to an end Alex put in the second movie to be watched. Trudy also watched the second movie with Alex. When that movie came to an end Alex and Trudy went to their respective beds.

Monday, October 25 at 9:50 A.M., Alex was leaving her first class of the day with her purse and book bag. Trudy was also in the class and walked out directly behind Alex while carrying her purse and book bag.

Trudy tapped Alex on the shoulder and asked, "Are you going to the library?"

"No," Alex said as Trudy began walking beside Alex. "I'm not going to risk running into Miles there. I am going to find a place to study though."

"You're really going to avoid Miles?"

"I can't be around Miles right now, and I'm going to stay away from places where he might find me."

"I was hoping to study with you, so do you mind if I come with you?"

"Sure, we can study together."

"So where are we going?"

"To the coffee shop just off campus. In my reality I would

study there more than anywhere else."

"So should we ride in the same car?"

"Actually, I'm going to be there for a while to catch up on all my studies so we better take two cars."

"All right; I'll meet you there."

Trudy followed Alex to the coffee-shop. There was a newspaper box in front, and after parking their cars, Alex bought a paper.

Alex and Trudy studied for an hour and a half and when Trudy noticed it was 11:40 A.M., she said, "It's time for me to leave. I have class in twenty minutes."

As Trudy was putting her books away, Alex said, "Okay. I'll see you on campus later."

"Well, don't forget you have a class at two."

Alex grinned before saying, "I won't."

Alex watched Trudy as she left the coffee-shop. Once Trudy was outside, Alex flipped to the horse racing schedule, and ripped out that section. After Alex collected her books she walked out while leaving the rest of the paper on the table. The paper was opened to the page that was missing part of its page.

Ten minutes later, Trudy was walking through the halls towards her classroom when Miles saw her.

Miles caught up to her and asked, "Hey, Sis, do you know where Alex is?"

Miles noticed a pause in Trudy's response before she said, "No. No I don't."

"Trudy, I know you're lying."

"Okay, fine. I know where she's at, but she doesn't want to see you."

"I just want to talk with her that's all."

"Miles, just let her be right now. She'll talk to you when she's ready."

"Trudy, please tell me where she's at."

"Alex will kill me if I tell you."

"Please."

Trudy thought for a second before saying, "If I tell you, you must act as if you ran into her by chance."

"I will."

"Alex is at that one coffee-shop just off campus. She's there studying, and if she asks, you just happened to be there for a Danish or something."

"I won't tell her that you told me; I promise." When Trudy nodded, Miles turned and walked away.

Trudy watched Miles for a second before going about her business.

Minutes later, Miles was looking over the seating area of the coffee-shop. When he didn't see Alex he walked up to the counter and asked the man working the register, "Have you seen a woman with long red hair? She's a college student and I was told that she was in here studying."

"There was a red headed woman in here, but she left about ten… maybe even fifteen minutes ago."

Miles showed a disgusted expression on his face and commented, "Great. I missed her. I wonder if she went back to Harvard."

"She went to the racetrack," the worker said.

Miles gave the worker a curious look before asking, "She told you that she was going to the racetrack?"

"Well, actually, that is where I'm assuming she went."

"Why are you assuming that?"

"She had a newspaper when she walked in, and when she left she left her paper on the table with the horse racing section ripped out."

"Thanks for the information."

As Miles walked away, the worker responded, "You're welcome." Miles just waved.

Fifteen minutes later, at the racetrack Alex had finally stepped up to the betting window after waiting in a good size line. When she stepped up she placed a twenty-dollar bet on White Dasher to show. White Dasher was a twenty to one long shot. She had also made a ten-dollar bet on the horse that was a favorite to win. The bet she placed was also to show.

Alex made her way through the crowd and walked to where she could see the track. She was there for a short time while waiting for the race to begin when Miles saw her.

Miles casually stepped up to her and asked, "So which horse are you betting on?"

Alex turned and glowered at Miles before asking, "Are you following me?"

"Not at all."

"So you always come to a horse track?"

"Okay, I'll admit that I did come here looking for you."

"And how did you know I was here if you weren't following me?"

Before Miles was able to respond, an announcement came over the speaker that the race was about to begin. Once the announcement was over, Miles asked, "Does it really matter how I found you? I found you and I really want to talk to you."

"Well, I'm not interested in talking to you."

"Why is talking to me a problem for you?"

"Miles, I do not belong here. I belong somewhere else and as soon as I get enough money I'm going to try to fix that fact."

"Is being here so terrible that you are gambling on horses?"

"It's not terrible; it's just that here is not where I belong, and I'm not going to pretend that it is."

"The odds of you making any money here are against you, you know. Most likely you'll lose the money that you have already."

"Yeah, well, short of robbing a bank, I can't think of any

other way to make money."

Miles said barely above a whisper, "Alex, I do understand that it is important to you for you to get back to your own reality, but you finding Randy might not happen right away. So why not enjoy yourself while you are here?"

Alex grinned and said, "Watching a horse race is fun to do."

"That's not what I mean and you know it."

"I do know, but I'm not the person you think I am," Alex said as she saw that the horse race was about to begin.

"Then tell me who you are."

Alex pointed to the horses at the gate while saying, "I really want to watch this."

"Fine, but can we talk after this race?"

"If I say 'no' to that will you go away without saying another word?"

"Alex, please talk to me."

"I'll take that response as a 'no'."

"Alex, I'm being serious."

"Fine, Miles, I'll talk to you after the race."

A short time later, the race got underway. Alex cheered for White Dasher. White Dasher was in fifth place for the first half of the race and moved into the fourth position while going into the final straightaway. As they were approaching the finish line White Dasher was trailing the third position horse by half a length. As the horses crossed the finish line White Dasher was inches from passing the third position horse. The horse that was the favorite to win came in first.

"Err, that was so close," Alex blurted out. "If the track was just a little longer, White Dasher would have come in third, and I would be a few hundred dollars richer."

"So how much did you lose?"

"Actually, I won a little on that race."

"Your horse didn't come in, so how did you win?"

"I put ten dollars on the horse that did win, but unfortunately the pay off wasn't as great."

"Ah."

"Well, I better collect my winnings."

Miles walked with Alex as she walked through the crowd towards the betting booth. As they walked Miles asked, "Now will you talk to me?"

"Let me get my money and place another bet and then we can talk."

Alex stood in line for a few minutes before stepping up to the betting window. Miles stood off to the side as Alex received her winnings and placed another bet.

As Alex stepped up to Miles, Miles asked, "Now can we talk?"

"Let's get somewhere where there aren't too many people around."

Miles looked around at how packed it was before saying, "That might be difficult."

"I know where. Follow me."

Alex walked to a spot that was relatively quiet. Miles followed and when they reached the spot Miles said, "Alex, living in this reality isn't half bad if you give it a chance."

"There are noticeable differences, but even with those differences this reality is much like mine."

"Then why don't you stick around? I know I would like it if you stuck around."

"We can only be friends even if I can't get back to my reality."

"What's so terrible about us being more than friends?"

"Miles, there is something about me that I'm trying to keep from you, but you are making it difficult for me to."

"Alex, I'm a big boy so you don't have to keep anything

from me."

Alex stared skeptically at Miles for a brief moment before sighing and saying, "All right, fine. I'll tell you. My name wasn't Alexandra in my reality."

When Alex stopped talking Miles asked, "What was it?"

Alex slightly hesitated to say, "It was Alexander."

Miles gave Alex a perplexed look while questioning, "Your... your name was Alexander?" Alex politely grinned and nodded. "You... you were a guy in your reality?"

"I was. That's why I say that we can't be more than friends. I didn't want to tell you because when Alexandra and I switch back, I didn't want you seeing her strangely."

Miles thought for a second before saying, "I... I need to go."

As Miles was turning to walk away, Alex said, "By you leaving the way you are, is another reason I didn't want to tell you."

Miles continued to walk away without responding. Alex slightly sighed before turning and going back to the track.

1:10 P.M., Trudy walked into the lunchroom for lunch. Miles was sitting at one of the tables in deep thought. When Trudy walked in and saw Miles she walked up to him and asked, "So how did things go with you and Alex? You didn't tell her that I told you where she was, did you?"

"She doesn't know that you were the informer. In fact, she wasn't even at the coffee-shop when I got there."

"So you didn't find her."

"Oh, I found her. She left a clue at the coffee-shop that she went to the horse track, and I met her there."

"So were you able to talk to her?"

"Oh yeah, I talked to her. I found out why she's not attracted to me."

"Miles, Alex is attracted to you."

"She's not because Alex in her reality is a guy. Alex is literally a man trapped in a woman's body. Alex hates being a woman so badly that she's at the track trying to win enough money to go to Mexico to find her friend."

Trudy sat down in the chair across from Miles before saying, "Miles, Alex is attracted to you. She is only in a hurry to get back to her reality because she is rapidly losing her identity as a man, and that is frightening the hell out of her."

"Wait, you knew she was a man in her… or his reality?"

"I had known from the beginning, or should I say the moment we discovered that she was from a different reality."

"You knew about it, and you didn't tell me?"

"It wasn't my secret to tell."

"Out of curiosity, how did you know? Did Alex tell you?"

"The moment when both Alex's switched bodies, Alexandra fell unconscious and when she awakened, she almost went hysterical that she was a woman."

"Now I know why you told me to refocus my attention to someone else, and you were right."

"Actually, I wasn't right."

"Of course you were right."

"Miles, I only told you that because I thought her mindset was of a man. Now I don't know if reality or Mother Nature… or whatever it is that's causing it is trying to correct itself, but Alex is losing her male identity by leaps and bounds. Both of you are seriously attracted to each other, so now I'm saying don't give up on Alex."

Miles gave Trudy a surprised look while saying, "I can't believe you just suggested that."

"Why?"

"Alex was a man."

"The only thing about Alex that's a man, are her memories and if this is her reality now then those memories will begin to fade over time as well. Everything else about her is definitely a woman."

"I will not be able to date Alex while knowing that she was a man in another reality."

"Aren't you a Star Trek, Deep Space Nine fan?"

"What does that have to do with anything?"

"The character Jadzia Dax had memories of being a man."

"That is science fiction and this is fact."

"I'm just saying that you should keep an open mind."

"I can't do what you are suggesting."

"Suit yourself," Trudy said before standing up. "Well, I'll be back after I grab some food." Trudy then hesitated before walking away. "You know, there's no reason that you can't be just a friend to Alex."

Miles looked at Trudy without responding as Trudy walked away.

Chapter Eleven

2:05 P.M., Alex was late for class and was rushing to get there. Before reaching her classroom, she and Miles met in the hallway. They both stopped and looked at each other.

As Alex took a step to walk away, Miles said, "Alex, I'm sorry for leaving you the way I did."

Alex stopped and as she faced Miles again she said, "You don't have anything to apologize for." Alex gestured down the hall. "I'm actually late for class, so I need to go."

"Did you win any money?"

"I lost twenty bucks."

"Well at least you didn't lose more."

"Miles, you don't have to do this."

"What am I doing?"

"You don't have to pretend to be interested in me."

With a mournful expression across his face, Miles said, "Alex, I would like for us to start over and for us to build a friendship on who you are."

Alex grinned before sticking out her hand to shake hands while saying, "Hi, I'm Alex Larson."

Miles grinned before shaking her hand and saying, "Nice to meet you, Alex. I'm Miles Appleby."

"Well, Miles Appleby, if I wasn't late for class, I would stay to talk so we can get to know each other better."

"Perhaps we can get together later and talk."

Alex grinned before saying, "I would like that." Alex then gestured down the hall. "Well, I better get to class."

"I have to be at the practice field at three, so I'll be there when you get out of class."

"Okay, I'll see you later."

Alex and Miles then went their respective ways.

A few minutes later, the instructor stopped lecturing the class when Alex walked in. He looked at the clock before saying, "Nice that you can join us, Ms. Larson. I hope attending my class wasn't too much of an inconvenience for you."

"I'm sorry I'm late," Alex said.

"Just take your seat, Ms. Larson."

"Of course." Alex then sat in the first available seat she came to.

When the class ended at 2:55 P.M. Alex went to the practice field to watch Miles. She sat where Miles couldn't see her. Her book bag and purse sat on the ground next to her.

When the practice ended at 4:30 P.M. Alex walked up to Miles.

When Miles saw Alex walking up, he curiously asked, "How long have you been here?"

"For a while. I didn't have anything going on so I thought I would watch you practice."

"You don't work today?"

"Sylvia's working today, not me."

Miles gestured towards his teammates and said, "Well, I need to..." Miles stopped talking when he saw Chad walking up behind Alex.

Alex was curious as to why Miles had stopped in mid-sentence and turned to look. When Alex saw Chad, Chad had a serious expression on his face.

When Chad stepped up Alex asked, "Are you okay, Chad?"

Chad shook his head before saying, "Chris' condition turned critical. The doctor said if a kidney doesn't get found soon, Chris won't live for another week."

"Oh my God!" Alex couldn't help blurting out.

"Chris asked me to try to persuade Trudy to visit him in the hospital. That's why I'm here, but I don't know where to find her. Miles, I just took a guess to come here to the field to find you."

"Miles, I'll take Chad to the dorm room," Alex said.

"Okay. I need to rejoin my teammates anyway before they get too far ahead of me. I'll catch up with everyone when I can."

"Okay," Alex said. Miles turned and rushed towards his teammates.

Minutes later, Alex and Chad were walking into her dorm room; however, Trudy wasn't there. Alex put her book bag down, but kept her purse. Alex then led Chad to the library. After walking in and looking around, Alex saw Doug's roommate Richard at a table studying.

Richard saw Alex and as Alex stepped up to him he asked, "So how's the prettiest woman at Harvard doing?"

"When I see her, I'll ask her," Alex responded. "In the meantime, have you seen Trudy?"

Richard gave Alex a curious look before saying, "I was referring to you."

"I know who you were referring to, but I didn't come here for you to make a pass at me. I'm looking for Trudy. Have you seen her?"

"A few people have been saying that you have changed, but you haven't, have you? You won't even let me give you a compliment."

"Richard, have you seen Trudy or know where she might be?"

"Most likely she's in her calculus class right now."

"Thank you, that's all I wanted to know." Alex then

hesitated to leave before telling him, "Richard, thanks for the compliment. I wasn't trying to shoot you down. I just need to find Trudy."

"Perhaps you have changed after all."

Alex grinned before saying, "Thanks again." As Alex turned and walked away, Chad walked beside her.

A short time later, Alex and Chad walked up to Trudy's classroom. While waiting for Trudy's class to end, Chad started a casual conversation, and their conversation ended when the students were leaving the room.

When Trudy stepped out of her classroom and saw Alex and Chad, she walked up to them. As she gave them suspicious looks, she asked, "What's going on?"

"Trudy, we met once last Christmas…" Chad said.

"Chad, I know who you are. What I don't know is why you and Alex are waiting outside my classroom."

"I'm here to talk to you about Chris…"

"Let me stop you there," Trudy quickly interrupted with. "I don't want anything to do with Chris."

"Trudy, he wants to apologize to you."

"He has apologized to me, but that doesn't change how I feel about him."

"Chris' condition turned critical," Chad quickly said. "He won't live another week if a kidney isn't found. Chris just wants to talk to you before he dies."

"Chad, I hate the idea of your brother dying, but I'm not…" Trudy was only able to get out.

"You would deny a dying man his last request?" Alex quickly interrupted with.

"Alex, I want to talk to you in private for a second," Trudy said.

"Sure," Alex said before she and Trudy walked away from Chad.

When they were out of Chad's earshot, Trudy said, "When Chris and I were dating, Chris treated me like I was his property. He was jealous of every guy that came near me and he had embarrassed me in public more times than I can remember."

"I'm not suggesting that you get back together with him, but the guy is on his deathbed. All he wants is to talk to you before he dies. I don't see the harm in talking to him."

Trudy sighed before saying, "Okay, Alex. I'll go see him, but you have to come with me."

"I have no problem with that."

"Good," Trudy said before gesturing towards Chad. "Well, we better let Chad know that I'll go see him."

"We need to talk to Miles before we go. I'm not really sure, but I think he wants to go too."

As Alex and Trudy walked towards Chad, Trudy asked, "You and Miles are talking?"

Alex grinned before saying, "We are."

When Alex and Trudy stepped up to Chad, Trudy said, "Alex talked me into seeing Chris, but I'm not promising that I will be visiting for any length of time."

"I believe Chris will be happy if you only visited for a minute or two."

Trudy pulled out her cell phone from her purse before saying, "Well, I'm going to call Miles to see if he wants to come."

"Miles just finished soccer practice, so he might be busy with his team," Alex said.

"Okay, well, I'll leave him a message on his voicemail that I'm going to the hospital and that he can join me if he wants to." Trudy then pressed the send button on her phone.

"I'll ride with you," Alex said.

Trudy nodded and when the phone went into voice mail she

left the message, "Hey, uh, Alex had talked me into visiting Chris, so that's where Alex and I will be. You can meet us at the hospital if you want; bye." She then put her phone away. "Okay; I'm ready."

Alex, Trudy and Chad then turned and walked towards the exit.

Minutes later at the hospital, Alex and Trudy followed Chad into Chris' room. Chris and Chad's parents were there visiting.

Chad stepped up to his parents and as he gestured towards Alex he said, "Dad, this is Alex. Alex, this is my dad, Raymond."

Alex stepped up and stuck out her hand to shake hands. When Raymond took Alex's hand, Alex said, "Nice to meet you, Mr…"

"Raymond," he interrupted with. "Please call me Raymond and it's nice to meet you, Alex."

"Okay, Raymond." Alex then waved at Linda. "It's nice to see you again, Linda."

"Nice to see you again as well," Linda said.

Raymond looked at Trudy before saying, "It's nice to see you again, Trudy."

Trudy slightly waved and said, "Likewise." Trudy then stepped up to Chris' bedside. Chris was lightly dozing off. When Trudy took hold of Chris' hand, he opened his eyes. "Chris, I'm here."

Chris looked at Trudy and said in a slur speech, "Trudy, hi."

Trudy slightly grinned before saying, "Hi."

"Trudy, I know I treated you poorly…"

"Chris, you don't have to apologize to me again." Everyone saw tears forming in Trudy's eyes before she continued to say, "I forgive you."

When Alex saw tears forming in Trudy's eyes, tears began to form in her eyes. She then stepped out into the hallway before anyone could see her.

As she wiped the tears from her eyes, Chad stepped out and saw her. He stepped closer before saying, "My mom has tissues if you need one."

Alex grinned before saying, "I don't know why I'm so emotional."

"These are emotional times. I've even shed a few tears over this. I've also been praying every night for a miracle. It doesn't seem to be enough... or it doesn't feel like it's enough. I feel like I should be doing more, but I just don't know what. Okay, I'm going to stop ranting before I start crying myself." Alex just grinned. Chad gestured towards the room. "Well, I'm going back in there." Alex just nodded.

Just as Chad was stepping back into Chris' room, Alex said barely loud enough for Chad to hear, "Maybe there's something that I can do."

Chad stepped back out to see what Alex had said. However, Alex had her back to Chad and her cell phone to her ear. Chad paused for a second, and he was just about ready to stepped back into the room when Alex continued to say, "Mom, it's Alex. I need your medical assistance on something." Chad stood still and listened to Alex's side of the conversation. "It's not me, Mom. I'm fine. It's a friend of mine who needs your help. His name is Chris Swan. He needs a kidney ASAP and I was wondering if you can check around to see if you can find a match for him." There was a short pause. "Yeah, I believe he's on the list to receive a kidney." There was another short pause before Alex told her mom the name of the hospital that Chris was staying in. Before hanging up Alex said, "Mom, thanks for doing what you can to help. Bye." Alex turned around and when she saw Chad standing there, she gave him in a surprise stare for a second. She then held up her phone. "My mom is a surgeon in St. Louis. Maybe she can help find a kidney for Chris."

"Thank you."

"I think it's a little premature to be thanking me. A kidney hasn't been found yet."

"True, but you did make that phone call to help and that's more than I expect of anyone. I'm also one who believes that a good deed shouldn't go unrewarded. If there's anything I can do for you just name it and I mean anything." Chad noticed a thought along with a grin coming across Alex's face. "There is something you want. What is it?"

"Oh, I think what I want is more than what you had in mind."

"I said name what it is you want and I'll get it for you. So what is it that you want?"

"I, along with five of my friends need to get to Mexico City, but we don't have the money to charter a plane."

"I won't give you the money for you to charter a plane…"

"I knew it was too much to be asking for."

"However, I will loan you a plane to use."

Alex gave him a surprise look before asking, "What?"

"My dad has planes at his disposal, and I will give you one to use."

"That is a generous offer, but my friends and I don't know a thing about piloting an airplane."

Chad laughed before saying, "I was planning on giving you a pilot as well."

"I really appreciate the offer, but…"

"There are no but's, Alex. You and your friends want to get to Mexico City, and I am going to make it happen for you. When do you and your friends need the plane?"

"Chad, your offer is more than I expected."

"So was that phone call you made to your mom. Now, when do you need that plane?"

Alex gave Chad a slightly skeptical stare for a moment before saying, "My friends and I will need to discuss it."

Chad pulled out one of his business cards and as he held it out for Alex to take he said, "When you decide when you want that plane, let me know."

Alex took the card and said, "I will. Thank you."

"My pleasure," Chad said as Alex's cell phone rang.

Alex looked to see who was calling before saying, "It's Miles."

"I'll give you some privacy."

Alex nodded. As Chad tuned to walk away Alex answered, "Hey, Miles, what's up?"

"Hey, Alex. I'm at my van in the hospital's parking lot. I was wondering if you can come down and meet me at the entrance."

"I'll be right down." As Alex was walking towards the elevators, she stuck her phone and Chad's business card in her purse.

A few minutes later, Alex stepped outside and saw Miles leaning against the walls with his eyes shut. He was taking deep breaths. Alex stepped up beside him before asking, "Miles? Are you okay?"

Miles looked at Alex before saying, "Yeah, I'm fine. I'm just trying to calm myself before going in there."

"Have you ever considered seeing a therapist about this phobia you have about hospitals?"

Miles said jokingly, "I would, but first I have to get over my phobia about seeing a therapist."

"Funny, but I'm serious. What if you get hurt and have to go to the emergency room?"

"Alex, relax. As long as someone is with me, such as a

friend, I can cope with the hospital. Even if that someone was a paramedic I'll be fine. I just can't walk into one alone."

"Well, are you okay enough to go in there?"

Miles nodded before saying, "Yeah, I'm okay."

Alex and Miles walked in. As they were stepping up to the elevator, Alex said, "I got good news." Miles was reaching for the button to call the elevator. "I have a way for my friends and me to get to Mexico City." Miles never pressed the button and with a grief-stricken expression across his face, he stood staring at Alex. Alex saw the look she was getting. "What's wrong?"

"Nothing. I'm happy for you."

"Then why are you looking at me as if I just told you that I ran over your dog?"

As Miles pressed the button to call the elevator, he said, "Alex, I am happy for you. So how are you getting to Mexico?"

"Chad is arranging it."

"So when will you be leaving?"

"I haven't talked to Doug and the others yet about it, so that part is still open. Actually I should call Doug now and arrange for us to get together in an hour or so." Alex reached into her purse. Just after getting out her phone she looked at Miles. Miles was looking at the elevator's lit up-arrow with a discouraged expression on his face. "Miles, what's wrong?"

"Oh, I'm just feeling the atmosphere of the hospital."

Alex stared at Miles for a brief moment before saying, "I'll talk to Doug later." She then put her phone away.

"Alex, when you do go to Mexico, I would like to go with you."

Alex grinned before saying, "Okay."

"Oh, and I even know Spanish."

"Then you're definitely going with me because I can't

speak Spanish."

Miles grinned before asking, "Alex, did you and Trudy both drive here?"

"No, I rode with Trudy."

As the elevator door was opening, Miles said, "So you'll be leaving in a few minutes with Trudy."

As Alex and Miles stepped into the elevator, Alex said, "I don't know how long Trudy is going to stay."

Miles pressed the button. As the door closed, Miles said, "I doubt she'll stay very long and I was hoping to visit for more than a few minutes, but I won't be able to if both of you leave."

"Most likely Chad will be staying so you won't be alone."

"Yeah, but Chad would probably start asking me questions as to why I suddenly became his shadow. You and Trudy are the only two who know about my phobia, and I would like to keep it that way."

"Miles, I'll ride back to Harvard with you, so you can visit Chris for a while."

"Thanks, Alex, for understanding."

"You're welcome." They were quiet for only a moment before Alex asked, "Miles, how many languages do you know?"

"Not counting English, I know three; German, Spanish and Italian. Maria's parents are actually from Mexico, and she was the one who taught me how to speak it."

"Interesting." There was again a short pause before Alex spoke again. "Miles, I hope you don't mind me asking, but what happened between you and Maria?"

"We spent too much time apart over the past three years. So I guess we just simply drifted apart; well she drifted apart from me anyway."

"Maria didn't attend Harvard?"

"No, she went to Kansas State College. We would see each

other on the major holidays and spend our time together during the summer, but that apparently wasn't enough for her. Her birthday is on September 28th and when I called her on that day to see if she had received her present from me, she informed me that she had refused the package, and that we were through. She then told me goodbye and hung up. That was it. That was the last that I heard from her."

"Miles, I'm sorry," Alex said as the elevator stopped.

As the door was opening, Miles said, "I'm pretty much over the grief of the break up, but thanks anyway." Miles then motioned for Alex to leave the elevator first. Alex grinned and stepped out of the elevator.

In the reality Alpha 0.0.0.0.0.0.0 at 5:30 P.M., at a local mental institution in Boston the psychiatrist Barney Gray opened the door to Alex's padded room. Alex was sitting on the floor wearing a straight jacket. He looked up at Dr. Gray as he walked in.

Dr. Gray observed Alex's behavior for a brief moment before saying, "You seem to be calmer today than this past weekend."

"Dr. Gray, I'm not crazy."

"I never made that claim, but something is causing you to have the illusion that you were born a female. Until you accept the fact that you weren't born a female, I'm afraid you will be here for a while. Since you are calm, can I trust you not to go hysterical if I arrange it for you to have that straight jacket taken off, and have you reassigned to a more comfortable room."

"I'm done going hysterical, Dr. Gray."

"Good. There is actually a room ready for you right now. Nurse Wyman will be in, in a few minutes to take off that jacket. I'll go and let her know, and I will see you in the morning for our session."

"Thank you, Dr. Gray."

Dr. Gray nodded and stepped out of the room.

Alex waited for a few minutes before Nurse Wyman stepped in and removed the straight jacket. The two then left the padded room and while they walked down the hall Alex looked around at his surroundings.

A young armed security guard was having a casual conversation with a nurse and wasn't paying attention to what was going on around him. Nurse Wyman was focused on the paperwork she had and was not watching Alex. Alex saw that he had the opportunity to take the security guard's gun and took it.

The guard felt the gun being pulled from his holster and quickly turned to face Alex. As Alex turned the gun towards his abdomen, the security guard grabbed quickly for the gun; however, before the security guard was able to grab the gun, Alex shot himself twice in the abdomen.

As Alex was falling to the floor, Nurse Wyman shouted out, "Get an ambulance! Quick!" Every staff member around Alex scrambled to Alex's aid.

In the reality Alpha 0.0.0.1.0.0.0 at 6:00 P.M., in Chris' hospital room, Alex, Trudy and Miles were standing between the bed and the windowsill. Chad and his parents were sitting in chairs on the other side of the bed. Alex's purse was next to Trudy's purse on the windowsill. Everyone was having a casual conversation when Alex's cell phone rang.

Alex got her phone from her purse and looked at who was calling. Before Alex answered she looked at the others before saying, "This is my brother Doug. I'm going to take it in the hallway." Alex walked towards the door and just before exiting the room she answered, "Hey, Doug, what's going on?"

"Where are you right now?"

"I'm at the hospital with Trudy and Miles. We're visiting

Gerald Pruett

Miles' friend Chris."

"Well, Ben is getting ready to go back to Atlanta. He wanted to say 'bye' to you before he leaves."

"Hey, I need to talk to everyone together, so don't let him go right now."

"What do you have to talk to everyone about?"

"Chad is going to arrange it for us to go to Mexico City. All we need is to tell him a definite date and it's set."

"Who's Chad?"

"Chad is the brother to Chris; the person we're visiting in the hospital."

"And why is he helping us to get to Mexico?"

"Actually he is rewarding my good deed towards Chris."

"What did you do for Chris?"

"Chris will be dead within a week if he doesn't get a kidney before then. I took it upon myself to call mom and get her involved in trying to locate a kidney. Chad overheard me talking to mom, and now as a reward for me getting another doctor involved, Chad is loaning us a plane and a pilot."

"And Chad has the means to do this?"

"Chad's dad is the president to a company with planes, and Chad has access to those planes."

"Okay, I'll tell Ben to postpone going back to Atlanta. When and where do you want to meet with everyone?"

"How about getting together in an hour from now?"

"Have you eaten since lunch?"

"Actually, I just realized I haven't even eaten lunch."

"Okay, well, meet us at the Chinese restaurant in an hour."

"Chinese sounds good actually. I'll be there; bye." Alex hung up the phone. She then walked back into the room and up to Trudy.

Miles was standing on the other side of Trudy and when Alex stepped up he asked, "Is everything all right?"

179

Alex saw that Chris was sleeping as she was saying, "Everything's fine." Alex turned to look at Miles. "I'm going to meet Doug and the others at a Chinese restaurant in an hour. You and Trudy are welcome to join us."

"I'm hungry, so sure. I'll join you," Miles said.

"Alex, do you mind if I join you?" Chad asked.

"I don't mind at all. Raymond; Linda, you two are also welcome to join us."

"Thanks for inviting us, but with how critical Chris is right now, I don't want to leave him," Linda said.

"I'll also be staying here," Raymond said.

"I understand," Alex said.

Trudy looked at her watch and said, "Hey, I'm going to get going. Alex; Miles... and Chad, I'll meet everyone at the restaurant in an hour."

"Bye," everyone said.

Trudy just waved as she was leaving.

Alex looked at Miles and said, "I'm going to the lady's room."

Before Alex had a chance to leave, Miles said, "Hurry back." Alex grinned before turning and walking out.

Chapter Twelve

6:55 P.M., Alex, Miles and Chad walked into the Chinese restaurant that had a buffet. Alex and Miles saw Doug and the others sitting at a table for six and walked up to them. Chad just followed the two.

When Alex saw that Doug was giving Chad an uncomfortable stare she said, "This is Chad." Alex pointed everyone out. "Chad, meet my brother Doug and my friends Brandy, Cindy, Kenny and Ben."

"Hi, Chad," everyone said.

Doug pointed to two empty tables that were next to each other that could both seat six and said, "We aren't going to fit at the same table so we should move to those tables over there."

As everyone was moving, Alex said, "Trudy is planning on joining us."

Brandy saw Trudy walking in. "She's here now."

Everyone looked at Trudy as they were moving. When Alex gestured towards the tables that they were moving to for Trudy to see, Trudy nodded.

When everyone stepped up to the tables, Chad suggested, "Alex, you and your friends should sit together to discuss my offer."

As Alex was hanging her purse on the back of her seat, she said, "All right; thanks."

Alex, Doug, Brandy, Cindy, Kenny and Ben sat at the same table. Miles and Chad sat at the other table. As Trudy stepped up, she sat at the table with Miles.

The waitress stepped up and asked, "Is everyone in your group here and ready to order?"

"Yes, we're all here, and I want the buffet," Doug said. "I'll take a cola to drink."

The others also ordered the buffet and their drinks.

When the waitress walked away for the drinks, everyone got up and went to the buffet.

Everyone was gone from the table for a few minutes before returning to his or her seat. After everyone had sat back down with his or her food, Alex asked, "Doug, have you spoken with everyone about when to go Mexico City?"

"I have, and we all think it would be best to wait until Saturday," Doug said.

"Why should we wait that long?" Alex asked.

Doug spoke loud enough for only his group to hear, "Alex, even you told me that we should minimize ruining the lives of our alternates. So we can't up and take off during the week when we're supposed to be attending classes."

"I don't like the idea of living out another week like this," Alex said.

"Alex, Doug is right; we should wait," Brandy said.

"I also agree with Doug," Kenny said.

"Cindy; Ben, what about you two?" Alex asked.

"There's a chance that Randy is coming here, so I also agree with Doug," Ben said.

"Ditto," Cindy said.

"Fine, that will give us five days to prepare anyway," Alex said. "I just hope I don't totally lose myself in the meantime."

"What are you talking about?" Kenny asked.

Alex shook her head before saying, "It's not important. Forget I said anything." Kenny gave Alex a confused look as Alex gestured towards the next table. "I'll tell Chad when we need the plane." Alex then got up and stepped over to the next table.

As Alex was telling Chad of what she and her friends had decided, Ben asked his group, "Hey, everyone, even if Randy is in Mexico, how are we going to locate him? I mean, in order to ask the locals if they have seen Randy, we are going to need a picture of him, and none of us has a picture."

Doug thought for a moment before taking his phone off of his belt and saying, "I have an idea for that." He then scrolled through his phone for his parents' number. Once he found it he dialed the phone. The phone rang twice when Beverly picked up from the study room on the first floor. "Hi, mom, is Michelle home?"

"Yes, hold on." Beverly laid down the phone and walked to the stairs. She then yelled up, "Michelle, Doug is on the phone and wants to talk to you."

"Okay, Mom," Michelle yelled back. Michelle picked up the phone in her room. "Hey, Doug. What's going on?"

Doug knew Beverly was listening in and made small talk.

Alex saw Doug on the phone and as she was sitting back down she asked, "Who's Doug talking to?"

"Michelle; whoever Michelle is," Brandy said.

"She's our younger sister in this reality," Alex said.

When Doug was certain that Beverly had hung up, he said, "Hey, Michelle, I'm actually calling to ask you for a favor, but I don't want Mom or Dad to know anything about it." Alex was focused on Doug as he continued to say, "There's a woman who lives on Victoria Place. Her name is Phyllis Miller. I want you to go to her house and ask Phyllis for a picture of her son, Randy."

"And Phyllis will give me a picture of Randy?" Michelle asked.

"Well, you may have to use a little persuasion on her, but I really need that picture."

"Does she know you?"

"Alex and I met her when we were in St. Louis last Thursday, so you can tell her that I sent you."

"What should I tell her if she asks why I want his picture?"

"Tell her that I may have met someone who had run into Randy recently, but the person I met needs to see what Randy looks like before he can verify it."

"Before I say 'yes' to this, why are you asking me to do it?"

"That's too complicated of a story to get into over the phone. So can you please do me this one favor?"

"If I do this, you are going to owe me big."

"You got it. If you get the picture, scan it and email it to me. And if you can't get it, call me and let me know."

"Okay, but you'll need to give me the address. Before you do, let me get a pencil and a piece of paper." Michelle put down the phone and went to get the items. When she returned she picked up the phone and asked, "Okay, what is it?" Michelle wrote down the address Doug gave her. "Okay, I got it. I'll borrow Dad's car and do it now."

"Hey, don't tell Dad or Mom what you're doing."

"I won't; bye."

"Bye."

After Michelle hung up the phone, she grabbed her purse and went downstairs to the living room. Avery was in the living room watching TV.

When Michelle stepped up to Avery she asked, "Dad, can I get the keys to your car?"

"Where are you going?" Avery asked.

Michelle thought quickly and said, "There's this movie that came out last week that I want to see. I tried to rent it Friday, but all the copies were out. Now I want to go back to the video rental and try again." Avery pulled out his keys from his pocket and handed them to Michelle. "Thanks, Dad."

"Well, just drive carefully, and make sure you obey the traffic stops."

"Dad, I've been driving since my sixteenth birthday and I think I'm a good driver. So when are you going to stop telling me to drive carefully?"

"Never, Sweetheart. I will still be telling you that when you'll be telling your teenagers that."

"That was what I was afraid of," Michelle said. Avery just grinned as Michelle walked towards the front door.

Beverly was in the kitchen and when she heard the front door closing, she stepped into the living room and asked, "Was that Michelle leaving?"

"Yeah, she went to the video rentals for a movie," Avery said.

"If I knew she was going out, I would have had her stop and pick up some milk."

"She might have her cell phone with her."

"I'll call her."

Before Beverly had a chance to walk away Avery asked, "So how much longer are you going to be studying that medical procedure?"

"At the rate I'm going, it will be another three hours. I told Mrs. Keller that I'm unfamiliar with the type of operation that she needs. I even tried for ten minutes to convince her to go with a surgeon more familiar with the procedure, but she refused to even consider another surgeon operating on her." Beverly then gestured towards the kitchen. "Well, I'd better call Michelle." When Avery nodded Beverly walked away.

Michelle was a short ways down the street when her cell phone rang. She immediately pulled over when she could and parked the car before getting her phone from her purse. The phone had stopped ringing before she was able to answer, and when she saw who had called she called back. When Beverly answered Michelle asked, "Mom, did you call?"

"I did. Why didn't you pick up when I called?"

"I don't want to be one of the drivers who talks on the phone as she drives, so I found a place to park before I picked up the phone."

"Okay, well, I'm just calling to tell you to pick up some milk while you're out."

"Okay, Mom. Do you need anything else?"

"No, that should do it."

"Okay. Bye, Mom." After Michelle put her phone away, she made sure that there were no approaching cars before driving off.

Ten minutes later, Michelle parked the car in front of Phyllis' house. When she got out she left her purse in the car and stuck the keys in her front pocket. She then stepped up to Phyllis' front door and rang the doorbell.

Phyllis opened the door and when she saw Michelle standing there, she asked, "Yes? May I help you?"

"Yes, are you Mrs. Phyllis Miller?"

"That's me. What can I do for you?"

"Mrs. Miller, my name is Michelle Larson. I was told that you met my brother Doug and my sister Alex last Thursday."

"Oh, yes, I remember. They came here looking for my son Randy, but Randy took off threes years ago and I haven't seen him since."

Michelle gave Phyllis a perplex look before asking, "Doug and Alex came here looking for Randy?"

"They did. Is there a problem?"

Michelle shook her head and said, "No; at least I don't think so. Anyway, Doug asked me to come here and ask if he could have a picture of Randy."

"Why does he need a picture of Randy?"

"Doug says that he had met someone recently who might have seen Randy. Doug wants to show that person Randy's picture to verify if it was Randy."

"God knows that I would like to see my son again after three years, but putting that fact to the side for a moment, I would like to know why your brother and sister are looking for my son."

"I was never told why, Mrs. Miller."

"Where are your brother and sister?"

"They both go to Harvard University. When they were in town last Thursday, they actually came back to St. Louis without telling anyone that they were coming. I never saw my parents so upset with them as they were that day."

"I'm not sure about this, but I'll get you a picture of him. Please come in." Michelle quickly gave Phyllis a wary look. Phyllis saw the look and said, "Honey, you came to me. I didn't come to you from off the street."

"Okay," Michelle said with a polite grin before following Phyllis into the house.

Michelle stepped into the middle of the living room, and looked around the room before Phyllis told her, "Just have a seat and I'll be right back with that picture."

Michelle looked at Phyllis before saying, "You have a lovely house, Mrs. Miller."

Michelle was in motion to sit down on the couch when Phyllis responded, "Thank you, dear." Phyllis then walked down the hall and entered a bedroom.

Michelle was sitting down for a short time when a cat named Tiger came into view. Michelle watched Tiger as Tiger walked up to her and sniffed her for a second. When Tiger rubbed up against Michelle's leg, Michelle petted him for a brief moment. After Michelle stopped petting Tiger, Tiger jumped into Michelle's lap.

Michelle resumed petting Tiger before saying, "I see that you like to be petted."

Phyllis was gone for a few minutes and when she returned she saw Tiger purring on Michelle's lap as Michelle petted him. Phyllis grinned at the sight before saying, "Well, I'll be. Other than me, dear, you're the only person Tiger will go to."

"I love animals," Michelle said. "I'm thinking of being a veterinarian."

"I can see that you have a way of gaining their trust." Michelle just grinned. Phyllis held out the picture of Randy for Michelle to take before she continued to say, "Here's that picture of Randy that you wanted."

As Michelle was taking the picture she said, "Thanks." Michelle then put Tiger back on the floor. After she stood up she gestured towards the door. "Well, I need to be going. My mom wants me to stop by the store and buy some milk."

"Dear, if your brother and sister do find Randy, I would like for Randy to call me."

"I will pass on your message, Mrs. Miller."

"My number is different from what it was a few years ago, so I wrote my number on the back of the picture."

As Michelle and Phyllis were walking towards the front door, Michelle looked at the phone number. When Phyllis opened the door Michelle said, "Thanks, Mrs. Miller, for the picture and I hope you have a good day."

"You're welcome, dear, and good day to you." Phyllis watched Michelle walking away for a brief moment before shutting the door.

After Michelle got into the car she stuck the picture in her purse. She then put on her seat belt and drove away.

As the minutes passed, Michelle went to a video rental and rented two movies. After leaving the video rental she stopped at a gas station that sold food items and bought a gallon of milk.

Michelle returned to the house at 7:00 P.M Central time and after putting the milk in the refrigerator, she went straight to her room and turned on her computer. Once the computer was on, Michelle scanned the picture and then emailed it to Doug. After that was done she called him.

When Doug answered the phone, Michelle asked, "Okay, Doug, what's going on?"

"Michelle?" Doug asked.

"Yes, it's me. What's going on? Why are you looking for a guy that ran off three years ago?"

"That's a bit complicated; especially to say over the phone. Were you able to get the picture?"

"I just emailed it to you, and Phyllis wants Randy to call her if you find him. How do you know Randy?"

"I met him several years ago, and I didn't know that he ran off the way he did. I think I know where he went though."

"Where did he go?"

"Michelle, I can't answer that. I'll talk to you later. Okay?"

"I have a feeling that something weird is going on."

"I can't really tell you anything over the phone, but I promise to explain when I see you again; now bye."

"Fine; bye." After Michelle hung up the phone she pondered the situation for a brief moment. She then picked the phone up again and dialed it. When the phone was answered, Michelle said, "Heather, it's me, Michelle."

"Hey, Michelle," Heather said. "What's going on?"

"Do you still want me to go to Boston with you this weekend?"

"I do, actually. Do you now want to go?"

"I do. So can you get your parents to talk to my parents about it?"

"Did you and Billy have a fight?"

"No; we're good."

"Then why are you now willing to skip going to Billy's football game and come with me?"

"I was thinking about the sales pitch you made."

"What sales pitch?"

"You said, how if I go to Boston with you, I can see Alex's and Doug's dorm rooms."

"Michelle, I know you, and I know there's more to what you're saying than what you're telling me."

"Okay, fine. Alex and Doug are up to something and I would like to find out what."

"Okay, Veronica, I will talk to my parents and get them to talk to your parents."

"Thanks, and stop calling me Veronica. I'm not Veronica Mars."

"You're right. Veronica Mars is a television character that will always be on top in the long run. You on the other hand are a real person and will not end up on top in the long run if you don't stop snooping in other people's matters."

"Heather, the position to be my mom is currently and permanently filled by Beverly Larson, so quit applying for it."

"Ha, ha, very funny, but one of these days you are going to snoop in the wrong place and things are going to blow up in your face."

"And when it does, you can tell me, 'I told you so.' Until then, I don't need a second mom."

"Fine. Bye."

"Oh, Heather, thanks again for talking to your parents about me going with you and your family."

"No problem. Bye."

"Bye." After hanging up the phone, Michelle turned on her TV and DVD player, and stuck in one of the movies she rented.

Tuesday, October 26, at 11:00 A.M. on Harvard's campus, Alex was studying while sitting on an outside bench. Stephen walked up to her and sat down beside her.

When Alex looked up from her book, Stephen said, "I understand that you called work last night and said that you won't be able to work this Saturday and maybe even Sunday."

"I did," Alex confirmed. "And why are you concerned about me not working Saturday and Sunday?"

"This is just typical of you."

Alex scowled at Stephen before questioning in a matching tone, "Excuse me?"

"I said, it's typical of you."

"I heard what you said, but how is not working Saturday and Sunday typical of me?"

"You only think of yourself and the parties you can go to."

"Stephen, I for one don't know what you're talking about. Do you?"

"Alex, when you applied for the job, did you stop and think that you might not be able to go to those parties that are coming up?"

"I don't know what you're thinking, and truthfully I don't even care, but I do not have plans to attend any parties of any kind today or anytime in the near future."

"So you're telling me that you're not planning to attend that Halloween Bash that will be happening this weekend? It's supposed to be the biggest bash in years."

"I don't know of any Halloween Bash, and although this is none of your business, the reason I took the waitressing job was to make enough money so I can go out of town to visit a friend. The means to visit this friend were actually fulfilled by another friend, so I'm leaving Saturday morning."

"So you're actually not attending any parties?"

Alex shook her head while saying, "No. You didn't want

me working there anyway, so why do you even care that I'm not working Saturday and Sunday?"

"Surprisingly you're actually the best waitress Victor has hired in years. Victor even said that the first night he watched you work. I just didn't want you blowing your job over a few stupid parties."

Catherine was walking up as Alex said, "Well, thanks for your concern for my... my employment status, but there's really no need for concerns."

"I just see a change in you for the better and I don't want to see you revert back to your previous self."

Before Alex was able to respond, Catherine stepped up and commented, "Doesn't this bring back memories from last year?"

Alex quickly looked at Catherine before saying, "No; it doesn't."

"I wasn't trying to imply anything," Catherine said. "I was just taking note about how you two are getting along. Anyway, Stephen, Becky just called me. She said that she has been calling you for an hour, but you're not picking up your phone."

"My phone was actually ripped off last night. I already reported it stolen."

"Well, Becky was out and had a flat tire."

"Becky is out stranded somewhere?" Stephen asked.

"No, a stranger stopped and helped her out. She's not happy with you at all though."

Stephen stood up and said, "Give me your phone, Catherine. I'll call Becky and tell her what happened."

"Do you want to borrow my phone?" Alex asked.

As Catherine was pulling out her phone, Stephen said, "Alex, will you stopped trying to cause trouble between Becky and me."

"What did I do?" Alex innocently asked.

"You know perfectly well what you are doing." Alex made a gesture as if she didn't know what he was talking about. "Becky knows your phone number and if I would use your phone, your phone number would show up on her ID. She would then be even more steamed with me for using your phone."

"Do you really want a girlfriend that you have to walk on eggshells to please?"

"Alex, please stop."

"All right; fine, I'll stop trying to help."

As Stephen took Catherine's phone, he echoed, "Help? You're being malicious. I guess some things will never change."

Alex gave him a distasteful smirk. Stephen ignored the look he got and walked away. He dialed the phone when he got a few feet from the bench.

Catherine sat down and said, "I see you're still holding a grudge over Stephen and Becky getting together."

"I'm actually over it."

"Yeah, I can tell," Catherine sarcastically said.

Alex grinned before standing up. As she was putting her books in her book bag, she said, "I'm going to get some lunch."

Alex was putting her purse over her shoulder as Catherine was saying, "If you wait a minute or two, I'll join you after Stephen returns my phone."

"All right." Alex retook her seat and placed her book bag on the ground.

"So have you received anymore flowers lately from your secret admirer?"

"Nope; last Saturday was the only time."

"When do you work again?"

"I'll be working tonight and every day this week. I'll then

be off Saturday and I might be off Sunday as well."

"Friday and Saturday would be the two days Victor would need you the most. So how did you manage to get Saturday off?"

"I basically told Victor that I had something important I had to do this Saturday and it might bleed over into Sunday and that I was taking those two days off. I told him that I would call in if I was able to work Sunday though."

"And he didn't say anything against you taking off those two days?"

"He did, but I then told him that he can fire me if he wants because what I have to do this weekend is worth losing my job over. He was silent for a brief moment. He then told me that he would need me to work next Monday."

As Stephen was returning, Catherine said, "Victor must like you. You are the only person I know who got by with taking off like that."

Stephen stepped up and as he held out the phone for Catherine to take, he said, "Here's your phone. Thank you for letting me use it."

"No problem."

Alex stood up and after she picked up her book bag she said, "Well, I'm going to the lunchroom for who wants to join me."

"I'm meeting Becky," Stephen said. "Thanks anyway."

"I'll see you later then," Alex said.

Stephen walked towards the parking lot while Alex and Catherine walked towards the building.

After walking a few steps, Catherine asked, "So what are you doing this weekend that you're taking Saturday and Sunday off?"

"I took the job at Little Bucks so I can solve a personal matter..."

"I remember you telling me that. What about it?"

"The opportunity has come up to where I can get closer at solving that personal matter, and I'm not passing up that opportunity."

"You never told me what needed solving."

Alex grinned before saying, "And I'm not going to either."

"I might be able to help if you confide in me."

"Sorry, Catherine, but this is something that you can't help me with."

"I just might be able to, but suit yourself. I won't ask again." Alex just grinned.

Minutes later, Alex and Catherine were stepping out of the food line with their trays. Alex saw Miles sitting with two others from the soccer team. As she pointed towards Miles she said, "Let sit with them."

Catherine stopped walking and practically demanded, "You want us to sit at the same table as Miles Appleby?"

"And that is bad because?"

"You know why I don't want anything to do with him, and I can't believe that you do."

"Perhaps you should refresh my memory."

Catherine gave Alex a curious look before saying, "The very first day at Harvard, he ruined my favorite blouse by dumping a tray of food on me. He says it was an accident, but I know he did it deliberately. From that day on, Miles and I have never gotten along. You even told me that you were going to support me by not having anything to do with him either."

Alex thought for a second before saying, "Catherine, the food tray being dumped on you would have happened regardless if it was Miles or another player from the soccer team."

"What are you talking about?"

"There was a dare made by the senior players for one of the

sophomore or freshmen players to dump a tray of food on the next freshmen student to walk through the cafeteria doors. You just happened to be that student."

"How do you know that when I don't?"

"I just do. Now I'm going to go sit with Miles and his friends. You can join me if you want."

As Alex walked towards Miles' table, Catherine sighed before following. When Alex stepped up, Miles and the other two stopped their conversation and looked at Alex. Miles slightly grinned before saying, "I think everyone here knows each other, so, Alex, have a seat."

Alex put her purse and book bag on the back of her chair. As she was sitting down, Catherine stepped up and asked, "Can I join you guys?"

Miles gave Catherine a surprise look before asking, "You want to sit at the same table with me?"

"Two years is a long time to hold a grudge, and I thought it's time to let bygones be bygones... unless you don't want me sitting here," Catherine said.

"I don't know why you are forgiving me now when you wouldn't forgive me before; however, I'm not complaining. Have a seat." As Catherine was taking a seat, Miles continued to say, "Catherine, in case you don't know, my two friends are Andy and Mark."

"I believe we all know each other," Andy said.

Miles looked at Alex before saying, "I wanted to make sure." Alex slightly grinned.

Mark continued the conversation at the point where he, Miles and Andy had left off. As everyone talked, Catherine felt a vibe between Alex and Miles.

Seven minutes later, Miles, Andy and Mark were done eating and had their trays stacked off to the side. Alex had eaten half of her meal before getting full. She then pushed the

Gerald Pruett

rest away. Catherine was swallowing the last bite she had. She then stacked her tray on top of the others.

As Andy was telling everyone about the worse date he had ever been on, Mark looked at his watch before interrupting with, "Hey, guys, we should get going. The coach wants us on the practice field in fifteen minutes."

"All right," Miles said. He then stood up and grabbed all of the trays. "Alex, I'll see you later."

As Andy and Mark were standing up Alex said, "Okay, bye. See you guys later."

As an afterthought Miles said, "Bye, Catherine. See you around."

"Bye," Catherine said

"Bye," Andy and Mark said.

After Miles, Andy and Mark were out of earshot, Catherine said, "Last Wednesday night I asked you to go somewhere with me on Thursday night, but you told me that you had a date and you wouldn't tell me with who. You went out with Miles last Thursday night and you wouldn't tell me because you knew what I would have told you. That is also how you knew that Miles spilled his tray on me as a dare."

"I didn't go on any dates last Thursday."

"And why don't I believe that?"

"Okay, you're right. I had a date with Miles last Thursday, but that date was canceled because Doug and I went to St. Louis Thursday evening."

"Why did you go to St. Louis?"

"Doug and I needed to talk to a friend of ours."

"You had to go there in person instead of picking up the telephone?"

"His phone number had changed since the last time we had spoken to each other, and it was very important to talk to him."

"Is that friend part of this personal matter that you're trying

197

to solve?"

"He is, and I won't tell you more than that."

"All right, fine. I'll change the subject back to Miles." Alex gave Catherine a curious look as Catherine asked, "Are you planning to make another date with him?"

"We won't be dating anytime in the near future. I do like his company though, so get use to me being seen with him."

"So if I still have a problem with Miles you would choose Miles as a friend over me; a person who you have been friends with since the second week of our freshman year?"

"I won't be choosing either one of you over the other, but if you stop talking to me or having lunch with me simply because I'm friends with someone who you don't like then you'll be the one to have chosen."

"It's good for our friendship that my problem with Miles isn't all that great."

"Well, I'm going to the library to study."

As Alex went to stand up, Catherine asked, "Do you have to study right now?"

"I don't have to. Why?"

"When I ran into you and Stephen, I was actually heading for my car to go to the mall. I was hoping that you would come with me."

"I have a class at three, so I have to be back before then."

"No problem."

As Alex picked up her book bag and purse, she said, "Well, I want to put my book bag up."

Catherine stood up and said, "I guess I can let you do that." Alex just gave her a smirk.

After Catherine grabbed her purse, she and Alex left the lunchroom.

Alex and Catherine met up with Trudy in the dorm room while Alex was putting her book bag up. When Trudy learned that Alex and Catherine were going to the mall, she joined them.

Catherine drove to the mall and during the two hours that Alex, Trudy and Catherine spent there, they went to several shops. Trudy noticed within the first thirty minutes that Alex was enjoying herself as they went from shop to shop. When they walked into a jewelry shop a pair of earrings caught Alex's eye. After a short coaxing by Catherine, Alex bought and put on the earrings. Before leaving the mall Alex had even bought two pairs of designer jeans. Alex, Trudy and Catherine returned to Harvard in time for Alex to get to class.

During the next three days, Alex was adjusting into a daily routine. In the morning she would shower, put on makeup, go to class and study. She had even started to wear her alternate's jewelry. In the evening she waited tables at Little Bucks. Becky and Catherine normally showed up at Little Bucks within a few hours after Alex started her shift. During Alex's free time, she spent most of that time with Miles and Trudy. Occasionally she would spend her free time with Doug, Brandy, Cindy and Kenny.

Chapter Thirteen

Saturday, October 30 at 8:10 A.M., Alex was showering. Trudy was in her dorm room preparing to put on makeup, but before she was able to do so, she heard a knock at the door.

Trudy left her bedroom and when she opened the door to the dorm room, she saw Michelle Larson standing at the door. Trudy gave Michelle a curious look before asking, "May I help you?"

"Yeah, I was told that this dorm room is where Alex Larson is living."

"I'm Alex's roommate, Trudy, and Alex is down the hall in the shower. Now who are you?"

"I'm her sister, Michelle. My friend and I came here for a surprise visit."

An amused grinned came across Trudy's face before she said, "Alex is gong to be surprised all right." She then gestured for Michelle to enter. "Well, you might as well come in and wait for her." Michelle walked into the dorm room and closed the door behind her. "You said that you had a friend with you?"

"Yeah, Heather saw the women's restroom on this floor and stopped to use it."

"Does Alex know Heather?"

Michelle gave Trudy a curious look before saying, "Of course Alex knows Heather. Heather and I have been friends since kindergarten."

Michelle saw a worried expression on Trudy's face as Trudy said, "I was just wondering."

In the women's restroom and shower, Alex was drying off. After she got dressed she walked to where the sinks and mirrors were. Women were at the sinks either brushing their teeth or blow-drying and combing their hair. Alex stepped up to one of the empty sinks and pulled out her hairbrush from her bag.

Alex was about done brushing her hair when Heather stepped up behind Alex and said with a sizable grin on her face, "Hi, Alex."

Alex looked at Heather through the mirror and said as she continued to brush her hair, "Hi. How's it going?"

While looking at Alex's reflection in the mirror, Heather gave her a curious look before saying, "You don't look shocked to see me."

"Should I be shocked?"

"Your mom told you that Michelle and I were coming to visit you and Doug this weekend, didn't she?"

With a surprise expression on her face, Alex jerked around and faced Heather before uttering, "Michelle? My sister Michelle? She's here?"

Heather gave Alex a confused look while saying, "Yes... to all of the above. Are you okay?"

"Of course I'm okay. Why wouldn't I be okay?"

"Because at the moment you're acting kind of strange."

"I'm fine. Where's Michelle now?"

"Well, since you are here, most likely she's outside your dorm room and knocking on the door to get in."

Alex put her brush back into the bag while saying, "I have to talk to her."

As Heather was following Alex out of the restroom, Heather said, "I'm confused as to why you didn't act surprised when you saw me, but you are surprised to hear that Michelle is here."

Alex quickly searched her thoughts for a believable response before saying, "There's actually a woman on campus who favors you, and I thought you were her."

Heather gave Alex a skeptical look before asking, "What is this woman's name?"

Heather noticed a hesitation before Alex said, "Natalie. Her name is Natalie."

"I would like to meet Natalie."

"I don't know where she's at right now, and we aren't really friends so I don't know where her dorm room is either."

Heather continued to give Alex a skeptical look before saying, "I hope we run into Natalie."

"Sometimes Natalie leaves on the weekend, so there's a good chance that we won't."

Heather said under her breath, "Something tells me that you are making Natalie up." She then shrugged it off.

In Alex and Trudy's dorm room, Michelle was telling Trudy about how Alex's dress was ripped off of Alex by accident while she was performing in a high school play. Michelle had laugher in her voice as she told the story and just as Michelle was finishing the story, Alex and Heather walked in.

Alex saw Trudy grinning and Michelle slightly laughing. As Alex gave them a curious look she asked, "What's so funny?"

"Oh, I was just telling Trudy about the high school play that you were in," Michelle said.

With laugher in her voice Heather questioned, "Oh, you mean the one where Alex got naked?"

Alex gave Heather a curious look while asking without thinking, "I got naked during a high school play?"

Heather gave Alex a confused look, as Michelle said, "You were practically naked when Kevin ripped off your dress. I mean you were standing on stage with only your bra and panties. Half of your dress was down at your ankles. The other half was shredded and hanging off of your shoulders. I've never seen you so embarrassed before."

Heather noticed that Alex's facial expression was as if Alex was hearing about the event for the first time. Heather was focusing even more on Alex's facial expression and body movement as Alex said, "Well, that was an embarrassing moment."

"Yeah, and how many days was it that you skipped school over that?" Heather asked.

Michelle gave Heather a confused look while Trudy gave Alex a worried look, just before Alex replied, "It's been a few years ago. I don't remember how many days it was."

Michelle suddenly shot Alex a confused look as Heather asked, "You can't remember the number zero?"

"Alex, you never missed any days," Michelle said.

"Back in the bathroom, you didn't know who I was," Heather said. "That's why you weren't surprised to see me. A person wouldn't be surprised to see someone she doesn't know."

"What are you talking about?" Alex asked. "Of course I know you."

"Then what's my name?"

When Alex didn't answer, Michelle asked, "Alex, what's going on? Why can't you remember things?"

When Alex looked at Trudy, Trudy just gave Alex a look with a gesture as if to say, "It's your call."

When Alex didn't answer, Michelle repeated, "Alex, what's going on?"

Alex sighed before saying, "Okay, Randy Miller, the person in that picture you got for us…"

"I know that part," Michelle said. "I'm not the one who

can't remember things."

"Well, the Randy Miller I know was an upcoming and inspiring scientist." Michelle and Heather gave Alex a curious look as Alex continued to say, "Randy's scientific focus was on alternate reality theory. He had even created a device that he thought would open up a wormhole so people could cross into another reality."

Michelle realized what was going on and blurted out, "Oh my God. You are from another reality, aren't you?"

Heather gave Michelle a confused look before asking, "What are you talking about, Michelle?"

Michelle looked at Heather, but instead of answering Heather's question she faced Alex again before saying, "Two Thursdays ago, when you were in St. Louis you told me that you dreamt that I was never born and that Dad wasn't dad and that your bedroom wasn't the same as it is now. That wasn't a dream, was it? That was your reality."

"Yes, but in my reality, I never lived on Wild Deer Road. I didn't even know where the road was until two Thursdays ago."

"What's going on?" Heather demanded to know.

"What's going on is that this woman isn't my sister."

"You can't be serious," Heather said.

"It's true," Alex said. "I'm not from this reality. I don't know your name because you and I never met before."

"My name is Heather."

"Well, hi, Heather."

"Where's my sister?" Michelle demanded to know.

"Randy was wrong about a wormhole opening up when he activated the device, but what did happen was that the Alex from this reality and I changed places. The same thing happened to Doug. The Doug from my reality changed places with the Doug from this reality."

"So my sister and brother are in your reality."

"They are, and the only way to correct this crossed reality is to find Randy."

"So the Randy from your reality had also switched places with the Randy from my reality?" Michelle asked.

"I haven't seen Randy since the switch, but I'm thinking that Randy was switched along with me, Doug and four others. Doug and I are in contact with the other four."

"If you can't find Randy, you and the others are stuck here, aren't you?" Michelle asked.

"We are, but there is a chance that I know where Randy is. In fact, in about two hours from now, the six of us who have switched realities will be on our way to search for him."

"Where do you think he's at?" Michelle asked.

"In my reality, I talked Randy out of going to Mexico City to look for his long lost dad. I believe he went to Mexico in this reality."

"You and the others are going to Mexico in two hours?" Heather asked.

"We are," Alex said.

"How are you getting there?" Michelle asked.

"We will be going by a private jet," Alex said.

"Can I go with you?" Michelle asked.

"No-no; you can't go," Alex said.

"Alex… or whoever you are; I can help. I have been taking Spanish lessons for three years, so I can speak to the people there."

"I am Alex, but from a different reality, and your Spanish would come in handy; however, if Mom finds out I took you to Mexico, she will kill me."

"Alex, Mom is going to kill you if she finds out that you went to Mexico and if you don't let me go, I'll tell her every-thing."

As Alex was giving Michelle an uncertain look, Trudy said, "Blackmailed by your own sister."

Michelle looked at Trudy before gesturing towards Alex and saying, "I don't know about her, but with my sister, Alex, I had to resort to blackmail from time to time for self preservation."

"All right, Michelle. You can come, but you must keep everything to yourself. Heather, you need to keep this to yourself also."

"Who would believe me even if I did tell someone?" Heather asked.

"Heather, I will need you to tell your parents that I will be staying here with Alex," Michelle said.

"Okay, but I sure hope you... actually I hope everyone knows what they are doing."

"So do I," Alex agreed.

"Alex, how is it possible for you and Doug to have a different father in your reality?" Michelle asked. "I mean since you are Alex and Doug is Doug wouldn't you two have the same parents still?"

"Michelle, you are a half sister to me and Doug or to Alex and Doug of this reality."

"What are you talking about?"

"My biological dad is named Nicholas Christopher O'Brien. In my reality and in this one too, my dad... Nicholas was injured on the job and had to go to the hospital. This happened before mom knew she was even pregnant with Doug and me. In this reality Nicholas was given an injection that he was severely allergic to and he died from his allergy. In my reality I don't know if my dad Nicholas was given the injection or not, but he never died."

"Two Thursdays ago, I heard Dad yelling, 'I'm your father.' So was Nicholas the topic that you, Doug, Mom and

Dad were discussing?"

"It was. Doug and I went to St. Louis to look for Randy, but when Mom and Dad caught us in town we used the knowledge of Nicholas for the reason why we were there. That was also when Mom told Doug and me about what happened to our biological dad."

"Trudy, are you from Alex's reality too?" Heather asked.

"No, but like you, I saw Alex acting as if she had amnesia," Trudy said. "My brother Miles and I were ready to drag her to the hospital when she told us about her being from another reality."

"Well, I'm going to finish getting dressed and then we can go find Doug and the others," Alex said. She then turned and walked into her bedroom.

Alex had stepped into her bedroom and shut the door when Doug knocked on the dorm door.

When Trudy opened the door, Doug said, "Hey, Trudy, I was going to the pancake house for some breakfast and I was wondering if you and Alex want to go."

"Well, Alex is in her bedroom getting dressed." Trudy then amusingly grinned as she continued to say, "You should come in and wait though."

Doug gave Trudy a curious look while asking, "Okay, what's up? Why are you grinning?"

Trudy backed up to allow Doug to enter while saying, "Come in and find out."

Doug walked in and when he saw Michelle, he demanded, "Michelle?! Why are you here?!"

"Heather's grandma lives only fifteen minutes from here. Heather and her parents had plans to visit her this weekend and I was invited to come to Boston too. While I'm here I thought I find out from you and Alex why you wanted Randy's picture, and what I found out is unbelievable."

"What all did Alex tell you?" Doug asked.

"I know you and a few others are going to Mexico City to look for Randy, and I'm going with you."

Without saying another word Doug stepped up to Alex's bedroom door and knocked hard on it. When Alex opened the door, Doug asked, "Did you tell Michelle that she can come with us?"

Instead of answering Doug's question, Alex said, "Good morning to you too."

"Alex, did you tell Michelle that she can come with us?"

"I did. I also told her everything about us, and I believe Michelle can be a big help to us in Mexico."

Michelle gave Alex a look as if she was pleasantly surprised by Alex's statement. Michelle grinned as Doug asked, "How is Michelle going to help to us?"

"When the two realities get straightened out, the Alex and Doug of this reality are going to need Michelle to understand what happened to them."

"I figure Trudy was going to help Alex and Doug to understand what happened."

"Trudy will," Alex agreed. "Trudy is a friend, but Alex and Doug might need a relative to share things with. Besides Michelle knows Spanish, so that alone will be a major help to us."

Doug sighed before saying, "Okay, fine, but I don't want anymore people involved in this."

"Neither do I," Alex said. "Now I'm going to finish putting on my makeup."

"Alex, before you do that, I came to say that I'm going to the pancake house for breakfast. I was wondering if you wanted to join me."

"Sure, give me about fifteen minutes," Alex said. She then walked back into her bedroom.

When Alex shut her door again, Trudy said, "I need to put on my makeup as well. Oh and Doug, I also want to go with you for breakfast."

"Okay." As Trudy was walking towards her bedroom Doug continued with, "Michelle, do you and your friend, want to join us for breakfast?"

"I'm in," Michelle said. She then gestured towards Alex's bedroom. "I'm going to talk to Alex."

As Michelle was walking towards the door, Heather said, "Doug, my name is Heather and I'm also in for breakfast."

"Okay," Doug said.

Michelle knocked on the door before asking, "Alex, can I come in?"

"Come in," Michelle heard Alex calling out.

Alex was at her desk and looking into a makeup mirror while putting on her makeup.

Michelle stepped up to where she could see Alex's face in the mirror before saying, "You took the blame by making Doug think that it was your idea for me to go."

As Alex continued to put on makeup, she said, "I don't think Doug has to know that I told you that you can go because you threatened to blackmail me. Besides, after I thought about it, I think you can help us."

"Well, thanks for being on my side."

"You're welcome."

Michelle thought for a moment before asking, "Alex, what is your reality like?"

"My reality is pretty much like this one, but in my reality, Randy and I were good friends, and Randy also attended Harvard."

"Were you and Randy a couple?"

"No, absolutely not."

"Besides me not being born and your biological dad being

alive, what are the differences between my reality and yours?"

Without mentioning that she was a man in the other reality, Alex went through a list of what she knew that was different between the two realities.

12:23 P.M. local time in Mexico City, at the airport, Alex, Doug, Michelle, Trudy, Miles, Brandy, Cindy, Kenny, Ben and a pilot named Leo stepped off the plane. Alex, Doug, Kenny and Ben had a copy of Randy's picture. On the back of each picture were Spanish phrases to what they were to say or ask as they searched for Randy. They broke into four groups and then left the airport in four cabs. Alex, Miles and Trudy were in one group. Doug and Michelle were in the second group. Kenny and Brandy were in the third group. Ben and Cindy were in the last group. Leo went to a restaurant that was near the airport.

As the minutes slowly passed each group entered several facilities all around the city and showed Randy's picture to the locals. Michelle roughly communicated with the locals who couldn't speak English.

Each group searched for three hours without finding a clue. As Doug and Michelle were leaving their latest facility, Michelle asked, "Is there any reason that we aren't talking to the Mexican police?"

Doug thought for a second before commenting, "Why not? Let's go and show them Randy's picture."

Doug and Michelle walked up to a cab and got in.

Ten minutes later, Doug and Michelle stepped out of the cab in front of the police station. As they were walking towards the door, Michelle asked, "What are we going to tell the police as to why we are searching for Randy?"

"I have been giving that some thought and we... or since you are the one who can speak Spanish, it will most likely be you who tells them that Randy has an identical twin, and that his twin brother is dying and to save his life, he needs a bone marrow."

"Okay. I can do that."

Doug held out Randy's picture for Michelle to take and said, "Here's the picture."

Doug and Michelle walked into the police station and up to an officer behind a desk. In Spanish the officer asked, "May I help you?"

Michelle held out the picture for the officer to take and roughly said in Spanish, "I'm looking for the man in the picture and I was hoping that you can help me find him."

Without taking the picture the officer said in English, "This is not a private investigator's office, so you two have to leave."

"How did you know I spoke English?" Michelle asked.

"Young lady, your espanol is okay, but it needs some work."

"How did you know I spoke English though?"

"Your accent gave it away. Now as I said, you and your friend have to leave."

"He's my brother."

Doug stepped up while saying, "Sir... officer, it's very important that we find this man as soon as we can. It's a medical emergency."

"I hate repeating myself, but I'm going to say this one more time," the officer said. "You and your sister didn't walk into a private investigator's office."

Before Doug was able to say anything else Michelle blurted out, "The man who we are looking for doesn't know this, but he is walking around your city with a contagious and deadly disease."

Doug gave Michelle a surprised look as the officer said, "Young lady, if you and your brother are coming in here crying wolf, you and him both will be in serious trouble."

"Officer, please excuse my sister, she doesn't know better.

However, it is very important that we do find this man. His twin brother is dying and the only thing that will save his life is this man's bone marrow."

The officer gave Doug an uncertain look before saying, "Young lady, let me see the picture you have." Michelle handed him the picture. The officer looked at the picture for a couple of seconds before handing it back. "The man who you are looking for is locked up in a cell in back."

"Randy is here?" Doug asked.

"He's been here for a while, waiting for his trial," the officer said.

"What did he do?" Michelle asked.

"He broke into a home of a respected person," the officer said.

"What will it take to get him released?" Doug asked.

"You will have to talk to the judge for that," the officer said.

"What is the possibility that I can talk to Randy?" Doug asked.

The officer moved a visitor's registry towards Doug and said, "Write your and your sister's names and you two can follow me."

"Where are you taking us?" Michelle asked.

Doug was about to say something when the officer said, "I'm taking you to a room to where you can visit, Senor Miller. Your brother did ask to see him, and I'm going to allow it."

"Cool," Michelle said.

After Doug wrote his and Michelle's names they were led to a small room with a table and four chairs. After stepping in the officer said, "You two have a seat, and I will have Senor Miller brought here."

"Thank you," Doug said.

After the officer left, Doug and Michelle took their seats.

Doug took his phone off of his belt and dialed a number.

Michelle gave Doug a curious look before asking, "Who are you calling?"

"I'm calling Alex to let her know that we found Randy so everyone can stop looking." When Alex answered the phone, Doug told Alex where he found Randy.

Minutes later, Doug and Michelle were sitting quietly when another officer escorted Randy into the room. Randy was twenty pounds lighter and had a full beard and mustache.

When Randy saw Doug, he said, "Doug, I'm glad to see you. But how did you find me?"

The officer stood at the door on the inside of the room. As Randy was taking a seat, Doug said, "Alex remembered a discussion about you coming here to look for your dad."

"I forgot about that. Where is he anyway?"

"He? What do you mean where's he?" Michelle asked.

Randy looked at Michelle before asking, "Who are you?"

"She's my and Alex's sister. Her name is Michelle and she knows everything."

"So you and Alex have a sister. Where is he anyway?"

"Are you calling Alex a he?" Michelle asked.

Randy gave Michelle a curious look before asking, "Alex isn't a he?"

Before Doug was able to say anything, Michelle said, "She's our sister." Michelle then had a thought. "Wait! Was Alex a guy in the other reality?"

Randy whispered, "Michelle, the man at the door doesn't need to hear about other realities, and yes, Alex was a guy."

"Okay, now Michelle knows everything," Doug said.

"Doug, does Alex still favor you?" Randy asked.

"She definitely doesn't favor me any more, oh and to answer your question of where she is, she's actually on her way here along with Kenny, Ben, Brandy and Cindy."

"So everyone at the table crossed?" Randy asked. Doug just nodded. "Do you know of anyone else who might've crossed?"

"It was just the seven of us," Doug said. "There are two more people who know about us. Their names are Trudy and Miles and they are also in Mexico with Alex and the others."

"Heather knows," Michelle said.

"Who's Heather?" Randy asked.

"She's my best friend," Michelle said.

"That's not important," Doug said. "We need to talk about how to get you out of here, so you can remake your device."

"Well, I was actually able to make diagrams of how to make the device, so if you guys can't get me released, you guys will have to create it," Randy said.

"You have the diagrams with you?" Doug asked.

"I do." Randy pulled out eight pages from his back pocket and held them out for Doug to take. Doug saw the officer staring at him as he took the papers. Randy noticed the officer staring too before telling him, "The papers are just those drawings I was doing. My friend here is actually who I wanted to mail them to, but you and your buddies wouldn't let me."

The officer didn't respond to Randy's comment and looked forward again.

When Randy faced Doug again, Doug said, "Well, I hope we will be able to get you out of here, so you can create the device. In any case Michelle and I should go and talk to the judge about getting you released."

"Okay, well now you know where to find me."

After everyone stood up, Doug and Michelle left the room first. As the two were walking back to the front of the police station, the officer escorted Randy back to his cell.

The officer from the front desk saw Doug and Michelle walking up and asked, "Did you talk to Senor Miller?"

"We did," Doug said. "Where do we go to find a judge?"

"Judge Carlos Torres will be the one who you want to talk to, and most likely he will be at his house. He also lives about thirty minutes from here. So do you want his address?"

"Yes, please."

"Oh and Judge Torres also speaks English," The officer said before giving Doug Judge Torres' address. Once Doug had the information, he and Michelle left the police station and waited for everyone to arrive.

Chapter Fourteen

Kenny and Brandy showed up first. Minutes later, Alex, Trudy and Miles pulled up in their cab.

As Alex, Trudy and Miles were walking towards Doug and Michelle, Michelle stepped up to Alex with a smile on her face. Alex saw the smile that she was getting and asked, "Why are you looking at me like that?"

"I found out why you and Randy were never more than friends," Michelle said.

Alex gave Michelle a skeptical look before asking, "What do you think you found out?"

Michelle whispered, "For someone who would have been a brother to me in even another reality, you are good with putting on makeup."

Alex grinned before saying, "Trudy and Brandy showed me how to do it and I didn't tell you because I was trying to respect the other Alex's privacy."

"I understand why you kept quiet, and you seem pretty mellow about your situation... well, more mellow than what I would be anyway. I'm also afraid that my sister Alex won't be as mellow as you are being either."

"Would Alex do anything rash?"

"I honestly don't know what Alex would do."

"Well, we need to correct this crossed reality before the other Alex does do something rash." Alex then stepped up to Doug before asking, "Doug, what did you learn about Randy's situation?"

"I was given a name of a judge to talk to, but if we can't get him released, we're going to have to create the device ourselves."

"Randy is the only one who can create the device though."

Doug pulled out the papers that Randy had given him before saying, "Randy gave me the diagrams to it."

"What did Randy do to get thrown into a Mexican jail anyway?"

"According to the officer at the front desk, he broke into someone's home."

"That doesn't sound like Randy to break into someone's home."

"The Randy of this reality was the one who broke into the home and we don't know anything about that Randy."

"Still, I don't believe Randy of any reality who searches for his dad would break into a home. I think there must be a misunderstanding somewhere. I'm going to talk to the officer. Does he speak English?"

"He does, but what do you need to talk to him about?"

"I want to know what home he supposedly broke into, and then I'm going to talk to the owner."

"Please don't go out there and play Nancy Drew, and get yourself thrown into an adjacent cell to Randy's."

"I have no intentions on playing Nancy Drew. I just want to talk to the owner that's all. And as I'm doing that, you can talk to the judge."

As Alex walked towards the door to the police station, Doug yelled out, "Please don't do anything stupid." Alex waved without looking.

Trudy and the others walked up to Doug. When Trudy stepped up she asked, "What is Alex doing?"

"She's planning to get the address of the person who got Randy arrested and then have a talk with him or her." Doug saw a cab driving up with Ben and Cindy in it. "Hey, guys, Michelle and I are going to grab that cab Cindy and Ben are arriving in and go talk to the judge. Someone needs to go with Alex to keep her from getting herself into trouble."

"I'll go with Alex," Miles said.

"Me too," Trudy said.

Inside the police station, the officer at the desk was watching Alex closely as Alex was walking up. The officer pleasantly grinned before saying in Spanish, "Hi, beautiful lady. How can I help you?"

"Do you speak English?" Alex asked.

"Si, Senorita. How can I help such a beautiful damsel as yourself?"

Alex slightly grinned before saying, "My brother and sister were just in here talking to a friend of ours, who is being held in a cell. Our friend's name is Randy Miller."

"Si, Senorita; Senor Miller is here. Are you an affectionate friend of his?"

"No-no, we're not affectionate friends. We're just friends. We knew each other since we were six. Anyway, I'm not really here to see him or talk to him."

"Why are you in here, Senorita?"

"I understand from my brother that Randy was arrested for breaking into someone's home and I was hoping that I can get the name of the owner of that home and the house address. I want to talk to the owner and perhaps I can persuade the owner to drop the charges with the promise that Randy will return to the U.S."

"I will give you the information, but the chance that the owner will drop the charges is remote." The officer took the time to get the information for Alex.

As Alex was receiving the information, she said, "Gracias."

"You're welcome, Senorita. Senorita, my shift ends in two

hours and I would feel honored if you would allow me to personally show you around our lovely city."

Alex slightly grinned before saying, "My boyfriend and I have seen a lot of your city already, but sure. You showing Miles and me around would be delightful. I bet there are plenty of sites that we haven't seen yet." Alex saw the officer searching his thoughts as she continued to say, "Miles is waiting for me right out front, so I'll go tell him of your kind offer."

"Senorita, wait. I actually just remembered a promise I made to be somewhere right after I got off."

"That's a shame. I bet the three of us would have a great time together. Hey, perhaps another time."

"Of course. Another time."

"Well, bye. I'll see you around."

"Bye, senorita."

Alex turned and had a smile on her face as she walked towards the door.

Miles and Trudy saw Alex smiling as she stepped out of the police station. As Alex stepped up to Miles and Trudy, Miles asked, "What happened in there for you to be smiling like that?"

"The officer at the front desk wanted to give me a personal tour of Mexico City," Alex said.

Trudy slightly grinned before asking, "The officer hit on you?"

"He sure did."

With a curious expression across his face Miles asked, "So how did you handle it?"

Alex grinned at Miles before saying, "I told him that my boyfriend Miles and I would be delighted for him to show us around."

"You told the officer that I was your boyfriend?"

"I did, and after I told him that, he seemed to have remembered something he had to do instead. You don't mind that I told the officer that, do you?"

"Oh no; I don't mind. You can tell every guy in Mexico that I'm your boyfriend if you want."

"Okay, thanks." Alex then noticed that everyone, but her, Trudy and Miles was gone. "So where is everyone?"

"Ben and Cindy went with Doug and Michelle," Trudy said. "Brandy saw a bargain store and she and Kenny went to that. They said to call one of their cell phones if we need them."

"Okay, well anyway, I have the address to the place that Randy supposedly had broken into. The owner's name is Catalina Mendez."

"Okay, we need a cab," Miles said.

Alex, Miles and Trudy walked up to the edge of the street and when a cab came by they hailed the driver.

Fifteen minutes later, Alex, Miles and Trudy were being let out in front of Catalina's house.

The house was slightly run down. The fence was broken in a few spots. The grass was tall and was filled with weeds. A car sat on the driveway that led up towards the house.

Alex, Miles and Trudy were quiet as they walked towards the front door. Once they reached the door, Alex knocked. Alex was about to knock a second time when Catalina, a sixty-year-old woman, opened the door.

When Catalina saw Alex and her friends, she asked in Spanish, "Can I help you?"

Miles said in Spanish, "Hi, ma'am. Do you speak English?" Catalina shook her head 'no'. "Well, anyway, ma'am, I'm Miles." He gestured towards the others. "They are Alex and Trudy. We are here to talk about Randy Miller, the man who was arrested for breaking into your home."

"What about him?"

"Alex is a good friend of Randy's and Alex believes that there was a misunderstanding as to Randy's intentions."

"There were no misunderstandings. My son Jose came to visit me while I was out and found him in my home."

"Yes, ma'am. I'm not arguing that part, but Randy is from the U.S. and the only reason he came to Mexico City was to find his father. The only reason Randy would have come here was if a clue to find his father had led him here."

"For whatever the reason he was here, he broke into my home."

Alex interrupted by asking, "Miles, what's being said?"

Miles gestured for Alex to wait before asking Catalina, "Ma'am, did you ask Randy why he had broken into your home?"

"His reason never interested me."

"Ma'am, if I promise that Randy will return to the U.S. and not return here would you drop the charges against him?"

"That man needs to pay for his crime."

"Can I offer you compensation in exchange for you to drop the charges?"

"What kind of compensation?"

"Name your price, and I will see if I can get it for you."

"I have been needing repairs done to my home, but neither I nor my son has the money to hire someone to do it. My son was going to do it, but he hasn't the time."

"So do you want me to hire a handyman to fix your home?"

"I want your friend, the one who broke into my home, to be the one to make the repairs. I have the money to buy the supplies. I just need your friend to do the labor."

"If Randy agrees to be your handyman, will you drop the charges?"

"Si. Once the repairs are done then he can go back to the

United States."

Alex gave Miles a curious look before asking, "Miles, what's going on?"

"Senora Mendez will drop the charges against Randy only if he agrees to stay in Mexico and make repairs to her house," Miles said. "Once he's done with her house then he will be free to leave."

"Tell Senora Mendez that Randy will do it or I'll personally kill him."

"What is she saying?" Catalina asked.

Miles grinned before saying in Spanish, "She said that Randy will do it or she'll personally kill him."

Catalina smiled and nodded at Alex.

"Miles, ask Senora Mendez if she can call us a cab so we can talk with Randy," Alex said.

"Senora Mendez, could you call us a cab so we can return to the police station?" Miles asked.

"I'll drive you," Catalina said. "I want to hear it for myself what Randy says."

Miles faced Alex and Trudy before saying, "Senora Mendez will drive us. She wants to hear it for herself that Randy will repair her house."

Alex looked at Catalina before saying, "Gracias."

Catalina grinned and nodded.

At Judge Torres's house, Doug, Michelle, Ben and Cindy stepped up to the front door and rang the doorbell.

Judge Torres opened the door and after seeing everyone at the door he asked in Spanish, "May I help you, people?"

Michelle looked at Doug and said, "He wants to know what we want."

"Judge Torrez, there's a man waiting for trial at the police station," Doug said. "He was arrested for breaking into someone's home; however, I think there was a misunderstanding as to why he was there."

"Who are you, people?" Judge Torres asked in English as Doug's phone rang.

Doug took his phone off of his belt. "My name is Doug." He glanced at the phone and saw that it was Alex who was calling. He then held out the phone for Michelle to take. "Answer the phone for me." Michelle took the phone and as she walked away she answered it. Doug turned back towards Judge Torres. "My friends are Cindy, Ben and my sister Michelle. The person I'm referring to in the jail cell is Randy Miller."

"I'm familiar with Senor Miller and his accusation, but why are you at my front door?"

Before Doug was able to answer Michelle said, "Doug, Senora Mendez, the person who filed charges against Randy is willing to drop the charges if Randy will stay on temporarily as her handyman. Alex, Trudy, Miles and Senora Mendez are on their way to the police station now."

"The person you are talking to is with Senora Mendez now?" Judge Torres asked.

"Si," Michelle said.

Judge Torrez stepped out of his doorway and said, "I want to talk to Senora Mendez."

Before Michelle handed over the phone she put the phone to her ear and said, "Hey, Alex, Judge Torrez wants to talk to Senora Mendez." Michelle then handed the phone to Judge Torrez.

Doug, Cindy and Ben watched Judge Torrez's facial expressions and movements as he talked in Spanish to Catalina. Michelle listened more closely at what was being said and was able to understand most of it.

Judge Torrez talked for a short time. He then handed the phone back to Doug and said, "I'll meet everyone at the police station."

"Okay," Doug said before he slightly held up the phone. "Oh, do you know the number for a cab? The cab we came here in is gone."

Judge Torrez gave Doug a skeptical look for a second before saying, "Since we're going to the same place, I'll give you and your friends a ride."

"Gracias," Doug said.

"Stay put and I will be back in a minute," Judge Torrez said before turning and walking back into his house.

At the police station, Alex, Miles and Trudy were in the visiting room while waiting for Randy. At the table Alex was seated between Trudy and Miles. An officer escorted Randy into the room and just after Randy stepped in, he gave Alex and the others curious looks.

The officer again stood by the door and as Randy stepped up to the table he asked, "Who are you, people?"

"Don't tell me that you don't recognize your best friend since the first grade?" Alex jokingly questioned.

Randy thought for a second before giving her a grin and asking, "Alex? Is that you?"

Alex smiled before saying, "It's me."

Randy sat down before saying, "Wow, you look awesome."

"Thanks... I think. Anyway meet two good friends of mine. Miles and Trudy. Miles; Trudy, meet Randy."

Randy and Miles shook hands while saying almost together, "Nice to meet you."

Trudy just waved and said, "Nice to meet you."

"Nice to meet you too," Randy responded before facing Alex again. "So, Alex, I doubt you came here just to say 'hi'. So, what's up?"

"I believe we're able to get you released from this police station on one condition," Alex said.

"And that is?"

"Senora Mendez will drop the charges if you remain in Mexico City and be her handyman for a short time."

"She wants me to be her handyman?"

"You broke into her home and she believes you have to pay for your crime. Miles offered to compensate her for her to drop the charges. You being her handyman is the only thing she would accept."

"One, I'm not the one who broke into her house and two, why is Miles making any offer to compensate her?"

Miles exclaimed in an agitated tone, "I was trying to help."

Alex took hold of Miles' arm near the wrist before whispering to Randy, "The Randy who belongs in this reality is guilty and like it or not, you have inherited his guilt. As for Miles making that offer, he's the only one of us who is able to speak Spanish and I told Miles before we met Senora Mendez that I wanted to do whatever it takes to get you released. And Miles did just that. All you have to do is accept the offer. Now do you want to accept Senora Mendez's offer or do you want to wait in jail for your trial to begin?"

"For how long do I have to be her handyman?"

"Her house is slightly run down and she just wants you to repair what needs repairing. Truthfully, I don't believe you will have to be the handyman for too long."

"Why do you believe that?"

"You gave Doug the diagram to build the device, so while you are repairing Senora Mendez's house, everyone else will work on building the device. Once we're done, we will come back here and activate it."

"All right, Alex; I'll accept Senora Mendez's offer."

"Good. I think you made the right choice." As Alex was standing up she continued saying, "Trudy, Miles and I will go out and tell Senora Mendez what you are going to do."

The officer turned and watched Miles and Trudy as they stood up.

As Randy was standing up he said, "Miles, thank you for your part with getting me out of here."

Alex gave Miles a pleasant grin as Miles said, "You're welcome."

As Alex, Miles and Trudy were walking back to the front of the police station, Randy was again being escorted back to his cell. After Alex, Miles and Trudy stepped up to the officer at the front desk, Alex told the officer that Randy accepted Senora Mendez's offer.

Senora Mendez called her son Jose and told him what was happening.

When Judge Torrez, Doug, Michelle, Cindy and Ben showed up, Judge Torrez used the computer and roughly wrote up a contract that stated that Randy had to work for Senora Mendez for either six months or when the job was complete. Meals, room and board were the only things Randy would receive for payment.

Before Catalina and Randy were able to sign the contract Jose walked into the police station and voiced his objections to it.

Miles and Michelle listened to what was being said with interest as the others watched in confusion.

Alex listened for a short time before tapping Miles on the shoulder and saying, "Miles, that guy looks irritated. What's going on?"

"That guy is Jose, Senora Mendez's son, and he is objecting to Randy being released and working for his mother," Miles said.

Alex faced Doug before asking, "Doug, does Jose Mendez look slightly familiar to you?"

Doug looked at Jose for a brief moment before shaking his

head and saying, "No. Does he look familiar to you?"

"I know he's not the guy I saw in Phyllis' picture, but he does have similar features to the one who is." Alex turned back to Miles before requesting, "Miles, ask Senora Mendez or Jose if Jose has a brother." Mile was about to respond when Alex continued with, "Oh and if Jose does have a brother, then ask if the brother was born with a cleft lip."

Miles gave Alex a curious look for a second before saying, "Okay." Miles then walked up to Catalina and Jose and asked them what Alex wanted to know.

Both Catalina and Jose said, "No."

Before Miles had a chance to walk away, Catalina suddenly had a thought and said, "Wait. My sister Francisca had a baby boy name Roberto who was born with a cleft lip. When Roberto was only six months old Francisca took him to a doctor in the United States. Francisca came back three years later without Roberto. She would never tell me what happen to Roberto, except that Roberto was with a nice family. Francisca died a few years later from AIDS."

Miles repeated what Catalina said in English for Alex to hear. Alex then said, "Miles, tell Senora Mendez that I have seen a picture of Randy's father and that he had a visible scar from having a cleft lip as a baby. I'm thinking that Randy's father is Roberto."

After Miles translated what Alex had said, the officer at the front desk said in Spanish, "Senora Mendez, Senor Miller was found with a photo of a man in his possession when he was arrested, and the man in the photo does look a little like Senor Mendez."

"Do you have that photo?" Catalina asked.

"Si." The officer walked to where Randy's personal belongings were kept. He searched through Randy's personal belongings and once he found the picture he handed it to

Catalina.

Catalina looked at the picture before looking at Jose and saying, "This man does look a little like you and from this picture I can also see a mark on his lip that could be a scar. So there's a chance that Randy might be my sister's grandson."

"Mother, just because the man in the picture may or may not have a scar from a cleft lip, you shouldn't be taken in by Randy Miller."

"Jose, Alex knew enough to ask about the cleft lip and this man in the picture can easily be a relative of ours." Catalina looked at the officer. "I want to talk to Senor Miller."

"You will need a translator with Senor Miller. He cannot speak espanol," the officer said.

"Okay. Please arrange it," Catalina said,

"Si," the officer said before stepping away.

Eight minutes later, Catalina was sitting in the visiting room as an officer who was able to speak English escorted Randy into the room. After stepping in the officer said in English, "Senor Miller, this is Senora Mendez."

"You can tell Senora Mendez that I accept her offer," Randy said.

After the officer translated what Randy had said, Catalina said, "Tell him to have a seat and that I'm actually here to find out what his father's name is."

After the officer translated what Catalina said, Randy sat down before saying, "I know his name by Robert Daniels, but according to my mother he was adopted by a couple when he was about two years old, so that's not his birth name and I don't know what his birth name is." The officer was about to translate when Randy continued to say, "I do know that he was born in Mexico City, and three years ago I was told by someone who used to work with him that he returned here."

The officer translated, but it wasn't verbatim. Catalina then said, "According to Alex, your father had a cleft lip at birth."

After the officer translated, Randy said, "He did. My mom told me that he had a few operations to correct it before he was three."

The police translated what Randy had said. Catalina then said, "My sister had a son named Roberto. He was born with a cleft lip. I now believe that your father is my sister's son." The officer translated what Catalina said. Before Randy responded Catalina said, "Tell Senor Miller that I'm rescinding the offer I made him, but I'm still dropping the charges against him."

The officer translated. Randy put out his hand to shake hands before saying, "Gracias."

After shaking hands Catalina stood up and walked out. The officer escorted Randy back to his cell.

When Catalina stepped back up to the front she told the officer at the desk, "I'm dropping all charges. There was no crime committed."

"That man broke into your house!" Jose uttered. "I caught him there myself."

"He is my sister's grandson. I believe Alex when she said that he was in my home looking for his father."

"Mother, you are falling for these people's con," Jose said.

Catalina turned towards the officer before saying, "There's been a mistake. Senor Miller committed no crime against me."

As Jose continued his objection, Alex asked, "Miles, what's going on?"

"Senora Mendez is dropping the charges against Randy, and Senor Mendez doesn't like it."

Catalina walked away from Jose and walked up to Miles. Michelle stepped closer to hear as Catalina said, "As you heard, I'm dropping the charges against your friend. When he gets released, he can return to the United States with you and the others."

"Gracias," Miles said.

"Tell Randy that if he is ever in Mexico City again, he's welcome to visit me."

"I'll tell him."

Catalina nodded and after she turned and was walking away, Alex asked, "What did she say?"

"Once Randy is released, he is free to leave Mexico," Miles said.

"Randy is also welcome to visit Senora Mendez if he ever returns to Mexico," Michelle added.

"Awesome. We're finally getting a break," Alex said.

"So I guess it is just a matter of days for you to go back home," Miles sullenly said.

Michelle caught the tone and gave Miles a curious look. Alex also caught the tone and responded with, "It looks that way. I think it's better if it happens sooner than later anyway."

"Yeah, you're probably right," Miles said insincerely.

Alex ignored Mile's tone and said, "Well, I actually need to use the restroom. So I can ask the officer where I need to go what is the word... or phrase for the lady's room?"

"It's servicio de senoras."

"Thanks," Alex said before turning and walking away.

Miles noticed Michelle looking at him and when he looked at Michelle, Michelle said, "You like Alex. I'm mean, the Alex who is here now."

"I like both of them actually."

"But you don't like both of them in the same way, do you?"

"How old are you again?"

"I'm sixteen, and I'm old enough to know when a person has a thing for another person. And you have a thing for Alex."

"I can't have a thing for Alex for a few reasons."

"Okay; whatever you say."

Miles gave Michelle a skeptical look before saying, "I'm

going outside for a bit of fresh air." Miles then walked away.

Alex stepped out of the stall and as she stepped up to the sink to wash her hands, Michelle entered the restroom. Alex glanced at Michelle long enough to see who was coming in as she turned on the water.

Michelle walked up to Alex and said, "Miles has a thing for you, you know."

"He did have a thing for me, but then I told him the truth about me... about how I wasn't Alexandra in the other reality." Alex turned off the water.

As Alex was reaching for the paper towels Michelle said, "From what I saw, Miles isn't concerned with who you were in the other reality."

As Alex dried her hands she said, "I think it's just that he is able to talk to me easier than he can with the other Alex, that's all. So I wouldn't read too much into it. We're just friends, and he knows that we can only be just friends. He'll miss me when I return to my reality, and honestly, I'll miss hanging out with him too." Michelle looked at Alex as if she was trying to make sense about something. "What?"

Michelle smiled before saying, "Oh my God. You have a thing for Miles too."

"Even if that was true, which I'm not saying it is, there is no way I can act on it." Alex threw the towels in the trashcan. "I don't belong here. I belong in the other reality with Bonnie, my fiancée."

"And what if you or the others can't get back? What if Randy's device working the first time was a fluke?"

"We'll know in a few days. We need to join the others."

"I need to use the bathroom first."

Alex nodded and as she was walking towards the door, Michelle entered a stall.

Minutes later, as Michelle was returning to the front of the police station, she could only see Doug. She walked up to him and asked, "Where is everyone?"

"The officer at the counter told us to clear out as we wait for Randy to be released, so everyone went outside to wait. I was about ready to walk outside myself when you walked up."

As Doug and Michelle walked towards the exit, Michelle asked, "Doug, do you know that Alex romantically likes Miles?"

"I do. In fact, she's losing her male identity rapidly and that has her scared. That's why she is so focused on getting back to our own reality."

"How long will it take Randy to re-create the device?"

"I'm thinking it will take him a week; two weeks at the most." Doug opened the door and motioned for Michelle to walk out first.

Chapter Fifteen

In the reality Alpha 0.0.0.0.0.0.0, Randy sat in the psychiatrist office of Dr. Martin Adams. Randy sat on the couch as Dr. Adams sat in the chair next to him.

Dr. Adams looked at his watch while saying, "I was hoping today will be the day you talk." Randy just looked at him without saying a word. "I can't help you if you don't talk to me."

"You can't help me," Randy said.

"If you give me a chance and talk to me, I might be able to."

"You say that I'm a student at Harvard and you want me to talk about that. How can you help me when you believe that?"

"Where am I making my mistake?"

"I never attended Harvard or any other college."

"What do you believe you were doing during the past three years?"

Randy uttered emotionally, "That statement... or that question that you just asked is exactly why you can't help me!"

"I don't understand. What was it about my question that makes you think that I wouldn't be able to help?"

"You asked me what do I believe I did during that time and not what did I do during that time. How can you help me when you have already made up your mind that I'm delusional?"

"I have copies of your college transcripts that prove that you are attending Harvard. Would you like to see them?"

"I don't care what you have. This life is a lie. This is not my reality."

"You are part of a group, and each person in that group is saying the exact same thing that you are."

"I don't know who those people are."

"And they are actually saying the same thing about you, but from what I understand from the people at Harvard, all of you were good friends."

"I don't care what those people are saying. I never attended Harvard."

"If you weren't attending Harvard for the last three years, what were you doing?"

Randy gave the doctor a skeptical look before saying, "During most of that time I was making my way to Mexico City to find my dad." Dr. Adams wrote down what Randy was saying. "I worked odd jobs here and there while traveling there."

"Did you make it to Mexico City and find your dad?"

"I made it there, but I didn't find my dad. My search was cut short when I was arrested for breaking into someone's house."

"You broke into someone's house?"

"No, I didn't, but I can't speak Spanish except for a few phrases, and the man who thought I broke in couldn't speak English, so I couldn't explain that the door was slightly open when I got there. And since the door was open I thought there was someone home so I walked in. I was only in there for a short time when the man found me there."

"Why were you at that house?"

"I was showing a picture of my dad around the city and a man told me that the woman who owns that house could help me find my dad. The person who pointed me towards the house said something else, but since I couldn't speak Spanish, I didn't know what he was telling me."

"How long where you in jail?"

"I lost track to how long it was. That was also where I was when I blacked out. When I came to, I was in Harvard's library."

Dr. Adams was about to say something when there was a knock on the door. He stood up before saying, "Excuse me for a moment." When Randy nodded, Dr. Adams left the room.

In the reality Alpha 0.0.0.1.0.0.0 at 8:00 P.M., Alex, Randy and the others were stepping off the private plane at the Boston airport. Chad was waiting at the airport and walked up to them.

Alex saw Chad approaching and waited for him to get closer before saying, "Chad, thank you for the use of the plane. I went there to look for a friend and I found him."

"You're welcome. Is there anything else I can do for you?"

"What you did for me already was a lot so you don't owe me a thing."

"Early this morning the staff members at the hospital where your mom works found a kidney for Chris. Chris is now in the recovering room after a successful operation, so yes, I do owe you something. You are the one who saved Chris' life. So what can I do to repay you?"

Alex thought for a moment before asking, "Would hiring a crew to make repairs to a house in Mexico City be too much to ask for?"

"Consider it done."

Alex gave him a shock looked before uttering, "Are you serious?"

"Yes I'm serious," Chad said with a slight laugh in his voice. "In fact, what you ask for is less than what I would give."

"Just repairs to the house is all I want."

"Give me the address and I'll arrange it."

"Thank you," Alex said before pulling out the information that the officer had given her and then giving it to Chad.

Randy stepped up while saying, "I don't know about anyone else, but I'm starving."

"Same here," Michelle said.

"I can go for a bite to eat myself," Brandy said.

"Ditto," Cindy said. "In fact, I'm actually hungry for some Adam's barbeque."

"That place has great barbeque ribs," Miles said.

"And barbeque chicken," Cindy added. "That's why I want to go there."

"Michelle, you should call Heather's parents and check in," Doug said. "Let them know that we're going to Adam's barbeque."

"Okay. Let me borrow your phone," Michelle said.

Doug handed Michelle his phone. As Michelle was making her call, she and the others walked towards the terminal.

Before they walked too far, Chad said, "Everyone, enjoy your meal, but I'm going back to the hotel."

"You're welcome to join us," Doug said.

"I would, but Alice is waiting for me at a hotel and I made dinner reservations for us at this romantic restaurant," Chad said.

"I hope you enjoy your meal, and what comes after it," Alex said. Chad just grinned.

A short time later, as everyone was walking through the parking lot Chad told everyone, "Bye."

"Bye," Everyone responded.

"I'll see you later," Alex added.

Chad just waved as he walked towards his car. Alex, Trudy, Michelle and Miles went to Mile's van. Doug, Kenny, Cindy, Brandy, Ben and Randy went to Doug's Jeep.

After Alex got comfortable in the van, she called Victor to let him know that she was able to work Sunday after all.

Several minutes later, Alex and her group were walking

into Adam's barbeque restaurant. The place wasn't crowded and the waiter put tables together to seat everyone. Heather and her parents' joined the group. An hour later, the bill was paid and everyone left. Michelle went with Heather and her parents. Randy went with Ben and checked into the same motel he was staying at.

Sunday, October 31, during the morning and early afternoon Alex, Doug, Kenny, Ben, Brandy and Cindy helped Randy to collect what he needed to create the remote.

After Alex left for work Doug, Kenny, Ben, Brandy and Cindy remained with Randy to help out where they could.

At Little Bucks, Victor was holding a costume contest and two-thirds of the customers entering were wearing costumes. By 5:45 P.M., the place was standing room only with barely enough room to move around and the noise level was deafening. Alex and another waitress named Miranda were the only two waiting tables. Miranda was dressed as Cleopatra while Alex was dressed normally.

Alex was waiting on a couple who were sitting not too far from the entrance. As Alex was writing down the food order Miles walked through the door. Alex was focused on trying to hear the couple and didn't notice Miles walking up behind her.

After Alex wrote everything down and was about ready to walk towards the kitchen Miles tapped her on the shoulder.

Alex turned to look and when she saw who it was, she loudly said, "Oh, hi. Are you alone?" Miles said something, but Alex was only able to hear a word or two. She shook head. "I can't hear you. You'll have to speak up."

"I'm here alone, but I came here to talk to you and not to eat."

"Whatever you came to talk to me about it will have to wait. I have tables to wait on." Alex held up the food ticket that she recently wrote out as she continued to say, "I have to turn this food ticket in."

"Can I tell you something right now? It will only take a minute and we can talk later tonight or tomorrow."

"Okay. What is it?" Alex saw Miles searching is thoughts for the right words. Miles had formed his mouth to say something, but when he didn't Alex said, "Miles, I can't stand around waiting for you to figure out what you want to say to me. So either say it, or I'll talk to you later."

Alex saw that Miles was nervous as he said, "I'll just come out with it." Part of crowd cheered that prevented Alex from hearing, "In this reality you are Alexandra. I don't care about any other reality."

Alex made a gesture that she couldn't hear. Miles repeated what he said, but Alex still couldn't hear. She then said loudly, "I can't hear you, so we should talk later. I need to go back to work."

Miles gestured for her to wait and tried to say over the crowd, "I'm saying that I don't care who you are in another reality. You are a woman. I like you and that's all I care about."

Alex again gestured that she couldn't hear. Miles was about to repeat himself again, but stopped and stared at Alex for a second.

When Miles hesitated to repeat himself, Alex held up the food ticket again and said, "Miles, I'm going..."

Before Alex was able to get too many words from her mouth, Miles gave Alex a passionate kiss. The people around them saw the kiss. Catherine and Becky were walking in and were able to see the kiss through the crowd.

It took a couple of seconds for Alex to realize what was happening. She pulled away before demanding to know, "What are you doing?!"

The noise of the crowd settled down slightly when Miles

said loud enough for Alex and a few nearby people to hear, "I don't care who you are in a different reality. I like you and I wanted you to know how much." Miles realized how much louder he was over the crowd and continued to say in a lower-volume voice, "Alex, I'm falling for you and in a hard way."

Alex gazed shockingly at Miles before she finally said, "Okay, I can't deal with this right now. I'm working." Alex then turned and walked away.

As Miles turned to leave, he saw the smiles on Catherine's and Becky's faces.

When Catherine and Becky stepped up to Miles, Catherine said, "That was an interesting sight that I witnessed."

"So how long have you and Alex been a hot couple?" Becky asked.

"The sight you saw was me trying to become a couple with her," Miles said.

"You're the one who sent Alex the flowers the other day," Catherine said. "You're her secret admirer."

"Guilty," Miles said. "Well, I'll see you two later."

"You're not going to stick around, so you can socialize with Alex?" Becky asked.

"Alex is working right now, and after that kiss I gave her, I got the impression from her that she doesn't want to deal with me right now."

"You can't retreat now," Becky said. "Stay and win her over."

"I would, but this is her place of work and as you can see she's slightly overwhelmed with customers. I would most likely make her mad at me if I stayed... if she's not mad at me already that is."

"Bye then," Becky said.

"Bye," Miles said.

Catherine just waved.

As Miles walked towards the exit, Catherine and Becky walked towards the bar.

After Alex gave the food order to Stephen, she walked towards the bar for the drinks. She stepped up just after Catherine and Becky sat down at the bar.

Catherine saw Alex stepping up and tapped her on her shoulder.

Alex turned to look and when she saw Catherine and Becky she said, "Oh hi. When did you two get here?"

"Becky and I walked in, in time to see you and Miles kissing," Catherine said.

"He kissed me. I had nothing to do with that."

"You seemed to have enjoyed it," Becky said.

"I enjoyed it?" Alex echoed. "I pulled away from him as he started the kiss."

"Alex, sweetie, I've seen turtles move faster than you did during that kiss," Catherine said.

"What are you talking about? I ended that kiss right after it started."

"It's obvious that Miles likes you and from that kiss I saw, you like him too, so go for it," Becky said.

Alex said in a defensive and aggravated tone, "I didn't step up to the bar to hear you two telling me to go for it with Miles. I step up to get my drink order filled before the customers start complaining. So I would appreciate very much if you would leave me and my relationships alone. Okay? Thank you very much."

"Okay, Alex, you can retract the claws before you hurt someone," Catherine said.

"Okay, I'm sorry. I have been on edge all day, so you two going on about me going for it with Miles is not a wise thing to do right now," Alex explained.

Catherine opened her purse and as she reached into it she

said, "Okay, first off, the way I feel about Miles, I would never tell you to go for it with him." Catherine pulled out a bottle of Midol. "Secondly, before you pull out an axe on someone, take a couple of these." Catherine held out the bottle for Alex to take.

Alex took the bottle and slightly grinned when she saw what it was. She then opened the bottle and took two tablets. After closing the bottle again she handed it back to Catherine while saying, "Thanks."

"No problem," Catherine said.

Alex gestured towards Bryon while saying, "I need to fill my drink order." Alex then walked up to the waitress' spot and placed the order.

Minutes later, Alex was giving the customers their drinks. Just before Alex stepped away, Devin, while dressed as a caveman, walked up to her and said, "I can't believe that I see you waiting tables."

Alex looked at Devin as if he was a stranger before asking, "Excuse me?"

"You're actually waiting tables. Venus must be out of sync with Jupiter."

"Okay, who are you?"

"I'm Maxine's husband, Devin." An expression of recognition came across Alex's face as Devin continued to say, "Maxine is going to be amazed when she walks in, in a few minutes and sees you waiting tables."

Alex gestured towards a group of four people who were sitting at a table before saying, "I have customers to wait on, so excuse me."

"Of course." Devin watched Alex for a brief time as Alex walked up to the group for their order. Devin then walked to the bar and bought drinks for him and Maxine.

When Maxine walked in, Devin handed her, her drink and

then pointed Alex out to her. As Maxine and Devin waited for a table to come available Maxine watched Alex as Alex performed her job. They waited seven minutes before getting a table in Miranda's section.

After taking their seats, Maxine told Devin, "I was actually hoping that one of Alex's tables would have opened up first. I'm curious to see how she is as a waitress first hand."

"From what I see, she seems to know what she's doing."

Maxine and Devin faced Miranda as Miranda stepped up to take the order.

As the time passed, Maxine would turn and watch Alex when Alex would walk near their table.

Within forty minutes, Maxine and Devin had eaten and paid their bill, but before they left, Maxine walked up to Alex. Alex noticed Maxine as Maxine was walking towards her. When Maxine stepped up she said, "I've been watching you."

"I've seen you watching me," Alex responded.

"Anyway, I wanted you to know that I'm impressed by what I saw. You don't seem to be the same Alex I met two years ago. In fact, from what I've seen tonight, you are actually a decent person."

Alex grinned before saying, "Thanks."

"I'm at O'Shannon's most Friday and Saturday nights, so you should drop in more often."

Alex continued to grin as she said, "I might do that."

Maxine nodded before waving and saying, "Bye."

Alex slightly waved before saying, "Bye."

As Devin and Maxine left, Alex went to check on a few customers.

At 12:20 A.M., Alex was entering her dorm. Trudy was sitting on the couch watching TV. There was a movie case on the coffee table.

When Alex stepped in, Trudy said, "Brandy brought a

movie by and said for you to check it out."

Alex stepped to where she could see the TV and asked, "Is that the movie she wants me to watch?"

"No. This is just regular TV." Trudy gestured towards the case. "The movie is there. I figured I would wait and watch the movie with you."

Alex picked up the movie and after reading the title she asked, "Why is she giving me this to watch when she knows I didn't like this movie?"

"According to Brandy, the movie is nothing like what you saw in your reality. She says that it is a hundred percent better. I haven't seen the movie yet, so I can't say if I like it or not."

"Fine, I'll watch it. At least this time I won't have to pay the box office price to see it." Alex gestured towards the TV. "So when is your show over?"

"Oh, I saw that show about half dozen times or more. So go ahead and put the movie in."

"Okay." Alex walked up to the DVD player; turned it on; put the movie in and then took a seat on the couch next to Trudy.

After Alex and Trudy saw thirty minutes of the movie, Trudy asked, "So how is it so far?"

"Brandy's right. This is nothing like what was shown in our reality."

"Are there different actors?"

"It's the same actors. I'm not sure, but it seems to me that in my reality, someone else wrote the screenplay. I was thinking that during the opening credits."

"Someone else writing the movie would make the storyline different," Trudy said as someone knocked on the door. Trudy looked at her watch and continued to say, "It's one o'clock." As Trudy was standing up, Alex paused the movie. "Who's knocking at this time of the night?" Trudy opened the door and saw Miles standing there. "Miles, do you know what time it is?"

Alex heard what Trudy had asked and stood up. As she walked towards the door, she heard Miles saying, "Yeah, I know. Is Alex awake?"

Alex stepped up behind Trudy to where Miles could see her before saying, "I'm up."

"Can we talk?" Miles asked.

"Sure. Trudy, I'll be back in a minute." As Trudy walked back to the couch, Alex walked into the hallway and shut the door behind her. She crossed her arms before asking, "So what's up?"

"I want to talk about what happened between us at Little Bucks."

"If you don't mind, I would like to pretend that what happened didn't happen."

"I do mind actually. Alex, I don't regret kissing you. In fact, I'm here because I can't sleep thinking about you and that kiss."

"Miles, Randy is pretty sure that he can re-create that remote of his in five to six days. This time next week, this crossed reality will be corrected. So save your passionate feelings for the other Alex."

"I don't like the other Alex in the same way that I like you and I know you have those feelings for me as well."

"No matter what I feel for you, nothing can happen between us. I don't belong here. The other Alex belongs here."

"You can always make this reality your home."

"I can't do that. That wouldn't be fair to the other Alex."

"You know there's a chance that Randy won't be able to duplicate his remote. And even if he can duplicate it, there's a chance that it will make matters worse."

"What do you mean?"

"Instead of correcting this crossed reality, you could cross over into yet another reality."

"That's a chance that we'll have to take."

"Alex, there may be an inconceivable number of realities and you are willing to take a chance and cross a portion of those realities?"

"Miles, Randy had come up with an address system, so we won't be crossing those realities like you think."

"And what if that address system is not perfect?"

"Miles, you're not going to say anything to talk me out of trying to get home, so give it up."

"Fine, I'll quit trying. Are you working tomorrow night?"

"I was supposed to, but that changed. Sylvia will be working and not me. Why?"

"Go out with me tomorrow night; on a date."

Alex looked at Miles as if he had lost his mind before uttering, "You can't be serious."

"Yes, I'm serious. You said it yourself that you have five, maybe even six days left before you and the others will attempt to correct reality. We both have feelings for each other, so let's spend that time together."

"That's not a good idea... for many reasons."

"Myself, I can't think of one reason not to date."

Alex said in a volume to where only Miles could hear, "I was a man in my reality."

"You're definitely a woman in this reality though."

"Fine, physically I'm a woman, but mentally I'm a man."

"No, Alex; you're not even a man mentally."

"What do you mean?"

"Alex, even you have to agree that your mindset right now is of a woman and not of a man."

"Even if that is true, we can't..." Miles didn't give Alex a chance to finish what she was saying and again gave Alex a passionate kiss. The kiss lasted for a few seconds before Alex pulled away and uttering, "Stop doing that!"

"Alex, give it a try. Give us a try. Go out on a date with me tomorrow night."

"As a friend, I'll go with you anywhere you want, but as long as there's a chance to correct this crossed reality, I'm not going on a date with you."

Miles gave Alex a curious look before asking, "So if Randy's remote fails to work, you'll date me?"

"No, I'm not saying that."

"Then what did you mean?"

"I'm not really sure right now what I will do if this turns out to be my reality, and... and I'm not going to guess as to what it would be either."

"If Randy's remote fails, will you please keep an open mind about going on a date with me?"

"That I can do," Alex said before gesturing towards her door. "Trudy and I were watching a movie, so I really need to get back in there."

"Do you mind if I come in and watch it with you and Trudy?"

"It's already thirty minutes into the movie."

"That's okay."

"Okay; you're welcome to join us."

Alex walked back into her dorm followed by Miles. The movie was two hours and fifteen minutes long and when it came to an end, Miles left the dorm. Alex and Trudy went to their respective beds. Before Alex went to sleep, she wrote in the diary; however, she left out the part about Miles kissing her.

During the next several days, Randy worked around the clock to re-create the remote. Ben helped Randy where he could. Alex, Doug, Kenny, Brandy and Cindy just focused on their studies. Alex worked her assigned shift and when she wasn't working or studying, Miles would talk her into going places with him. Trudy tagged along with Alex and Miles to a few of those places.

Thursday, November 4 at 9:20 P.M., Alex, Miles and Trudy were returning to Harvard just after doing laundry at a Laundromat. Miles was the one driving, and he had pulled into a gas station and food mart for some gas. Most of the pumps were busy, and inside the station the customers were standing in a good size line while waiting to check out. Other customers were picking out the items they were going to purchase.

As Miles was pumping the gas, Alex and Trudy went into the station to use the restroom and to get sodas. Alex and Trudy were still in the restroom when Miles stepped in line to pay for the gas.

Miles was standing in line for a short time when a pretty eighteen-year-old woman stepped up to him while questioning, "Miles? Miles Appleby?"

Miles looked at the woman as if she was a stranger before saying, "That's my name."

"From the expression on your face, I see you don't recognize me. Of course I was only ten years old when you saw me last. And I had the biggest crush on you then."

Miles thought for a second before asking, "Mindy?"

"I knew that hint would tell you who I was."

"Wow, you certainly grew up into a lovely woman."

Mindy slightly curtsied while saying, "Thank you."

"How long has it been since we saw each other last?"

"Well, I'm eighteen now, so it was eight years ago when your dad was transferred to a different base."

"Do you live in Boston?" Miles asked as the line in front of him moved forward.

As Miles and Mindy were moving up slightly, Mindy said,

"I do. I still live at home, just a few minutes from here."

"How long have you been living in Boston?"

"Three years after you moved away, my dad was injured and had to take a medical discharge. Since my parents are from Boston, we moved here after his discharge. What about you? Are you living here or are you visiting?"

"I'm actually in my fourth year of Harvard."

"Oh my God, that's great. My dad believes that I have a good shot in going to Harvard next year."

"How are your grades?"

"My grades are great. In fact, the school counselor just recently told me that I will be graduating before my class."

"That's great. I wish you luck with going to Harvard."

"Thank you. Oh, how's Trudy?"

Miles briefly gazed around the room before saying, "Actually, she's here somewhere. I guess she and Alex are still in the restroom."

"Trudy's here?"

"Yeah; she is in her third year at Harvard."

"I was thinking Trudy was more than a year younger then you."

"Oh she's twenty and I'm twenty-two. She skipped a grade, which put her a year behind me in school."

"Cool. Is Alex Trudy's boyfriend?"

"Oh no; Alex is short for Alexandra and she's Trudy's roommate," Miles said before seeing Alex and Trudy stepping into view as they were getting sodas. "Oh, there they are now."

Mindy turned to look. She then faced Miles again before asking, "So are you and Alex an item?"

Miles shook his head and sullenly said, "No. I'm not seeing anyone."

"Really," Mindy said delightfully. "You know, I still think that you're still the cutest boy around."

Alex saw the delightful expression on Mindy's face and the smile on Miles' face. Miles was about to respond, but stopped when he saw Alex and Trudy stepping up. Instead of responding, he asked, "Trudy, you remember Mindy, don't you?"

Mindy noticed Alex's serious and curious gaze towards her, but ignored it as she faced Trudy. Trudy was curiously gazing at Mindy too, but she was searching her thoughts.

When the answer finally came to Trudy, Trudy said, "Oh, yes. I remember you." Mindy pleasantly grinned. Trudy then gestured towards Alex. "Mindy, this is my roommate and good friend, Alex. Alex, this is Mindy. When my dad was stationed in New Mexico about seven... eight years ago, Mindy and her parents lived next door to us."

Mindy took hold of Miles' arm and as she held it, she said, "And I had the biggest crush on him then. I couldn't act on it then, but I can now."

Trudy saw the jealousy in Alex's eyes as Alex watched a grin coming across Miles' face before he said, "A woman as pretty as you, you must have a boyfriend."

Mindy shook her head while saying, "Nope; I've been boyfriend-free for a few weeks now." Mindy let go of Miles' arm and faced him. "In fact, there's a party tomorrow night and I would love it if you would come with me as my date."

When Alex saw a delightful expression coming across Miles' face, Alex said disgustedly and loudly, "I'm going to wait in the van." Alex put down the bottled soda that she was holding on the closest shelf and stormed towards the exit.

Miles and Mindy curiously stared at Alex as Alex stormed away. Before Alex was able to get too far away, Miles called out, "Alex, what's wrong? Alex!"

Alex ignored Miles and kept walking. Everyone in the place watched Alex as she angrily shoved open the door and left the station.

When Miles gave Trudy a confused look, Trudy said, "Alex's problem is that you are currently the biggest jerk on Earth."

"What did I do?"

"Oh, God," Mindy blurted out. Miles gave Mindy a curious look. "If I had known that Alex had feelings for you, I wouldn't have asked you to that party."

Miles whispered in Trudy's ear, "Alex doesn't want to date me. You know that. So why would she be upset with me when Mindy asked me to a party?"

Trudy whispered, "Alex still likes you, and you are flirting with Mindy in front of her. No woman would want to see that."

Miles pulled out the money to pay for the gas, and as he handed it to Trudy he said, "Here's the gas money. I'm going to talk to Alex." Miles then turned towards Mindy. "Mindy, it was good to see you, but I'm going to have to pass on that party." He then turned and walked away.

As Miles was leaving, Mindy asked Trudy, "Can I give you my number to give to Miles... just in case things don't work out between him and Alex?"

Trudy just looked at Mindy as if Mindy had lost her mind.

Chapter Sixteen

Out at the pumps, Alex had climbed into the back seat of the van and shut the door. After getting comfortable in one of the back seats, she saw Miles walking towards the van.

Alex watched as he walked up to the driver's side. After he climbed in and sat down, he looked back at Alex and said, "Alex, I'm sorry. I thought since you didn't want to…"

In an annoyed tone Alex quickly said, "Miles, I don't want to talk about it."

"I want to explain why I…"

In the same annoyed tone, Alex interrupted Miles with, "Miles, please don't."

"You're mad at me, and…" Alex didn't let Miles finish. She quickly opened the door and climbed out. Miles quickly got out also and as he walked towards Alex he demanded to know, "Why are you acting like this?"

Alex said though clinched teeth, "I don't want to talk about it."

"I'm trying to apologize."

"You said that you were sorry in the van, and I believe you. I also don't want an explanation or the details as to why that… that floozy is throwing herself at you."

Miles gave Alex a confused look before demanding to know, "What is your problem?"

Without realizing as to what she was saying Alex quickly and angrily rattled out, "The guy I love enjoys being fondled by a bimbo and I'm not supposed to get upset over that?!"

Miles was surprisingly taken back for a moment before asking, "What?"

Alex realized what she had said and responded, "I didn't mean that. I'm confused. I have been confused since I've been in this reality and this confusion seems to be growing each day."

Miles delightfully grinned before asking, "You love me?"

Alex gave Miles a disgusted smirk before saying, "I like you. I over-spoke myself a minute ago. In fact, now that I think about it, it's good that you have a date tomorrow."

Miles continued to delightfully look at Alex as he said, "I told Mindy 'no'. I passed on the party."

"Well, you should go back in there. Tell her that you've changed your mind."

Miles continued to give Alex a delightful look and as he shook his head he said, "I'm not interested in Mindy."

"Stop looking at me like that, and... and you're wasting your time being interested in me." Alex faced the entrance to the station before she continued to say, "Before your friend leaves, you really should go back in there and accept her invitation."

"Alex, I'm not going to do that, and I now believe that it isn't a waste of time to be interested in you."

"Miles, most likely in a couple of days I will be returning to my reality, and this confusion I'm having will cease... hopefully."

As Alex watched Trudy leaving the station, Miles said, "Well, we'll see what will happen in a few days." Miles then turned to look at what Alex was staring at. "I guess it's time to return to Harvard now though."

Alex turned and watched Miles for a second as he walked towards the driver's door. She then opened the back door again to climb in.

After Miles got comfortable in the driver's seat he started the van. When Trudy was close enough to the van, Alex saw that she was carrying two sodas.

Seconds later, after Trudy sat down in the front passenger seat, Trudy faced Alex and held out one of the sodas for her to take before saying, "I bought the soda you put down. I thought you would eventually want it."

Alex slightly grinned and while taking the soda, she said, "Thanks."

Minutes after Miles drove off, Trudy realized that Alex was very quiet. Trudy glanced back at Alex and saw that she was thinking hard about something while holding the unopened soda. A slightly concerned expression came across Trudy's face; however, without saying a word, she faced forward again.

A short time later, just after Miles parked his van on Harvard's parking lot, Alex quickly opened her door. As she was getting out while carrying her unopened soda, she said, "I'll get my laundry later."

After Alex had shut the door and was walking away in a haste, Trudy looked at Miles before saying, "You really have her mad at you."

"Yeah," Miles said in a slightly mournful tone. "I guess I do."

Minutes later, Trudy walked into the dorm and saw Alex's unopened soda on the coffee table. She then saw that Alex's bedroom door was shut. Trudy walked up to the door and knocked. When Alex opened the door, Trudy said, "I'm a good listener if you want to talk."

"Thanks, but I really want to be alone right now."

"Alex, Miles was an insensitive jerk at the gas station, and he knows it."

"Miles told me that he was sorry for what had happened and I believe him, so I'm over it."

"Then why are you acting like this?" Alex gave Trudy a look as if she was debating on saying anything or not. "Alex, I consider you a good friend, and…"

Alex walked passed Trudy and as she stepped into the common room she said without looking at Trudy, "Trudy, I've been in this reality too long." Alex then faced Trudy. "I was totally jealous when I saw how that… that girl was clinging onto Miles."

"You liking Miles is no secret, so your reaction was normal."

"Well, I should have been able to control my emotions and what I said to Miles, but I failed at both."

Trudy gave Alex a curious look before asking, "Did you say something to Miles that you shouldn't have?"

"I was extremely angry at Miles and I said something without thinking."

"What did you say to him?"

"I told him that I loved him. I then told him that I didn't mean it. I told him that I'm confused."

"Are you confused?"

"I'm totally confused." Alex gave Trudy a nervous look before she continued to say, "But not about my feelings towards Miles."

"Alex, do you love Miles?"

"I think I do and seeing that girl all over Miles made me realize how much."

"That girl's name is Mindy."

"Trudy, I don't care what her name is!" Alex uttered. Trudy gave Alex a curious look. "What matters is that I'm at the edge of losing my male identity completely and… and if it takes more than another twenty-four hours for Randy to get done, I'm scared that I will. Even now I'm feeling the temptation of staying behind to be overpowering."

"Are you thinking about staying?"

"I'm feeling myself wanting to stay. The only reason why I even want to go back to my reality is because I know it wouldn't be fair to the other Alex if I stayed."

"Alex, my advice is for you not to worry too much about the other Alex."

"Why shouldn't I worry?"

"Cross reality is an unknown territory to everyone, and I'm willing to bet that you are not the only one who is being conformed to the different reality."

"Are you thinking that the other Alex is being conformed as a man?"

"I think everyone who changed realities is being conformed. It's noticeable with you because you were the one who went through the biggest change when everyone was switched. If it takes another month or so, I'm willing to bet that your brother and the others will start showing signs of that too."

Alex echoed with a slight laugh, "Another month? In another week, if even that long, there will be nothing left of my old identity."

"In any case, I believe what is happening to you is most likely reality trying to correct itself, and I'm willing to bet that the other Alex's mindset is also being conformed."

"What you're saying does make sense, and our talk helps. Thanks."

Trudy smiled before saying, "I'm just glad I can help. Now what do you say about watching TV with me and getting your mind off of your situation?"

Alex grinned before saying, "I'll watch TV with you, but I doubt I can get my mind off of this."

"A good movie just might do it, and I know where there's a good movie."

Alex gave Trudy a curious look before asking, "Where is there a good movie?"

"Sarah has a huge video collection and she lets me borrow one anytime I want. She has one that is side splitting funny and if this movie doesn't get your mind off your situation for at least a short time then I say nothing will."

Alex gestured to the door before saying, "Go get it. I could use something other than the last two weeks of my life to laugh about."

Trudy grinned before saying, "It's good that you think of your situation as being funny."

"Well, it's either that or go nuts. So go get the movie."

Trudy nodded before turning and walking away. As Trudy was walking out the door Alex sat down on the couch. Alex then picked up her soda and opened it.

During the early morning of Friday, November 5, Alex, Doug, Kenny, Brandy and Cindy attended their classes as usual. At the motel, Ben was working to put the remote together by Randy's diagram. As he picked through the resisters to be soldered he had trouble determining the strength of one of the resisters. Ben glanced at Randy for a second and saw that he was busy writing on a flip chart while working through an equation. Ben then made a choice to which resister to use without asking Randy for help.

At 11:03 A.M., Alex drove to the motel and knocked on Randy's door. When Randy opened the door, Alex spouted out, "I need you to tell me that the remote is about ready."

"Good day to you too, Alex." As Randy backed up he continued to say, "Will you please come in."

As Alex walked in she said, "I'm having a bit of a crisis, so excuse me if I skip the pleasantries." Once the door was shut behind Alex, she saw the remote pieces on a table in front of Ben with resisters around the pieces. "Please tell me that the remote will be ready today."

"I could tell that, but it wouldn't be true."

"So when will it be ready?!"

"With any luck, Sunday." Randy saw a disgusted expression on Alex's face before asking, "What kind of crisis are you having anyway?"

"If you don't mind, I..." Alex saw the equation on the flip chart and stopped in mid-sentence. As she pointed to the flip chart she demanded to know, "What's that?!"

"Oh, I'm just trying to figure out the best address to our home reality."

Alex gasped before uttering, "Are you telling me that you don't know the address of our home reality when I distinctly heard you telling Prof. Blumberg that all you have to do was use the same address?"

"Alex, that address wouldn't be valid for this long."

Randy heard the tone in Alex's voice and saw in her body movements that she was controlling her rage as she asked, "And why isn't it valid?"

"Alex, most likely our home reality, as well as this one, has multiplied itself by more than a hundred times during the past two weeks. So when we attempt to return to our reality, we will be jumping into one of those many versions of our reality that has also been crossed by our original jump."

"Are you saying that we can't get back to the reality that we came from?"

"Alex, I'm sure that you have stepped in-between two mirrors before that were facing each other, and I want you to imagine what you would see when you look into one of those mirrors."

"Okay, I'll imagine it."

"You're only one person standing in-between two mirrors, but you would see your mirror image too many times to count.

Now pretend that each one of those images is a reality that mimics your life at the point that you looked into the mirror. You belong to each one of those realities and you can make a claim on anyone of them. When we had switched realities, the us in our mimic realities had also switched. Now since we have switched realities, not all, but some of our mimic realities have slightly diverged from each other. We still hold a claim on all of those realities though, and when we attempt to switch back, we will be attempting to switch back to one of those realities."

"Okay, I think I understand what you're telling me. Is there anyway that you and Ben can speed up with building the remote though?"

"We all want to get back to a version of our own reality, Alex," Ben said. "For some reason though, you are in more of a hurry then us."

"Ben, there's a chance that when Sunday gets here, I won't want to go home," Alex said.

"What are you talking about?" Randy quickly asked.

"You asked me what my crisis was earlier. At the time I wasn't going to tell you, but now I'm going to tell you anyway. I am quickly being taken over by this reality. I am already feeling the urge to stay and if it takes two more days for that remote to get done there's a chance that I'll be staying behind as everyone else goes home."

"Alex, you have a fiancée whom you love. You asked me to be your best man."

"I no longer care about that. I'm a woman in this reality and I'm having female urges. At first I was able to keep these urges in check, but now, I'm feeling myself wanting to give in to these urges."

"Doug has mentioned to me about how you are attracted to Miles, but I didn't realize how serious it was," Randy said.

"It's more than attraction. I have strong feelings for Miles and those feelings are becoming more deeply rooted each day. Trudy thinks that what is happening to me is reality trying to correct itself, and what's happening to me is happening to everyone, but in a lesser degree."

"That's interesting," Ben said.

"Alex, I'll see what I can do to speed things up," Randy said.

"Thank you."

Randy grinned before saying, "No problem."

"Before I go back to campus do you need me to run an errand?"

"We're good for now," Randy said. "Thanks anyway."

Alex nodded before saying, "Well, I'll see you two later."

"Later," Randy and Ben said.

Alex waved 'bye' as she walked towards the door. She then opened the door and walked out.

Miles, while heading away from Harvard's campus, was sitting in his van and was waiting for the traffic light to turn green.

One block away from Miles and traveling towards the intersection among the cross traffic was a fifty-year-old man driving a pick-up truck.

As the man was a half a block away from the intersection and approaching the yellow light he had a massive heart attack.

When Miles' light turned green, he failed to see the approaching truck and started through the intersection. Miles was in the middle of the intersection when the truck, while traveling at thirty-five miles per hour, plowed into Mile's van near the back tire. The airbags in both vehicles were deployed and the back end of Mile's van was shoved sideways for a few feet.

Just as the two vehicles were coming to a rest an officer, approaching in his squad car, saw the scene and turned on his lights. Other drivers came to a stop at the sight, and a small crowd of spectators began to form.

Miles jumped out from his van and rushed to the truck only to find the man slumped over in his seat.

"Oh God!" Miles uttered before turning towards the forming crowd. "Someone, call for an ambulance! The driver's injured!" Miles then noticed the squad car pulling up.

"I just called nine-one-one!" a woman called out.

"Thanks," Miles said before rushing towards the squad car. As the officer was getting out Miles was uttering, "Officer! Officer, the driver to the pickup truck is seriously injured!"

The officer gave Miles a nod before pressing the button on his radio to speak. As he was informing dispatch of the situation he ran towards the truck. Miles followed closely behind. The officer ended his transmission as he reached the truck. He then quickly checked the man's pulse and when he couldn't find it he said, "This man is dead."

"Oh God!" Miles blurted out. "I can't believe this is happening!"

The officer faced Miles before asking, "Who are you and how are you involved in this accident?"

"My name is Miles Appleby and I was driving the van. Officer, I swear the light was green and the man was nowhere in sight when I started through the intersection. I'm a good and safe driver. As a driver, I was never involved in an accident before."

"Calm down, Mr. Appleby. I don't know what caused this man's death, but it wasn't from this accident."

"Are you saying that this man was dead when he plowed into me?"

"From what I see I believe it's likely. I've seen this once before and the driver suffered a heart attack while driving. That is probably what happened here. Regardless of what happened we will find out more when the paramedics get here. But until then, I'll need to see your driver's licenses and insurance card."

"Of course," Miles said before pulling out his wallet and opening it up to get out the requested items.

A short distance from the motel, Alex had pulled behind five other vehicles in a drive through line at a fast food restaurant. It took Alex several minutes to go through the line and get her large size chicken meal. Just after getting back on the road towards Harvard, she began to leisurely eat her food. As the minutes slowly passed, the traffic became heavier as she got closer to the accident scene.

As Alex approached the intersection of the accident scene she still had more than half of her sandwich and most of her fries left. Alex took a bite of her sandwich, but hesitated to chew when she saw that Mile's van was involved. Alex then saw the paramedics wheeling a body away on a gurney with a blanket covering the body. Alex quickly pulled her Jeep to the side of the road and as she was quickly getting out of her Jeep she swallowed the bite she had.

As Alex approached Miles' van an officer blocked her way while saying, "Ma'am, get back in your vehicle and continue about your business."

"I know the driver to the van." Alex then demanded to know, "Was he the one on the gurney?!"

Before the officer was able to reply, Miles called out, "Alex!"

Alex quickly turned to face Miles and saw that he was walking towards her. While acting on impulse Alex rushed up to Miles and hugged him tight. As she hugged him she said, "When I saw your van and then the dead person on the gurney, I thought the worse."

As Miles embraced the hug, he said, "As you can see, I'm fine." When Alex and Miles ended the hug, Miles saw that

Alex had tears in her eyes. "Alex, I'm okay. So why the tears?"

Alex wiped her eyes while saying, "I see that you are okay. It's just that... I'm not over the thought of you being on that gurney." Miles grinned and then gave Alex a passionate kiss. Alex allowed the kiss at first, but after a few seconds she pulled away. "Miles, this isn't right."

"Alex, you're a woman. What's not right about it?"

Alex thought for a second before saying, "I don't know anymore. The reason now seems to be hollow to me." Miles again gave Alex a passionate kiss. Alex never pulled away and the kiss ended after several seconds. "I can't believe we just did that."

"It felt right though."

Alex grinned before saying, "It did feel right."

Miles grinned before kissing Alex again. While they were kissing the original officer on the scene walked up to them and cleared his throat. They quickly ended the kiss and looked at the officer.

As Alex and Miles were holding hands, Miles said, "Officer, I have a ride."

"Good. The tow truck will be here in a few minutes. You'll need to stick around so you can tell the driver where to tow your van."

"Yes, Officer."

The officer turned and as he was walking away, Alex asked, "So what happened?"

"The driver of the pick-up had a heart attack and most likely died behind the wheel."

"Oh my God! That's awful!" Alex uttered. "I guess it was good that you were the one who got hit and not a pedestrian or even someone in a small car."

Miles grinned before saying, "That's an optimistic approach at looking at what happened."

"What? I'm just saying…"

"Alex, you're right. That's a good way of looking at what had happened."

Alex stared delightfully into Miles' eyes for a moment before giving him another passionate kiss. When the kiss ended she said, "My Jeep is right over there. We can wait for the tow truck there."

Miles nodded before saying, "Sounds good."

"I can finish eating my chicken sandwich while we wait too."

"I thought I tasted mayonnaise when we kissed."

Alex defensively said, "Well, I didn't know that we were going to…"

Miles took hold of Alex's hand while interrupting with, "Alex, it's fine. I really didn't mind the mayonnaise." Alex just grinned, and as she and Miles walked to her Jeep they held hands.

After Alex and Miles got into the Jeep, Alex held out the container full of fries for Miles while asking, "Do you want any fries?"

"That's your lunch."

"Well, I ordered a large combo when I shouldn't have because there's no way I'm going to eat all of these fries."

"Are you sure?"

"Yeah, I'm sure. I'm about full on what I ate already."

Miles looked at how much food she had left before saying, "You only ate half of your sandwich and maybe a few fries."

"Well, I thought I was hungrier than this when I ordered the food. So do you want some fries or not?"

As Miles was taking some fries, he said, "Alex, I wasn't meaning anything by what I said."

As Alex was putting the fry container down, she said, "Oh, I know. With all the food I have been wasting for the past two weeks, I should know better by now than to order the same way I did in the other reality."

"Since I have known about you, I have noticed that you do eat about the same amount as the other Alex would eat."

"That's good I guess." Alex then picked up her sandwich and took a bite.

Alex and Miles waited ten minutes for the tow truck and once the tow truck driver got there the driver took a few minutes to hook up Miles' van. After everything was set, Miles instructed the driver to tow the van to Harvard, and when the tow truck driver drove off, Alex followed behind him.

Several minutes later, Alex and Miles watched as the tow truck driver was putting the van in a far parking space in the Harvard's parking lot. As the driver was unhooking the van, a Harvard security officer pulled up and got out of his car.

Miles and Alex saw the officer and when he stepped up, Miles told him, "The van won't be here like that very long. The accident happened less than an hour ago and I need to locate a shop to have an estimate done and have it fixed."

The officer looked closely at the van before saying, "If this van isn't out of here by Tuesday morning at the latest, you'll be written up."

"I'll get right on searching for a shop to have it towed to," Miles said.

The security officer nodded before walking away.

The driver of the tow truck stepped up before saying, "The tow is seventy-five bucks."

Miles pulled out his wallet before saying, "My car insurance pays for the towing." Miles pulled out his insurance card and handed it to the driver.

"I'll be back with your card once I write down your information."

"No problem."

As the driver walked away, Alex nudged Miles while asking, "Speaking of your car insurance, did you report the accident?"

"I was getting off the phone with my insurance company when I saw you talking to the officer."

"So all you have to do is find a shop and have an estimate done on it?"

"That's right." Miles then leaned in and gave Alex a kiss.

Doug was walking through the parking lot and saw Miles kissing Alex. Doug was bothered by the sight and rushed up to them. When the kiss ended Alex saw Doug rushing up and before she was able to acknowledge his presence, Doug grabbed Miles by his collar and reared back his fist.

Alex quickly grabbed his arm while demanding to know, "What the hell are you doing?!"

While holding onto Miles' collar, Doug said, "I saw him kissing you."

"And you were what?! Jealous?"

"No, I'm not jealous!"

"Well turn Miles loose and tell me what is going on."

Doug turned Miles loose before saying, "I'm not going to let Miles take advantage of your vulnerability."

Alex gave Doug a confused look before uttering, "What?!"

"You're my sister, and I'm not going to let him take advantage of you."

"Okay, first of all, Miles wasn't taking advantage of me. Secondly, where did you get the idea that I need your protection?"

"Alex, you are not thinking clearly right now. You said it yourself."

"By me being a woman and having female desires, you took that as I wasn't thinking clearly."

Doug said in a volume loud enough for the tow truck driver

to hear, "You're not a…"

Alex quickly hissed, "Lower your voice! The tow truck driver can hear you!"

Doug said in a lower voice, "Alex, you're not a woman in our reality."

"And you're not an overly protective brother either like you're being now."

"Because I don't want Miles taking advantage of the situation, I'm being overly protective?"

"You came charging in with the taste of blood on your lips, so yes; you're being overly protective. Trudy was right."

Doug gave Alex a curious look before asking, "What was Trudy right about?"

"Trudy believes that what had happened to me is happening to you, Randy and the others, but in a lesser degree."

Doug continued to give Alex a curious look while asking, "What happened to you?"

"This is my reality now."

"Alex, you can't give in now."

"I have already decided and I'm set on my decision."

Doug looked at Miles before saying, "Miles convinced you to stay."

"Doug, we're the same age, so stop acting like an older and protective brother."

"Well, technically, I'm the older one by five minutes."

"And you think you're wiser than me just because you were born minutes before me?"

"I was just pointing out that I was actually older."

"Let me point something out to you," Alex sternly began. "My thoughts are very clear. Miles didn't do anything to convince me to stay and I do not need an overly protective brother threatening my boyfriend."

Doug saw a slight smugness on Miles' face. He then faced

Alex again, but before he was able to say anything, the tow truck driver stepped up and said, "Okay, Mr. Appleby. Here's your insurance card."

As Miles took the card, he said, "Thank you."

"Well, I hope your day gets better."

Miles glanced at Alex before saying, "It has already, actually."

The tow truck driver just nodded with a slight grin before turning back towards his truck.

As the tow truck driver was walking away, Alex said, "Doug, I want you to back off and stop being protective of me."

Doug slightly sighed before saying, "Fine, I'll back off."

"And apologize to Miles."

Before Doug could respond, Miles quickly said, "Alex, that's really not necessary."

"Yes, it is," Alex quickly said.

"All right; fine," Doug said. "Miles, I overreacted and I'm sorry."

"Your actions were understandable."

Doug nodded before turning towards Alex and asking, "So, is everything good now?"

"It is for now, and as long as you don't charge in again it will remain that way." When Doug slightly chuckled, Alex gave Doug a curious look. "What?!"

"Your actions just remind me of mom."

"And that's bad?"

"No-no; that's not bad. I'm just noticing it, that's all."

"If things are settled, we should get off the parking lot," Miles suggested.

Alex took hold of Miles' hand and when she looked at Doug, she saw Doug staring at her and Mile's embracing hands. Alex then gave Doug an inquisitive look before asking,

"Everything's settled, right, Doug?"

Doug looked into Alex's eyes before saying, "Of course." He then gestured towards the direction of his Jeep. "Well, I'm supposed to be meeting Liz. I better get going before I'm late."

Before Doug was able to walk away, Alex said, "You had about six dates with Liz."

"Somewhere around there. What about it?"

"You have the hots for Liz and she wouldn't date you in the other reality. You will lose that when you go back."

"I'm planning to use what I have learned about Liz when I ask her out again in our reality."

"It might work if the other Doug hasn't alienated you with Liz already."

Doug thought for a second. He then shook off the thought before saying, "Oh no, you're not going to talk me into staying with you."

"I'm not trying to. Well, you better get going. You don't want to be too late."

Doug gave Alex a curious look before saying, "I'll see you and Miles later."

As Doug turned to walk away Alex and Miles said, "Bye."

As Doug was walking away, Alex asked Miles, "Where were you heading anyway when you got ran over?"

"I was going to the store for shaving cream and razors. Why?"

"Well, I knew you were heading away from Harvard, and I thought I can give you a ride if need to be somewhere."

"Well, I don't need to be somewhere, but I would appreciate a ride."

Alex stared delightfully at Miles while saying, "Okay."

Miles grinned before giving Alex a kiss. The kiss lasted for only a couple of seconds. Once they turned and began walking towards Alex's Jeep, Miles asked, "Oh, aren't you off tonight?"

"I am. Is there something you want to do tonight?"

"I was thinking that we can go to dinner after my soccer game; I even know what restaurant that I would like to take you to, and then we can go somewhere where there's a dance floor."

Alex grinned before saying, "All right. It's a date... our first date." Miles just gave Alex a delightful smile for a brief moment.

While Doug was on the road to Liz's house, he called Randy and told him the news about Alex and Miles.

After hearing the news, Randy asked, "So are you going to give up on Alex and allow her to stay?"

"No, but trying to convince her to return with us is definitely not an option, so we'll have to take a more strategic approach."

"What do you have planned?"

"Once your remote is ready to be activated, we'll trick Alex into being in the same room with us."

"Let's hope that Alex won't kill you afterwards."

"I'm thinking everything will return to normal after we fix reality."

"Okay, well I'm thinking that the remote will be ready by Sunday at the latest."

"All right; bye."

Chapter Seventeen

Later at the grocery store, Alex and Miles turned down an aisle while heading for the check-out line. Miles was carrying a can of shaving cream and a package of disposable razors. Alex was talking about a movie that she saw when Miles saw boxes of condoms on the shelf. Miles abruptly stopped at the condoms and picked up one of the boxes. Alex stopped and turned to see what Miles was doing.

When she saw what Miles was holding a surprised expression and somewhat of an amused grin came across her face before asking, "Isn't that rushing things a bit?"

Miles gave Alex a curious look. Alex just responded by looking at the condom box. When he realized what Alex was referring to, he said, "Oh, uh, I wasn't thinking about getting this for tonight, but eventually I'm hoping that we can... when you're ready that is. In fact, I don't have to get these today."

Alex gave Miles a kiss that lasted a couple of seconds before telling him, "Buy them. In fact, I need to look into getting birth control."

"Should we go to the feminine products before we leave?"

"I think I should talk to a doctor before buying anything."

"Okay. Then I guess we're set; unless you have something to get."

"I don't need anything."

"Let's go check out then."

Alex slightly grinned before the two continued towards the registers. After Miles paid for the items, they left the store.

Alex drove back to campus and as the afternoon progressed, she helped Miles by calling auto repair shops. However, before they were able to locate a shop that would look at Miles' van before Tuesday Alex had to go to class.

6:45 P.M., Alex and Trudy were taking their seats in the bleachers to watch Miles' game. During the game Trudy noticed how much Alex was enjoying herself.

Near the end of the first half, Trudy got Alex's attention before saying, "Your mood has certainly improved a lot since you decided to give you and Miles a chance."

"I am in a good mood," Alex agreed. "I don't feel stressed out like I was."

"It shows. Perhaps Doug will realize as to how happy you are and not try anything to force you to return with him."

"Until you mentioned it earlier I didn't even think that he would try something to force me back with him. After thinking about it though, I agree that he might try something. Whatever he might try, I won't have to worry about it until Sunday."

Trudy stood up and when Alex gave her a curious look, Trudy said, "I'm going to the concession stand. Do you want anything?"

Alex grinned before saying, "No, thanks. I don't want to fill up on anything before Miles and I go out to dinner."

"All right; I'll be back."

Alex just nodded. When Alex turned back towards the game, Trudy made her way to the aisle.

As the game progressed Miles was able to prevent the other team from scoring and when the game ended Harvard won by a score of four to zero. As the spectators were dispersing and the players were leaving the field, Alex and Trudy positioned themselves to where the Harvard's team would pass them.

When Miles saw Alex and Trudy waiting, he stepped up to Alex before saying, "You are definitely my good luck charm."

Alex grinned and while giving him a confused look, she asked, "Why do you say that?"

"We were the underdog in this game by two goals, and we just skunked them."

"I doubt that my presence here has anything to do with you winning the game."

"Thinking about our date tonight had put me in the spirit to stop those balls coming my way."

Alex smiled before saying, "Well, I'm glad I was able to inspire you."

Miles gestured towards his team before saying, "I need to go with them."

Alex nodded while saying, "I'll be with Trudy in our dorm when you get done."

Miles gave Alex a quick kiss before saying, "I'll see you in a few minutes."

Alex delightfully grinned before saying, "All right."

As Miles turned to rejoin his team, Alex and Trudy walked away.

Forty minutes later, as Alex and Miles were walking towards Alex's Jeep, Alex gave Miles her keys for him to drive.

Miles took Alex to a romantic restaurant where they dined by candlelight. They spent an hour at the restaurant and as Miles was paying the check, Alex saw a basket full of peppermint candy near the register.

As Miles was receiving his change he noticed Alex dropping several peppermints in her purse. Before starting for the exit, he nudged Alex while saying, "You must like peppermint."

Alex gave Miles a grin before saying, "Actually, they're for morning breath for the mornings that I can't brush my teeth right away."

Miles gave her a grin followed by a passionate kiss. After the kiss they left for the exit.

When they left the restaurant they went to a nightclub. Neither one of them drank very much as they spent most of their time dancing. When the club closed at three in the morning, Alex and Miles got into the Jeep and drove off. Alex was driving.

When Alex had pulled onto the street from the parking lot, Miles said, "I'm having such a good time that I hate for this night to be over." Alex gazed at Miles as if she was debating something over in her head. He got nervous as to how long she had her eyes off the road. "Alex, face the road. I don't want to get into another accident less than twenty-four hours apart."

Alex turned back towards the road before saying, "Sorry; I was thinking that this night doesn't have to end."

"What do you have in mind?"

"Do you have any of those condoms with you?"

Miles gave Alex an interested stare before saying, "I do."

"There's a motel a couple of miles from here. Let's go there."

"Alex, we don't have to do this."

"Are you against the idea?"

"No-no; I'm not against it. It's just that… I don't want you to feel that you're being rushed into anything."

Alex looked at Miles before saying, "I'm the one who brought it up."

Miles pointed towards the road while saying, "Alex, the road."

Alex faced forward again before saying, "Miles, I'm not being rushed. I have been thinking about it since I saw you holding the box of condoms, and I want to do this."

Miles smiled before saying, "Okay; let's go to the motel." Alex took hold and held Miles' hand.

Several minutes later, Miles was in the office and paying for a motel room for the night as Alex waited in the Jeep. After getting the key, he went back to the Jeep. Once Alex parked her Jeep, she and Miles entered the motel room.

Saturday, November 6, 11:50 A.M., Alex and Miles were returning to the dormitory after being out all night.

Just after reaching the entrance, Alex said, "Give me an hour to get a shower and for me to change my clothes, and I'll meet you in your dorm."

"You still want me to order a pizza, right?"

Alex nodded while saying, "Yeah. Pizza sounded good since you mentioned it. No mushrooms though."

"I'm getting mushrooms on half of it and you can eat the half without it."

Alex grinned before saying, "Fine." Alex then gave Miles a quick kiss. "I'll see you in an hour."

As Alex was walking away, Miles said, "All right."

As the hours passed, Alex, Miles and Miles' roommate Dennis watched a couple of movies. At 3:45 P. M., Alex left for work.

At 6:35 P.M., Doug was eating dinner with Liz and her grandparents at Liz's grandparents' house. Midway through the meal Doug's cell phone rang. Doug looked at who was calling. When he saw everyone staring at him, he said, "It's just Randy... a friend of mine. I'll call him back after this delicious meal."

"We're not against accepting phone calls during dinner," Liz's grandfather said.

"I doubt what he has to say is important enough that it couldn't wait for another ten minutes or so."

"Okay," Liz's grandfather said. He then picked up the conversation of where they had left off.

Doug put his phone back on his belt, and took a bite of

Gerald Pruett

food. Doug had finished his meal and a dish of apple pie within fifteen minutes. As he got up from the table and was walking towards the living room, he dialed Randy.

When Randy answered, he said, "Doug, I'm glad you called me back."

"So what's going on?"

"The remote is finished."

"Well, right now Alex is at work, and she won't get off until after one."

"We can do it bright and early in the morning then."

"That's sounds good. I'll get Cindy to make up some excuse to get Alex in Harvard's library at nine in the morning."

"If it wasn't for Trudy being on Alex's side, it would go a lot smoother if we all met at Alex's dorm."

"Even if Trudy wasn't on Alex's side, that would be too obvious of what we have planned."

"You still believe that Alex will be looking for us to try to trick her."

"If the situation was reversed, I believe that Alex would do what she can to get me to go back."

"Okay, well Ben and I will be hiding out in the library before nine; bye."

"All right, bye," Doug said before putting his phone away.

At Little Bucks, Alex was finishing up at taking the food order from a group of six when Becky and Catherine walked in.

Becky and Catherine stepped up to the bar and took their seats while Alex was turning in her food order. After Alex walked up to the bar and placed her drink order, Catherine tapped Alex on the shoulder. When Alex looked at Catherine, Catherine asked, "So do you want to bite someone's head off today?"

Alex had a big grin on her face before saying, "I'm actually in an excellent mood today."

Becky grinned while saying, "You had sex last night."

Alex looked at Becky and as she continued to grin she asked, "What makes you think that?"

"I know you and your moods, and you had sex last night," Becky said. "Am I wrong?"

Alex smiled before saying, "You're not totally wrong."

Catherine grinned before saying, "It was this morning."

Alex continued to smile as she said, "Actually, it was last night and this morning."

"So tell us the details," Catherine said.

"Was it with Miles Appleby?" Becky asked.

"It was with Miles, and that's all the details you two are getting from me," Alex said.

"Well, I'm happy for you," Becky said.

"Becky, you're just happy to know that I'm not trying to rekindle things with Stephen," Alex said.

"Stephen is with me, so I'm not worried about you attempting to rekindle anything with him," Becky said.

"Oh, so you don't come here when I'm working to keep an eye on me?" Alex asked.

"Maybe I did on the first day you worked, but I missed our friendship, and so I come here in the hopes that we can be friends again," Becky said. "So can we put the last two months behind us and the three of us go back to the way that things were before?"

Before Alex was able to respond, Bryon called out, "Alex, your drinks are up."

Alex looked at Bryon before saying, "Okay, thanks." Alex then faced Becky again. "Becky, our friendship will never be the way it was before, but I would like it if we could rebuild our friendship."

"Rebuilding our friendship is good too," Becky agreed.

Alex nodded with a grin before she turned; placed the drinks on her tray and walked towards the customers with the tray of drinks.

An hour later, Miles walked in and before he was able to find a seat, Becky invited him to sit with her and Catherine. As the hours passed Becky, Catherine and Miles talked. Alex talked with them between waiting on and serving the customers. When the kitchen closed, Stephen sat next to Becky and joined in on their conversation.

Sunday, November 7, at 8:45 A.M., Miles was walking near Harvard's library and saw Doug, Randy, Kenny, Ben and Brandy walking into the library. Miles also saw something in Randy's hand, but he couldn't make out what it was. After seeing what he did he turned and walked towards the dormitory.

Meanwhile, at Alex and Trudy's dorm room, Trudy woke Alex up from her sleep before telling her, "Hey, Cindy is here and wants your help on something."

Alex turned over on her back before asking, "With what?"

"She didn't say. She's carrying a book on Roman Mythology and I think it has something to do with that."

"Okay, thanks. I'll be out in a minute."

As Alex was getting out of bed, Trudy went back into the common room.

Cindy and Trudy were casually talking in the common room when Alex opened her door to step out. Cindy was in a middle of her sentence and when Alex stepped out, she stopped talking.

Cindy turned towards Alex before telling her, "Alex, I'm sorry to wake you, but I would like to get your help on an assignment for my class." Cindy held up the book. "Is this the mythology book you used when you wrote that paper in Dr. Carson's class?"

Alex was still sleepy and she sluggishly answered, "No. The book I used was on Greek Mythology."

"I was thinking it was this book."

Alex shook her head before saying, "It's not, but it does have a similar cover to the one I used."

"I really would like to use that book you had. Can you go to the library with me and help me find it?"

"Sure. Let me put on some shoes and we can go," Alex said before going back into her bedroom.

A short time later, Alex and Cindy were walking down one stairwell as Miles was walking up another. As Alex and Cindy were leaving the dormitory, Miles was knocking on Alex and Trudy's door.

When Trudy opened the door and saw who it was, she asked, "What's up, Miles?"

"Where's Alex?"

"She went with Cindy to help her find a Greek Mythology book."

Miles, with a worried expression across his face, dreadingly asked, "Did they leave for the library?"

Trudy gave Miles a perplexed look before saying, "They did." Trudy then saw the disgusted expression that appeared rapidly across Miles' face. "Alex is going to find that book for her."

"When did they leave?"

"Just a short time ago. I'm surprised you didn't pass them in the hallway."

"They must have gone down the other stairs. Come on, we have to warn Alex."

"What are you talking about? Warn her about what?"

"Cindy is leading Alex into the library, so come on."

As Miles made a gesture for Trudy to come with him, Trudy uttered, "Miles, wait! Tell me what you're talking about."

"I just saw Doug, Kenny, Brandy, Ben and Randy walking into the library and Randy had something in his hand... it could have been a remote. Now Cindy is leading Alex into the library."

"Oh God; we have to get to Alex before something happens."

"If you would have followed me when I said, we could have been halfway down the hall by now."

Trudy grabbed Miles' hand and as she began to pull him along she said, "Shut up and let's go."

9:02 A.M., at the library, Doug and the others were standing between bookshelves and out of sight from the entrance. When Alex and Cindy walked in, Cindy pointed towards the bookshelf that held the mythology books before nervously saying, "I got this book from over there."

Cindy saw that Alex was giving her a curious look before Alex said, "Let's see if we can find the book." After taking a couple of steps towards the shelf, Alex noticed how nervous Cindy was acting. "Are you all right, Cindy?"

In a snappy reply Cindy said, "Of course. Things couldn't be better. Randy's remote is supposed to be ready today and all of us can return to our home reality." Alex abruptly stopped. Cindy stopped and looked at Alex. "Is there anything wrong?"

"You wouldn't be looking for a specific book knowing that you'll be returning to your own reality."

As Alex was looking over the room, Cindy nervously asked, "What do you mean?"

Alex looked at Cindy before saying, "You made a good attempt, but I'm staying here."

As Alex was turning to leave, Cindy grabbed Alex before crying out, "Doug, help! Alex knows!"

As Doug and the others rushed to help stop Alex from

leaving, the librarian also walked towards Alex and Cindy to investigate the commotion.

Alex was just about to break free when Doug and Kenny ran up and grabbed hold of her.

"Alex, you're not going anywhere so settle down," Doug quickly said.

The librarian stepped up and demanded to know, "What's going on here? Why are you holding this young lady?"

"This young lady is my sister, Alex, and she's a kleptomaniac," Doug said.

Alex gave Doug a surprised looked before blurting out, "What?!"

Cindy held up the mythology book that she had while saying, "I found this book in her possession and if you check your records, this book was reported missing yesterday."

"And Alex was making such progress at getting better these last few months," Doug added.

The librarian took the book before saying, "Hold her until I can check my records."

As the librarian was walking away Alex said, "You guys are my friends and I can't believe that even one of you would sink so low as to resort to this."

Randy pulled out the remote that was preset to an address that he thought to be the correct one before saying, "Because you are our friend is why we resorted to this."

"The book was actually checked out by my roommate, and I was returning it for her," Brandy said. "We just told the librarian what we did so he would walk far enough away from us."

"It's time to go home," Randy said.

Alex watched Randy's thumb as he pressed the remote.

Sunday, November 7, at 9:06 A.M., in the reality Alpha 0.0.0.0.0.0, Randy and the others were in their respective rooms at the mental institution. As agreed upon by the parents, each one of them was being monitored by a camera. When each one of them fell to the floor unconscious at the exact same time, the staff members who were monitory the cameras became overly alarmed. Dr. Jacob Tyson, Dr. Martin Adams and Dr. Barney Gray, the three psychiatrists who were assigned to their cases, were called in.

In Randy's room, Randy was just waking up when Nurse Palmer and two orderlies rushed in. Both orderlies were holding the ends to a stretcher.

Randy noticed the white uniforms that they were wearing and as he was standing up, he asked, "Am I in some kind of hospital?"

"You are in a mental institution in Boston," Nurse Palmer said.

The nurse saw the confused expression on Randy's face just before he asked, "How long have I been in here?"

"Since the first time you blacked out at Harvard." Nurse Palmer pointed to the monitor as she continued to say, "We were watching you and we watched you black out again. We were going to take you to the infirmary by a stretcher, but since you are awake and seem to be coherent you can follow me."

Randy read the nurse's name tag before saying, "That won't be necessary, Nurse Palmer. There's really nothing wrong with me."

"Mr. Miller, I can give you a sedative and have you carried to the infirmary as I had originally planned," Nurse Palmer pointed out.

"Now that you put it that way, let's go."

"I thought you would see it my way," Nurse Palmer said before leaving the room. Randy followed behind her as the orderlies followed behind him.

As Randy, Nurse Palmer and the orderlies were walking

down the hall, Randy asked, "Do you know anything about my friends, Alex, Doug, Kenny, Brandy, Ben and Cindy?" Nurse Palmer stopped walking and quickly faced him with an astonished expression across her face. Randy and the orderlies had stopped walking as well. "Did I say anything wrong?"

"On the contrary. Until now, you haven't acknowledged knowing them."

"Do you know where they are?"

"They're also in this facility."

"Can I see them?"

"I can't allow that right now, but I will inform Dr. Adams of your request. Now we need to get you to the infirmary and see if we can find the answer to why you had blacked out."

"There's nothing wrong with me, but let's go and let your medical staff verify it."

As everyone continued walking Nurse Palmer said, "There are a few patients here who feel that they don't belong here."

Randy gave Nurse Palmer a grin while slightly shaking his head. A minute later, Randy, Nurse Palmer and the orderlies were walking into the infirmary; however, before Randy was able to be examined, Doug, Kenny and Cindy also were being escorted into the infirmary.

Two hours later, Randy was being escorted to Dr. Adams' office. Randy walked into the office alone and after he walked in Dr. Adams said, "Mr. Miller, please have a seat." Dr. Adams watched Randy as he sat down. "Mr. Miller, two hours ago you and your friends had simultaneously fainted for no apparent reason in the same manner as all of you did at Harvard. The first time when all of you fainted, all of you remember events differently, and now after fainting again you remember everything has it had happened. I'm reluctant to call this a miracle…"

"It's no miracle, Doctor."

"You talk as though you know what happened."

"I do know what happen. In fact, I'm the one who caused all of this."

"What did you cause?"

"I'll tell you, but you won't believe me. And because you won't believe me, I'll most likely be in this facility for years while you and your staff try to convince me that what had happened was all in my head. However, what's going to throw you into confusion is that all my friends will tell you a similar story."

"Mr. Miller, what did you cause?"

"When my friends and I woke up the first time, was I found with a remote in my hand... or was there a remote near where I had fallen?"

"I have no knowledge of a remote, Mr. Miller."

"Well, there should've been, and that remote was a device that I created to open up a wormhole that would take whoever who would enter into another reality. It worked, but unfortunately it didn't work as I had planned."

"Explain what you mean by, it didn't work as you had planned."

"A wormhole never opens, but what does happen is that me and the me from the selected reality would switch bodies. After pressing the remote the first time, I found myself in a Mexican jail cell..."

Randy continued to tell his story in great detail.

Chapter Eighteen

As Randy was telling his story to Dr. Adams, Dr. Gray opened the door to Alex's padded room. Alex was sitting in the floor while wearing a straight jacket.

Alex looked up at Dr. Gray as he walked in before saying, "This straight jacket isn't necessary."

"I thought that about two weeks ago and when I had it removed, you put two bullets in your abdomen," Dr. Gray said. "It was really short of a miracle that you even survived."

"So Michelle was right."

"Who is Michelle?"

Alex shook his head before saying, "She's no one important. Doctor, there's probably nothing I can say that would convince you that I won't attempt to commit suicide. However, I will say though that I'm not the same Alex who had attempted suicide."

"What do you mean?"

"You won't believe me."

"If you don't tell me then you are not even giving me a chance to believe you."

"All right. I will tell you everything." Alex told Dr. Gray what had happened from the beginning to end.

As the days passed, the psychiatrists didn't know what to make of the story that was told to them. The parents to Alex's group were even called in.

Thursday, November 11, at 9:00 A.M., the parents were sitting in a conference room with the doctors and were told of the story.

After hearing the entire story Nicholas O'Brien said, "I'm also at a loss at what to make of the story, but there were some facts in Alex and Doug's part of the story that I never told anyone."

"What kind of facts, Mr. O'Brien?" Dr. Gray asked.

"When I was injured on the job and had to go to the hospital, a nurse was about to give me a shot that I was allergic to. However, before the nurse injected me with it she asked me if I was allergic to any medicine. When she asked, she asked me as if it was an afterthought. I can still remember the look on the nurse's face when I told her what medicines that I was allergic to."

"So the nurse almost gave you a shot that you were allergic to?" Dr. Adams asked.

"As I said, the nurse asked me only as an afterthought, and my mind wasn't on that either, so yes if other realities are real, I might've been given that shot. And also like my sons' story goes, I had taken out a life insurance policy and made Beverly the beneficiary."

"Did Alex or Doug know any of that?" Dr. Gray asked.

"I was the only one who knew about any of it."

After Nicholas spoke his piece, Cindy's mother said, "Eighteen years ago, I came extremely close to going to an abortion clinic when I found out that I was pregnant with Cory."

With a surprised expression across his face, Cindy's father uttered, "What?!"

"We were separated and I didn't want you to think that I was trying to get you to come back by saying that I was pregnant."

"What stopped you from having an abortion?" Cindy's dad asked.

"My mom told me as I was leaning towards an abortion that she had an abortion when I was about five years old. Having that abortion caused her to not be able to have any more kids. I saw the regret of that decision in my mom's eyes, and I didn't want that to be me in twenty years."

"Why didn't you ever tell me this?"

"I didn't feel it was important enough to tell you."

"Okay, obviously there are facts in your sons' and daughters' stories that are true to a degree, but for them to trade realities with their other selves from another reality sounds more like a science fiction story," Dr. Tyson, the leading doctor, said.

"My sons knew about Avery Larson and his sister Melissa," Beverly said. "They never met those two people before, and the story of how Avery and I would have gotten together if the reality of Nick dying would have come true does fit."

"Dr. Gray, I believe my sons' story and I would like them released," Nick said.

"Mr. O'Brien, at this point in time, I don't see that to be a wise move."

"I don't care. I want Doug and Alex released," Nick said.

The parents of the others spoke up and said the same thing about their kids.

"Other than Alex, the others never displayed any dangerous tendencies towards themselves or towards others, so I have no problems with releasing them," Dr. Tyson said. "I do have a problem with…"

Nick interrupted with, "I want Alex released also."

"I really don't see that as a wise decision," Dr. Gray said.

"It is my final decision on this and if you don't release Alex, I will be contacting a lawyer."

Dr. Tyson sighed before saying, "Okay, Mr. O'Brien. Alex

will be released; however, I strongly suggest that Alex... and even the others be placed in an out patient therapy treatment. My recommendation is for them to go to therapy at least once a week for the next eight weeks."

"We'll agree to that," Beverly said. Beverly looked at Nick. "Right, honey."

"Them going to therapy sounds like a reasonable suggestion and an alternative to staying here."

"Okay, give me about two hours to get the paper work in order and all of your sons and daughters will be released."

11:35 A.M., outside near the entrance of the facility, Alex, Doug, Randy, Kenny, Ben, Cindy and Brandy were gathering for the first time in days as their parents were signing the papers.

Alex saw Doug and Randy walking up to him and when they stepped up, Doug asked, "So, bro? Are you mad at us for forcing you to return with us?"

Alex shook his head before saying, "Actually, I'm slowly returning to my former self. I mean I would have been okay if I was living my life in the other reality, but I am finding myself with my old opinions again... oh and my attraction to women is back."

Brandy grinned before asking, "Are you certain about that?"

Alex grinned while saying, "I'm certain. In fact, there's a beautiful nurse in there who I am definitely attracted to." Alex pointed to a spot on the right side of his lip. "The nurse I'm talking about has a dark freckle right about here."

"I saw her too and she is pretty," Kenny agreed.

"Well, it sounds like you're returning to normal," Doug said.

"Alex, I heard that the other Alex attempted suicide while she was living your life," Cindy said.

"That's true," Alex said. "I have half healed bullet wounds just below my rib cage. According to Dr. Gray, the other Alex came very close at committing suicide."

"What would've happened to you if the other Alex had committed suicide?" Ben asked. "Would you have jumped along with us?"

Randy was the one to say, "No. Alex wouldn't have jumped with us."

"How can you be sure?" Brandy asked.

"Using the term Alternate Reality Traveler... or ART for someone who swaps realities, the only way an ART can swap realities is if the person traveling exists in both realities. In Alex's case where he is a man in this reality and a woman in the other reality; the moment when Alex was conceived, the exact egg was fertilized in both realities, but by different sperm. The same would be true with all of us in other realities as well."

"So there's a reality out there that I wasn't able to jump along with you guys, isn't there?" Alex asked Randy.

Randy looked at Alex for a long moment before answering his question.

Sunday, November 7, at 9:02 A.M., in the reality Alpha 0.0.0.1.0.5.0, at Harvard's library, Doug and the others were standing between bookshelves and out of sight from the entrance. When Alex and Cindy walked in, Cindy pointed towards the bookshelf that held the mythology books before nervously saying, "I got this book from over there."

Cindy saw that Alex was giving her a curious look before Alex said, "Let's see if we can find the book." After taking a couple of steps towards the shelf, Alex noticed how nervous Cindy was acting. "Are you all right, Cindy?"

In a snappy reply Cindy said, "Of course. Things couldn't be better. Randy's remote is supposed to be ready today and all of us can return to our home reality." Alex abruptly stopped. Cindy stopped and looked at Alex. "Is there anything wrong?"

"You wouldn't be looking for a specific book knowing that you'll be returning to your own reality."

As Alex was looking over the room, Cindy nervously asked, "What do you mean?"

Alex looked at Cindy before saying, "You made a good attempt, but I'm staying here."

As Alex was turning to leave, Cindy grabbed Alex before crying out, "Doug, help! Alex knows!"

As Doug and the others rushed to help stop Alex from leaving, the librarian also walked towards Alex and Cindy to investigate the commotion.

Alex was just about to break free when Doug and Kenny ran up and grabbed hold of her.

"Alex, you're not going anywhere so settle down," Doug quickly said.

The librarian stepped up and demanded to know, "What's going on here? Why are you holding this young lady?"

"This young lady is my sister, Alex, and she's a kleptomaniac," Doug said.

Alex gave Doug a surprised looked before blurting out, "What?!"

Cindy held up the mythology book that she had while saying, "I found this book in her possession and if you check your records, this book was reported missing yesterday."

"And Alex was making such progress at getting better these last few months," Doug added.

The librarian took the book before saying, "Hold her until I can check my records."

As the librarian was walking away Alex said, "You guys are my friends and I can't believe that even one of you would sink so low as to resort to this."

Randy pulled out the remote that was preset to an address that he thought to be the correct one before saying, "Because you are our friend is why we resorted to this."

"The book was actually checked out by my roommate, and I was returning it for her," Brandy said. "We just told the librarian what we did so he would walk far enough away from us."

"It's time to go home," Randy said.

Alex watched Randy's thumb as he pressed the remote.

Seconds after Randy pressed the button, Alex watched her brother and friends as they fell to the floor unconscious.

Alex gave her friends curious and confused looks while saying barely above a whisper, "Okay; now this is weird."

The librarian saw Alex's friends fainting and rushed back over to them. As he rushed up he worriedly asked, "What going on? What happened to them?"

Alex confusingly stared at the librarian and searched her thoughts for a believable response before responding with, "What do you mean what happened? You didn't feel that?"

With a confused expression across his face, the librarian quickly asked, "Feel what?"

"Some kind of shock wave came through here; perhaps a sonic boom."

The librarian gave Alex a skeptical look before saying, "Young lady, if there was a sonic boom, windows would be broken out."

"Well, some kind of wave came through here because I almost fainted from it myself."

"I didn't feel a thing."

"Yeah, that's weird that you were the only one who didn't feel it. You don't have any inner ear defects, do you?"

"There's nothing wrong with my inner ear," the librarian insisted.

"Well, I was born with a slight inner ear defect and I was thinking that my defect was what kept me from fainting."

"Well, I don't have any inner ear defects," the librarian repeated.

"Are you sure? Have you ever been tested?"

"This discussion is over. And I'm going to call nine-one-one."

Alex gave the librarian a concerned look before uttering, "No; don't do that... not yet anyway. They should wake up any second now."

Alex saw Trudy and Miles rushing in as the librarian was backing away. Just before he turned to walk away he said, "I'm calling nine-one-one."

Alex looked at the librarian and slightly cringed. She then turned towards Trudy and Miles.

As Trudy and Miles stepped up, Trudy gave Alex an inquisitive stare before asking, "Alex, do you know what happened?"

"Something's not right. Randy was standing right next to me when he pressed the remote. I'm glad that I didn't, but I should have switched realities with them."

"So you are the Alex who was here for the past two weeks?" Trudy asked.

"I am. Oh and I told the librarian that I felt some kind of shock wave come through at the point they fainted as an explanation as to why they fainted. He doesn't believe me, so I need you and Miles to help me convince him."

"I'll do what I can," Miles said.

"Yeah, same here," Trudy said. She then saw Doug stirring and pointed. "Alex, look."

Alex turned to look and saw Doug moving. Doug opened his eyes and when he saw Alex, he quickly sat up and delightfully blurted out, "Alex, is it really you?"

As Doug was quickly getting on his feet, Alex said, "Yes... and no."

Doug glanced at Trudy and then at Miles. As he scanned the room he sullenly said, "I'm dreaming. This isn't real."

"Doug, you're not dreaming," Alex said.

Doug looked at Alex before saying, "Then I entered the twilight zone again."

"You never entered the twilight zone... well, not exactly anyway," Alex said.

"You talk as if you know what's going on."

"I do."

"How could you? I mean, you were just as confused as I was just before...."

Alex gave Doug a curious look before asking, "Just before what?"

Doug said barely above a whisper, "Just before you committed suicide."

A stunned expression came across Alex's face just before she looked at Trudy while saying, "That must have been why I didn't switch. The me in my reality is dead."

Doug gave Alex a confused look before asking, "What are you talking about?"

"Doug, I am Alex, but I'm not the same Alex you know."

"Again what are you talking about?"

"Multiple realities exist and my friends and I were switched with the us of your reality. Except for me, the two realities should be corrected."

"You can't be serious."

"Doug, Alex is telling you the truth," Trudy confirmed.

"How? How can what you say be possible?"

Alex looked down at Randy and saw that he, Brandy and Ben were stirring. She then pointed to Randy before saying, "In my reality that man is my best friend since childhood. He is also the most brilliant scientist Harvard has seen in a long time. Unfortunately, his theories were so far ahead of the professors that the professors saw him as a joke. He built a device that was supposed to have opened up a wormhole so he could travel into other realities."

Brandy and Ben opened their eyes and as they looked up, Doug said, "There was no wormhole."

"Yeah, that was where his theory went awry."

Ben sat up and looked around before uttering, "Oh God, not again!"

Brandy also sat up before saying, "We're back at Harvard."

Alex saw the others moving around just as she was saying, "I will explain what had happened once everyone is back on his or her feet."

Doug saw the librarian walking up and as everyone was getting back on his or her feet, Alex turned to see what Doug was looking at.

The librarian stepped up and informed everyone, "An ambulance in on its way."

"We don't need an ambulance," Alex said before giving Doug a look as if for him to play along. "My friends had blacked out because of a shock wave that came through here."

"Again, there was no shock wave; sonic boom or a wave of any kind," the librarian strongly insisted.

"Are you telling me that you didn't feel that?" Doug asked.

"God, I was walking down the stairwell and I almost fainted from it," Miles said.

"I don't know what's going on, but I'm not buying it, and I hope you don't think that the paramedics will buy it also," the librarian told them.

Trudy glanced at Alex before asking, "Buy what?"

With a confused expression across his face, the librarian answered, "Buy your guys' excuse as to why these six fainted."

Trudy looked at Doug and the others before asking, "Did anyone in here faint or blackout?"

Doug looked at the librarian before saying, "I don't know of anyone who fainted."

"I saw you and your friends faint," the librarian insisted.

"And who will the paramedics and the police believe?" Miles asked. "You or the nine of us?"

"Okay, I don't know what's going on, but obviously I will be looking like a fool when the paramedics get here," the librarian angrily hissed. "I can't do anything about this incident; however, you nine consider yourselves warned. I will be watching each one of you from this point forward." The librarian turned and walked away.

"Okay, would someone like to tell me as to what is really going on?" Randy quickly asked. "The last thing I remember was being in a mental institution for supposedly having delusions."

"So was I," Kenny, Ben, Brandy and Cindy proclaimed.

"All of you were institutionalized?" Alex quickly and incredulously questioned. .

"We were," Randy confirmed. "The doctors there were trying to convince me that I knew each and everyone of you. And I was in a Mexican jail just before waking up in this room the first time."

"I heard that you committed suicide," Brandy told Alex.

"You were also changed into a man somehow," Cindy added.

"Multiple realities exist, and two of the realities, your reality and mine, were crossed," Alex explained.

"Are you saying that you don't belong to this reality?" Kenny asked.

"The Alex who belongs to this reality committed suicide in my reality, and therefore I was unable to switch back along with everyone else."

"How was the reality crossed?" Randy asked.

"Randy, in my reality, you were the one who had caused this," Alex answered.

Kenny gestured towards Randy while angrily demanding to know, "This man caused it?"

"Obviously this Randy didn't do it," Miles told him. "He was in a Mexican jail cell for breaking and entering."

Randy gave Miles a curious look as Alex said, "Kenny, the Randy from my reality loved science and he's destined to be a great scientist..."

"In other words the Randy from your reality was showing off," Kenny interrupted with.

"Not exactly," Alex told him. "Prof. Blumberg was giving Randy F's for his alternate reality theory research papers. Randy decided that he was going to prove to the Professor and everyone that his papers weren't science fiction nonsense. So he shut himself up in his rented house, and created a remote that he thought that would open a wormhole into an alternate reality. Obviously it didn't work how he thought it would. In my reality, each one of us was with Randy when he tested his remote."

Ben looked down and saw the remote on the floor. He then pointed to it while asking, "Is this the remote that caused all of this?"

"The remote would stay in its own reality, so that remote is the remote that Randy had to re-create to fix the crossed reality," Alex said.

Kenny stepped up to the remote and crushed it. As an afterthought he looked at Alex while saying, "I hope you didn't have a problem with me doing that."

An amused grin came across Alex's face just before Alex shook her head while saying, "I had planned to do that myself.

You just beat me to it."

"Hey, Red, how did I get out of that Mexican jail?" Randy asked.

"Randy, my name is Alex and I'll tell everyone everything. But can I do it on the way to the cafeteria? I'm actually starving."

Doug gestured for her to walk before saying, "After you."

As everyone left the library they saw paramedics entering the building. They ignored the paramedics as they continued to walk away.

While walking to the cafeteria, Alex explained to Randy and the others as to how she knew who Randy was and how she knew to look for Randy in Mexico City. Alex even mentioned to Doug about Michelle's involvement and that Michelle has knowledge of the crossed reality. Everyone was walking up to the end of the food line in the cafeteria when Alex was finishing the story on how everyone was able to get to Mexico and on how Randy was released from the Mexican jail.

Once Alex's explanation was finished, Doug tapped Alex on her shoulder before asking, "Okay, who is Nicholas O'Brien?"

"He is our biological father," Alex said.

Doug, with a shock expression across his face, quickly demanded to know, "What are you talking about?"

"In this reality, a month before mom knew that she was pregnant with us, Nicholas O'Brien had died from a severe allergic reaction to an injection that he was given. Mom then met Avery. Two days later and in front of Avery, a doctor tells mom that she's pregnant. You know the rest better than I do."

"I can't believe that, that was kept from us... I mean, the Alex who belongs here and me."

"They actually had no intentions in telling you or Alex.

Mom and… well, I guess dad to me now, had acted as though Doug and I had literally resurrected the dead when we brought up the name Nicholas Christopher O'Brien. In fact, when Doug and I were busted for being in St. Louis, we had told mom and dad that we were there looking for Nicholas. That was when Mom told us how he died."

"Trudy, how long have you known about this crossed reality?" Doug asked.

"Pretty much from the beginning," Trudy said.

"The day after the switch, Trudy and Miles were insisting that I go to the doctor for severe memory loss. So it was either go to the doctor or take my chance and tell them the truth. As you already know, I told them the truth and after telling them, they helped me out so no one else would think that I was having severe memory loss. That and I have been reading Alex's diaries every chance I got."

Kenny was behind Alex by three people and as they were moving through the food line he angrily grumbled, "At least you knew what was happening to you and you also knew what to do to fit in. We were oblivious of the whole thing."

Alex stopped and jerked around to look at Kenny before she defensively shot back, "Including the Randy who created the remote, there were fourteen victims here."

Doug and Miles stepped between Alex and Kenny just as Doug quickly uttered, "Time out! Kenny, I do believe that the Randy who created the remote didn't know that we would all switch as we did. So any more accusations towards Alex, you will have to deal with me."

"I wasn't accusing Alex of anything," Kenny quickly proclaimed.

"So that wasn't hostility towards me that I heard?" Alex questioned.

"Alex, I'm upset over the situation and not with you,"

Kenny assured her. "So I'm sorry if I sounded hostile towards you."

Alex nodded before saying, "I'm sorry too." Alex then faced forward and continued to step through the line.

A short time later, as everyone was walking towards the table with his or her meal, Cindy asked, "Alex, since you weren't able to switch back, can you adjust to being in this reality?"

Trudy chuckled before saying, "She's already adjusted to this reality."

Alex, while slightly annoyed, looked at Trudy before sarcastically saying, "That didn't make me sound bad at all."

"Alex, that isn't bad," Trudy assured her as they stepped up to the table. As every was placing his or her tray on the table Trudy continued to say, "As I told you before, I believe as to how fast you had been assimilated into this reality, was this reality correcting itself."

As everyone was taking his or her seat, Doug said, "A few days before the second switch, I felt myself adjusting to my new... to the other reality."

"I was too," Randy said.

Cindy had readied a bite to eat, but before she took it, she asked, "So, Alex, are you okay with living your life as a woman?"

Doug, Ben and Cindy noticed the slight grin that Alex had given Miles before she answered with, "I'm okay with living my life this way."

When Miles returned Alex's grin, Doug casually asked, "So, Alex, how long have you and Miles been a couple?"

Alex gave Doug a 'caught red handed' look before she finally answered with, "Only two days. I knew I was being assimilated into this reality just before I was even here a whole week. I tried to resist it, but my feelings for Miles dramatically grew each day until resisting didn't make any sense anymore."

"And Alex is a woman with woman's desires," Miles added.

"I'm not judging either one of you," Doug assured them.

"Alex, even though this reality had assimilated you as you and Trudy put it, you still tried to return to your reality with the others?" Randy asked.

Everyone saw that Alex's expression was as if she didn't want to answer, and after taking a deep breath, she finally said, "Doug and the others didn't give me the chance to decide what to do. They tricked me into being in the library without even trying to convince me to be there on my own."

Doug grinned before saying, "That's exactly what I would've done."

Alex smiled at Doug before taking a bite of food. After Alex swallowed the bite she said, "Doug, when we get back in St. Louis, I'm going to need your help to fit in."

"I'll help you where I can," Doug said.

Alex grinned before saying, "Thanks."

When Doug nodded, Ben said, "Alex, I was at work when the first switch happened. Do I still have a job?"

"I honestly don't know. Ben... the other Ben never said how he handled things when he was in Atlanta."

"Ben, what kept you from going to Harvard when the Ben in the other reality did?" Cindy asked.

"The Ben in the other reality won the scholarship, and I didn't," Ben said. "And I would love to know what he did differently to get it."

"You may not have done anything differently," Alex told him. "For each crossroad event that a person comes to in his or her life, that event will spawn multiple realities."

"An interesting theory you have," Randy said.

Alex, while pleasantly grinning, looked at Randy before

saying, "The theory isn't mine; it's yours."

"So even in another reality, you would've switched along with the others?" Cindy questioned.

"I believe so," Alex said. Alex then saw that Brandy was just sitting there without joining the conversation. "Brandy, why are you so quiet?"

"I'm just listening to what you have to say," Brandy said. "After I get done eating I'm going to attempt to get my life back to normal."

"Brandy, I know you and the other Alex weren't friends, but in my reality everyone at this table... except for Trudy and Miles who I didn't even know until I came here, have been friends and study partners since our freshman year. I would like it if all of us can be friends."

"I didn't like Alex because she was an arrogant and a fastidious person," Brandy proclaimed. "You, I don't even know."

"I know all of Alex's shortcomings, Brandy. In fact, I'm the one who inherited her reputation, but what you need to realize is that Alex had a good heart. She never meant to alienate herself the way she did."

"I can only take your word for that. As for us being friends, it's not going to happen right away."

"I wasn't expecting it to."

"Good."

"Oh, I do owe you a good sum of money, and I will pay you back."

"Why do you owe me money?"

"Yours and the other Brandy's realities were basically identical. The other Brandy was able to get into your bank account. She gave Doug and me the money to get to St. Louis to look for Randy."

"The money given to you was in an effort to fix the two

realities, right?"

"It was. Randy was the only one who could correct them, so we needed to find him."

"Then you don't have to pay me back."

Alex pleasantly grinned before saying, "Thanks; that's sweet of you." She then took another bite of food.

"You're welcome."

"Alex, if each crossroad event would spawn multiple realities, then would there be a reality where there's another alternate group of you and your friends who didn't correct things, but disrupted yet another reality?" Randy asked.

Alex looked at Randy and thought for a second before saying, "I don't know for sure, but I would say 'yes'."

Sunday, November 7, at 9:02 A.M., in the reality Alpha 0.0.0.1.0.1.2, at Harvard's library, Doug and the others were standing between bookshelves and out of sight from the entrance. When Alex and Cindy walked in, Cindy pointed towards the bookshelf that held the mythology books before nervously saying, "I got this book from over there."

Cindy saw that Alex was giving her a curious look before Alex said, "Let's see if we can find the book." After taking a couple of steps towards the shelf, Alex noticed how nervous Cindy was acting. "Are you all right, Cindy?"

In a snappy reply Cindy said, "Of course. Things couldn't be better. Randy's remote is supposed to be ready today and all of us can return to our home reality." Alex abruptly stopped. Cindy stopped and looked at Alex. "Is there anything wrong?"

"You wouldn't be looking for a specific book knowing that you'll be returning to your own reality."

As Alex was looking over the room, Cindy nervously asked, "What do you mean?"

Alex looked at Cindy before saying, "You made a good attempt, but I'm staying here."

As Alex was turning to leave, Cindy grabbed Alex before crying out, "Doug, help! Alex knows!"

As Doug and the others rushed to help stop Alex from leaving, the librarian also walked towards Alex and Cindy to investigate the commotion.

Alex was just about to break free when Doug and Kenny ran up and grabbed hold of her.

"Alex, you're not going anywhere so settle down," Doug quickly said.

The librarian stepped up and demanded to know, "What's going on here? Why are you holding this young lady?"

"This young lady is my sister, Alex, and she's a kleptomaniac," Doug said.

Alex gave Doug a surprised looked before blurting out, "What?!"

Cindy held up the mythology book that she had while saying, "I found this book in her possession and if you check your records, this book was reported missing yesterday."

"And Alex was making such progress at getting better these last few months," Doug added.

The librarian took the book before saying, "Hold her until I can check my records."

As the librarian was walking away Alex said, "You guys are my friends and I can't believe that even one of you would sink so low as to resort to this."

Randy pulled out the remote that was preset to an address that he thought to be the correct one before saying, "Because you are our friend is why we resorted to this."

"The book was actually checked out by my roommate, and I was returning it for her," Brandy said. "We just told the librarian what we did so he would walk far enough away from us."

"It's time to go home," Randy said.

Alex watched Randy's thumb as he pressed the remote.

Sunday, November 7, at 9:10 A.M., in the reality Alpha 0.0.0.2.1.0.0, Alex woke up in her bedroom at the dormitory. She quickly got to her feet and looked into the mirror and saw that she was still a woman. She then rushed out and saw Doug who was also a woman named Denise lying in the floor. Except for the hair and eye color, Alex and Denise again looked much alike. Alex quickly went to her aid.

When Denise came to, she sat up. As she looked at Alex she said, "Randy's remote didn't work." She then grabbed her throat. "What's wrong with my voice?"

Alex gave Denise a curious look before asking, "Doug?"

"It's me. What's going on?"

Alex amusingly grinned while saying, "You have to look in the mirror."

As Denise was getting on her feet she became aware of her female physique and what she was wearing. As she gazed down at herself she blurted out, "I'm a woman?! I'm going to kill Randy!" She quickly entered the second bedroom. As she was looking at her reflection, she saw Alex pulling out a wallet from a purse. "What are you doing?"

Alex looked at the driver's license while saying, "Your name is Denise O'Brien and the street name on your driver's license is Victoria Place. Hey, since our last names are O'Brien and we live on Victoria Place, there's a good chance that Randy is attending Harvard in this reality."

Denise stared at her reflection in the mirror while blurting out, "And here we go again; once more from the top."

~ THE END ~